QUICKSAND

BY THE SAME AUTHOR

Plays

Loose End
Striking
Silence
The Aquarium

Fiction

Simone

QUICKSAND

LOUISE HIDE

Honeyglen Publishing

First published in the UK in 1989 by Honeyglen Publishing Ltd.

British Library Cataloguing in Publication Data:

Hide, Louise, 1957
Quicksand.
I. Title
823'.914 [F]

ISBN 0 907855 07 5

Typeset by Preston Editions, 01-979 5960
Printed and bound in Great Britain by The Bath Press.

To Anna

With special thanks to Bertrand

All characters in this novel are fictitious. Any resemblance to actual persons, either living or dead, is purely coincidental.

PART ONE

'Thirty is a good age for a woman,' said Vera of V.G. Stores. 'It means you're on your way.'

'On your way where?'

'Well . . . to wherever you're going of course.' She hit the total button of the till and the cash drawer came flying out with a ping. 'Twelve eighty-five,' she said.

I rummaged around in my purse and handed her a couple of notes. She was always coming out with these statements, they sounded quite profound at first. Until you thought about them. And realised what nothing remarks they were.

'Got a cake?' She handed me my change and sank her hands into her cardigan pockets, stretching it down over her droopy breasts.

'I made it myself.'

'Well that's no good. You can't make your own birthday cake.'

'No one else is going to.'

Vera cocked her head to one side and thought for a moment.

'Well,' she said slowly, 'there's some that do and some that don't.'

'Very true,' I replied, and left the shop.

When I got home the plumbers were still in the kitchen, pulling out pipes and filling the place with such a putrid smell I could hardly breathe. I didn't want to breathe. I breathed out and then tried to breathe in, in short sharp snatches. I started to feel dizzy.

'It's your smell,' said the plumber. 'Your shit. It might

be a bit old but it's still your smell.'

'Thanks.'

He waggled his little finger around the inside of his ear and then flicked a tiny ball of wax into the air before disappearing under the sink again.

Everyone was very upset because I blew out the candles before they arrived. The cake, made by me, sat on the table, laid by me, with its thirty candles, arranged by me, waiting to be lit. And it was my birthday.

'There's no point doing anything now.'

'No. You can't light them up again. It just wouldn't be the same.'

'Well I'm very sorry. I didn't mean to spoil things.'

'It was meant to be a surprise.'

'But I made it.'

'We were going to bring it in, all lit up, with the lights off.'

To be honest, I hadn't wanted a cake at all. I hadn't wanted a celebration. I wanted to keep this birthday to myself. But of course I couldn't. I wasn't allowed to. Everyone wanted to make a big deal out of it, so I had to as well.

I apologised. Sorry, sorry. Tickle, tickle. Kiss, kiss. Coodgy coo. We all raised our eyebrows and clicked and frowned and finished off with a good laugh.

Then, as I rocked back on my chair, I went flying over and landed on the floor with a thud.

Of course, they all thought it hysterically funny and rolled around hooting with laughter. I was shocked at first. But when I pulled myself up, I laughed too, for being so bloody silly as to fall off the chair in the first place – at the age of thirty.

That's what made me decide to write this.

Not Vera. Or the plumber. Or falling off the chair. But

turning thirty. At thirty I can look back and see what happened. What really happened.

I can see change.

Change within. Change without. Change in the world. Rapid change we cannot keep up with, understand or justify. Change we instigate and perpetuate in the name of freedom. Change that keeps us guards and prisoners within ourselves.

* * *

Even though I was born in Portsmouth (in a draughty pre-fab that was hastily erected after the maternity ward was bombed), I have always considered myself a Saltingford girl.

Soon after I was born, Mum scooped me up, slung me over her shoulder and continued the nomadic wanderings she had taken to ever since my father cleared off with all our money and unworldly possessions.

One day, we landed in Saltingford. We just turned up, out of the blue, from nowhere. And the next day Mum found a live-in job at one of the large houses in Swingate Lane.

Two weeks later she was fired; the mistress of the house had found her with the master of the house, in the greenhouse.

It was all very confusing, but we decided to stay nonetheless.

A kind fisherman called George Jarvis let us have his caravan for a very nominal rent. Prior to our moving in there, he had used it for storing his tackle, so when Mum humped me and her battered old brown suitcase up the steps, she let out a long wail as the smell of the place hit her. But the caravan was ship-shape in a matter of weeks, sitting at the head of the beach like a giant, pale blue blancmange. 'Only temporary,' Mum always assured me when I was old enough to complain. She couldn't see what a tip it was. It had grown on her like a large wart.

Saltingford lurks in the fog on the east coast of Suffolk. It is remote, isolated and on the way to nowhere. As a tourist attraction it has nothing to offer: no pubs, no miniature golf courses, no amusement arcades or candy floss or ice cream parlours. Nothing. It can be a very bleak place.

The village itself is divided into two parts: the High Street, which is the main hub of the village, and the beach. The two parts are joined by about half a mile of winding coast road that is lined by a ragged hedge which belongs to no one when crisp packets and cloudy white milk bottles have been stuffed into its wiry tentacles, yet to everyone when the question of land and its ownership arises. Usually Mum cleaned the hedge. Picking away at its tatty brambles as she strode along the road. She never thought anything of it. Why shouldn't she tidy it up? She was passing.

The main centre of activity in the village has always been the King's Head. In the evening, the male members of our small community gathered together between the four bare whitewashed walls of the public bar, creating a microcosm of village life. The only woman who ever went into the King's Head was my mother. The only woman who ever got booted out of the King's Head was my mother; but that was for being drunk, not for being a woman, they said.

Randalls owned the King's Head. Like Mum and me, he too had turned up in Saltingford out of the deep blue sea, an ex-chef from the merchant navy. Randalls had squinted at the world through the steamy window of the ship's galley and, after fifteen years of tossing around the ocean, he packed up all his earthly knowledge and perched himself on a stool behind the bar with a book on his lap and a scowl on his face.

Only visitors to the village were thrown by Randalls' filthy moods. The locals were used to him, they logged the growth of his large bulbous nose as he consumed vast quantities of port. Once, while I was sitting behind the bar with Mum, I counted twelve curly black veins crawling across it like tiny worms. A month later there were fourteen.

Why should Randalls care what people thought of him? Or worry about the veins on the end of his nose? There was nowhere else to drink in Saltingford. And with only a fortnightly meeting of the W.I. to compete with, he held a monopoly on entertainment in the village.

A couple of hundred yards further up the High Street was the church. At one time, it may have been well situated near the pub for the convenience of the congregation. However, those who visited the church these days rarely turned up at the King's Head, and vice versa. That is with one exception, Father Armitage.

Father Armitage spent a great deal of time in the King's Head, desperately trying to cling to his diminishing flock. If they would not go to the church, then he must go to the people. The family, the church, society itself was disintegrating around him. He had heard the most appalling stories at the monthly diocese meetings held in the Bishop's drawing room. He had heard about a degeneration in moral standards to a point where there were almost none left at all. He had heard about sex, drugs and rock and roll and couldn't imagine any of it. He claimed never to have experienced a sexual feeling in his life.

Nestled behind the church in a great wad of dry, overgrown jungle sat the Rectory. It was a massive, red brick house that was festooned with turrets and gabled windows and ivy that was so brittle it turned to dust at the slightest touch. Everything around the Rectory seemed dead: the windswept sheaves of dry grass; the overgrown brambles that lay in massive tangled clumps, interwoven and impenetrable; the garden furniture that had been left out on the patio for years, its white paint chipped and stained, its cast iron skeleton rusting and discoloured. To us children, the Rectory was a Hammer House of Horrors surrounded by a deadly aura that hung in the air as though Armitage were cultivating mortality to dish out to his flock with communion. We were convinced the place was haunted.

Although Father Armitage could barely have reached forty-five years of age, he looked sixty to most people and well over a hundred to me. His hair had been grey for years, yet his face was not wrinkled. Running down either side of his face were two thick sideburns which he had lovingly cultivated ever since he first began to shave. He didn't realise it, but sideburns were very much in fashion at the time and those who had never met him before took him for one of those new fangled 'trendy' vicars. Apart from the sideburns, there was nothing remotely memorable about Father Armitage. We only noticed him because of his cassock, a filthy black thing that trailed along the ground giving him the air of the Prima Donna as he flounced down the High Street, his long thin nose almost poking the pavement as he steered himself resolutely down the road.

Saltingford has always been very closely knit. Everyone knows everyone else and, as is common in these parts, many of the villagers are related. Over the centuries, families have united, multiplied and united again; woven together to form a tapestry of fragmented local colour that has frequently concerned the local authorities. 'Idiocy' is no longer permissible. Instead the social services have had to resign themselves to the fact that part of the Saltingford population is just a bit 'thick'.

The two other main streets in the village were Swingate Lane and Mead Close. Swingate Lane hosted a collection of large houses that lay comfortably lodged in several acres of ground. Mead Close, on the other hand, was quite a different matter. We all hated it and everyone who lived there. At one time, Mead Close had been an idyllic green field that sprouted wild daffodils and primroses. Then, one day, a convoy of bulldozers arrived and after much noise and shifting of muck, attached Mead Close to the High Street like an artificial limb.

Dotted around the close were eight horrible boxes. They were all the same, without a single original feature amongst them (even the crazy paving that led up to the front door was the same, each slab as crazy as the next). And the day before the close was opened, I sat on top of a large tractor dropping and watched the contractor empty three goldfish into each ornamental pool as a welcoming gesture.

New people must have moved into Mead Close, but no one noticed them. They just blended in with the ordinariness of it all.

Opposite the church and next to V.G. Stores were the Alms Houses, which were over 400 years old and sat toppling over the pavement like four creaky old men. And next to the Alms Houses were the Council Houses, less admired and only just tolerated by many in the village.

Stumble out of the King's Head, turn right, follow the coast road and about half a mile further along, another collection of houses comes into view. This is where we lived. In our caravan.

Strangers to the area are often surprised when they turn that last corner because a vast expanse of surging grey water suddenly comes into sight, spanning the view from north to south to east. It's alive, manipulated by invisible currents, undulating, lurching, pulsating like a huge animal. White, frothy crests deceiving us. I knew because that sea had devoured people I'd known, people I had seen the lifeboat bring in, reduced to sagging, drowned corpses.

From the shore, the stony beach climbed steeply, forming two banks of slithery wet shingle. Then it levelled out and finally reached a row of white cottages. There were five cottages in the row, each identical except for the last where the lifeboat was kept. Here a pair of runners mounted on a steep launching pad swept down to the shore, sending the lifeboat on its way with a surging explosion.

A few yards from the cottages lay the prime residence of the beach, a long, one-storey building called the Boat House. This was owned by Miss Stiff-finger, a middle-aged woman who had lived in Saltingford for some years with her 'friend' Martha and who owned a string of butchers around Suffolk. A matronly person, Miss Stiff-finger was called in to deal with every disaster. She always seemed to know what to do. And if she didn't, she pretended she did, and it worked just as well. People sniggered as they watched her striding up the High Street in her sensible shoes and thick grey hair yanked up in a bun. But face to face they held her in great awe. She was an awesome woman.

A little further along the beach was the Martello Tower, one of hundreds built at regular intervals on the east coast to protect us from Napoleon.

Between the tower and the Boat House was a dip in the land, and it was here that our caravan nestled. The wind skimmed over the roof and rattled the loose telegraph poles behind us. On a blowy day we would sit inside listening to the creaks and groans as the wind tugged at the straining joints of the caravan. Had the main structure not been firmly fixed to a large slab of cement, we would almost certainly have been blown into the ditch behind us like a bundle of hay.

The only other building on the beach was owned by George Jarvis' brother. This was a very grim little bungalow which lay in a plot of waste land a hundred yards from the cottages. George's brother was a simple (idiot) man who had been married to a simple (idiot) woman who had gone out in a boat one day and drowned. No one knew how she had drowned, or even why she was in the boat in the first place, but since her death, George's brother had let the place go. The garden was overgrown and strewn with rubbish and at night I could hear the wind playing with an old swing that dangled from its rusty frame round the back, hurling it into the air and shaking it. The bungalow was filthy, inside and out. No one could see through the windows (we all tried but with no success). And no one saw much of George's brother either. The family just took him out of the bungalow for Christmas, plonked a hat on his head, stuck a cracker in his mitt and thought he was happy. No one knew what he got up to the rest of the year.

One cold November morning while I was plodding along the top of the beach, bent over and battling against the wind, I found my father lying dead behind one of the fishing boats.

I knew it was him. I had had a glimpse the night before when a man woke us up by banging loudly on the caravan door. My sister Margaret and I were in bed and terrified until we heard Mum shouting at him.

'Bugger off you,' she yelled, opening the living room window.

But he was such a poor starved creature that she finally let him in, yet only for a minute and only to say his piece and then he could piss off again because she'd had a belly-full of him eight years ago and she'd sworn then that if she ever saw him again she'd cut his balls off.

There were two rooms and a WC in the caravan. The main living room had a sink, a fridge and a cooker and served as Mum's bedroom. The other room, the bedroom, contained a three-quarter size bed that Margaret and I shared. So there was no room to do anything there unless it was done on the bed itself. Play was conducted in a squishy, bouncy sort of way or under Mum's nose – and on her nerves – in the living room.

'Go and see who it is,' I hissed at Margaret.

'I can't,' she wailed. 'I'm scared.'

'Don't be so wet.' I clicked and scrambled out of bed. Margaret immediately followed and crouched down behind me, peering through the crack of the living room door.

'What's up with you then?' Mum said, leaning against the sideboard and folding her arms to cradle her huge bosom.

She was wearing a faded brushed nylon nightie over which she had pulled her mauve cardigan. Her face was red and bloated. She'd had a few that night.

'I've come back,' said my father, hanging his droopy head. He looked filthy, as though he hadn't bathed or shaved for weeks. His hair was streaked silver and brown, greasy and stained by tobacco smoke. And his face had at least a week's growth of beard on it, patchy and uneven, decorated by bits of food.

'Huh!' my mother laughed. 'That's a joke. Whatever makes you think you can do that?'

'It's the only decent decision I've made for years.'

'Don't make me laugh. Everyone else has had enough of you and now you've nowhere else to go, you think you can come swanning back whenever it pleases you.'

'I wouldn't call it swanning' he mumbled.

'That's true. You look bloody awful. What's this thing? A piece of old carpet?' Mum grabbed my father's tatty old herringbone coat and gave the lapel a tug. 'Oh God, you stink like a skunk. There's some baths in Ipswich, you'd better get yourself down there fast.'

'Couldn't I stay here?'

'No you bloody well can't.'

'But it's late. Freezing out there.'

'You should have thought of that before. I didn't invite you.'

'But the child needs a father.'

'You should have thought of this eight years ago. It's your own bloody fault.'

Suddenly my father began to wobble; he threw out his knobbly hand and slammed it on top of the fridge to keep his balance. Mum glared at him. 'Still up to your old tricks I see. Well you can't fool me, so bugger off.'

A groan began to surge from his belly and rumble up his throat until it finally burst out of his mouth like the cry of a wounded hyena. He began to shudder inside the layers of clothing that swamped his spindly body, lurching every second as though something were prodding him inside.

Margaret and I looked at each other, holding our hands over our mouths, and then scampered back to bed and threw ourselves across it, screeching with laughter.

'Shut up you two,' shouted my mother. 'And you can get out.' She went to the door and pulled it open. A freezing blast of air swept through the caravan. 'Out,' she snapped again at my father. 'You look pathetic. Now get out. Out, out out.' The last three words rose in pitch as Mum began to prepare for one of her hysterical outbursts that could have left us all anywhere between here, Heaven and Kingdom Come.

My father must have remembered. He left very quickly. And the door was slammed and bolted behind him.

'Who was that man last night?' I asked the following morning. Of course I knew who he was. I had guessed before he said a word about me. But I still asked the question, to see what my mother would say.

'Just your father,' she answered, plonking a bowl of cereal down in front of me. 'Now get that down you before I shovel it in.'

The visit had obviously disturbed her. Her mood in the morning was always a reflection of the night before. If she went heavy on the booze, she was bad-tempered and grumpy. If she stayed sober and got an early night, everyone's life was a lot easier. She was tolerant, patient and loving. She was herself.

That November morning was particularly cold and windy; the sky was a dirty white sheet draped from one side of the world to the other, without a single gap to let the sun through. The muddy grey sea crashed into the shore, its waves welling up in frothy crescendos before being sucked back into the currents below.

When I saw my father sitting against George Jarvis' blue

boat, I carefully laid down the seaweed I had been collecting on the beach and tip-toed over to him. My God, he looked dead, sitting there, slumped against the side of the boat. He must have been trying to take shelter from the wind. Why hadn't he climbed inside the boat? It might have saved him. Instead, he was dead.

His skin was yellow and wrinkled, like a corn-fed chicken's. His mouth open, gaping, with a grisly old tongue hanging over a few rotten teeth. I didn't touch. I wanted to shut that mouth but didn't dare. He might have come alive and swallowed me up in one.

I decided to sit down next to him. Not too close. I didn't think he would mind. After all, I was his daughter. I did have my rights. Even though the boat sheltered us from the wind, it was cold. Icy gusts of wind wound their way around the bows and lashed against us. My hands were numb and I couldn't feel my bum at all. It seemed inevitable that I would catch piles.

I only sat there for a few minutes and, to be honest, nothing happened. I couldn't believe that this man was my father and even if he was, so what? My mind was blank. All I could think of was my cold bum.

And then I suddenly became very aware that I was sitting next to a corpse. It didn't seem to matter who it was any more. 'I think I'd better go now,' I mumbled, beginning to feel afraid. 'Mum told me not to be too long. I've been collecting seaweed, you see. For my pictures.' I struggled up and took one last look. Were those the beginnings of his brains I could see in his mouth, I wondered. Or did brains go to Heaven with your soul? I stood there for a moment; I expected a sign, a bow, a grin, a blink, anything. But nothing happened. He really was dead.

Terrified, I suddenly turned tail and scuttled off along the beach, forgetting all about the seaweed which was still lying in a neat little pile beside him.

By the time I got back to the caravan, the sky had begun

to turn grey and the wind was whipping itself up into a storm. The waves swelled, glistening in a strange light that made everything seem unreal, like a dream. I didn't feel there at all. Some great force was about to engulf us, swallow us up. The end of the world was nigh, the caravan a figment of my imagination, its rotten, chipped body gleaming like an alien as it sat there on the beach.

As I climbed the rusty steps to the door, my mother grabbed the handle from the inside and yanked me in. She'd been cooking; the caravan was warm and smelt of biscuits browning in the oven. 'I thought I told you not to leave today,' she said, hauling me into the living room. 'There's a storm coming up and you know damn well you shouldn't be out.'

'You never said anything.'

'I did.'

I griped in protest and then sulkily shuffled over to a small table where my sister had once again done the carthorse jigsaw. I was fed up with the wretched thing. Did she never tire of it? I knocked the edge of the table and the whole thing went flying. Margaret was in the other room.

That morning, while the wind raged around us, we sat in our battered space bubble listening to the caravan groan and strain. It was very cosy. A fire crackled in the stove, giving out a wonderful glowing heat that disappeared up a metal funnel and out through the caravan roof. Next to the stove were two shelves on which there stood a collection of books, mainly reference books, books of value. Mum always threw away the rubbish she read. With the books was a small collection of silver antiques: a pepper pot, a salt dish and spoon, a couple of napkin rings, a mirror and a hairbrush with a silver-plated handle. Next to the silver was a mahogany writing box and next to that was a large Art Deco clock in the shape of a stumpy coffin with a very loud tick.

As the clock ticked, I lay on the grubby beige hearth mat

and read. Margaret was putting the carthorse jigsaw back together again and kicking the leg of the table in a very irritating way.

Mum was cooking. Making a stew, chopping onions and swearing as a stream of tears came running out of her little brown peepers. Neither Margaret nor I took any notice of her: everything had to be a drama for our mother. Otherwise she barely knew she was alive. That's what she said.

I hadn't mentioned finding my father at all. I probably would have, had my mother not hauled me into the caravan so viciously when I got back from the beach. But she hurt my arm and then finished me off with a clout round the back of the head so I decided not to tell. Why should I? And then, of course, as my mood improved and Mum became more even-tempered with the rhythmic chopping of the onions, it became too late to say anything.

So I decided to leave it and not do anything at all. Someone would find him eventually. When the storm died down, the fishermen would be out and they'd certainly trip over him. I put down my book and went over to the window. Kneeling on the bench and resting my chin on my folded arms, I stared out and watched the squall hurl bundles of seaweed across the stony beach. The white tips of the waves soared and fell, climbed and crashed into the chilly mass of surging grey washing-up water. I could see the end of the world. I could watch the tiny black freighters, miles out, tumbling and rolling along the horizon, drawing an invisible line between the sea and the sky. What was on the other side of the horizon? Surely no one goes to sea just to see the sea. You can see the sea on the shore.

And that was the hum of the day.

They didn't find my father until the next morning.

Margaret and I sat at the table, laboriously shovelling spoonfuls of cornflakes into our mouths. She would not stop imitating me. I couldn't even eat my breakfast in peace; when I looked up she was sitting in exactly the same position as me, one elbow on the table and a spoon sticking out of her mouth. I scowled. She waggled the spoon with her tongue. I took my spoon out and stuck out my tongue. She did the same. It was the school holidays and, as usual, after the first week we all began to get on each other's nerves, like three goldfish cooped up in a bowl.

Margaret was three years younger than me, a plain child with straight brown hair and a pallid complexion. She was by far the plainer of us two and even though people took me for a gypsy, I was proud of my thick dark hair and olive skin. It gave me a rather continental look. Whilst I had inherited some of Mum's looks, Margaret had the same tendency to get fat. At six she was a real roly-poly, a little dumpling that strutted around after me, never giving me a moment's peace. There's nothing worse than a fat child, I used to think, nothing quite so ugly. Sometimes I tried to get them to diet. They just wouldn't stop eating.

Of course no one liked Margaret. Not so much because she was fat, but because she turned into a spiteful little brat. She told tales at school, she lied incessantly, she made up stories, it was impossible to tell what was fact and what was fiction because most of her stories contained some minute grain of truth which was then blown out of all proportion.

The favourite was her father who, it is true, was a G.I. from the nearby American Air Force base. The G.I., who Margaret insisted was an officer, was conveniently posted to Germany shortly after Margaret was born and took no interest in either Mum or the baby. In fact, he had several children dotted round Europe, all with different mothers, all little more than a symbol of his virility. Many times I caught Margaret holding forth about her American parentage, swearing that one day her father would return for her and they would go 'home' to the States, where she belonged. All this at six. I had to laugh.

Mum was sitting at the table with us, leafing through a magazine as she munched a piece of buttered toast. She quickly flicked through the pages, barely looking at them, then sighed and flung the whole thing on the floor. We always had a battered collection of magazines strewn about the place. Mum used to pick them up from the surgery and accidentally walk away with them. The receptionist saw, but she was a young woman in her first job and too afraid to say anything. Mum stretched out her legs under the table and threw her arms up behind her head clasping her podgy hands together. She then let out a windy sigh, looked around her, mumbled 'pigsty' and proceeded to eat. And eat and eat and eat. Often for an hour or so, rummaging through the cupboards like an animal, devouring all she could find, ripping biscuits from their packets, shovelling handfuls of crisps, cereal, cake, anything to fill the bottomless hole inside her.

At that time my mother's real problem was food. Often she would gorge into the night and spend the next day feeling guilty about it. I'd seen her try to make herself sick a couple of times, her vast body squeezing out of the window as she frantically poked her finger down her throat, retching until huge slimy chunks of food flew out of her mouth like cannonballs. She had binges, good times and bad times. Sometimes she was fine and the pounds dropped off. And then something would happen, the most trivial thing, and it would trigger off another binge. It was a vicious circle. She stuffed it down, felt guilty, then she ate more to smother the guilt. Sometimes she was happy, usually grumpy. She didn't like the way she was, didn't like the way she looked, and that was hardly surprising. She was fat and bloated most of the time, with long wispy hair spreading down over her podgy shoulders to where her bra strap cut a fatty wedge into her back. She nearly always wore black or, worse still, brown. And she seemed to be immune to the cold, wandering around in the middle of winter wearing a T-shirt and nothing on her feet. We thought the fat kept her warm.

And then there was my father. Lying there in his brown herring-bone coat against the bows of a bright blue fishing boat.

Suddenly there was a rap on the window and the witch-like face of Molly Johnson loomed like an apparition. We all looked up, startled, and then Mum shoved a couple more biscuits into her mouth and crashed over to the front door, knocking the stool over.

'They've found a goner down on the beach,' said Molly as fast as her lazy Suffolk drawl could take her. 'Just now. Just ten minutes ago. It were George Jarvis that found him.' Molly stood outside on the step, drowned by a heavy brown mackintosh and a purple woolly hat pulled down over her ears. The storm had left us with its sediment, grey sky and drizzle that fell miserably, constantly, blurring every outlook. Molly turned her head and tried to peek inside the caravan; no one except George Jarvis and Miss Stiff-finger had ever been in there. Everyone in the village wondered what sort of state it was in and how a woman could possibly bring up two children in such a confined space. They didn't know my mother.

'Who is it then?' Mum asked, standing in the doorway, her mouth clogged up with a pulp of biscuit. She moved slightly to the right to block Molly's view.

Molly twisted her mouth, annoyed, and then returned her thoughts to the drama in hand. 'That's the thing. No one knows him.'

'Well is he young? Old?'

'I don't know. I've only just heard myself. And I was passing, so I thought I'd drop in on the way.'

'Right. I'm coming with you.' Mum slammed the door, leaving Molly standing on the step, her wrinkled face screwed up in fury.

As drama came all too infrequently to Saltingford and death made her nervous, Molly had to wait. She wasn't going to miss out, even if she did have to go with my mother.

Margaret and I were off our chairs and diving under the table to find our boots and coats in a second.

'Where do you think you're going?' my mother snapped.

'We're coming.'

'You're not.'

'Why? You're going.'

'That's different. You're children.'

'We're not.'

'You are.'

Margaret found one of her boots and flung it across the floor in anger. Then she slammed her fist on the rug and, twisting over onto her belly, lay on the floor and wailed. As I had no intention of missing out, I calmly laid my boots on the floor and sat on the bench watching Mum get ready and Margaret in her tantrum.

Mum knew. She glared at me for a second, raised her eyebrows and continued to blunder around the house pulling on her sheepskin jacket and boots. Her face was pale and anxious, her hands shaking as she fumbled with the zips on her boots. In the end she gave up and stumbled out of the caravan with the leg of one boot hanging over itself, flapping around her shin.

I left half a minute later.

As soon as I had shut the door behind me, a tremendous wail reverberated from the inside of the caravan. It was Margaret. She was too young to go, only six. I was nine and it was my father. A totally different matter. I jumped down the steps, pushed my hands into my pockets and, walking briskly towards the beach, turned back to wave at a red blotchy face that was pressed against the caravan window, staring morosely after me.

I began to crunch across the beach as fast as I could. The

wind was against me and a sheet of white mist hung in the air like blotting paper. I couldn't see much; boats loomed ten yards ahead, inky blobs on the clean white sheet that enveloped us. I couldn't even see the sea; I could only hear the waves crashing onto the shore sending a fine carpet of shingle shimmering across the sand. A muffled foghorn was blaring away; it came from somewhere, a long way out, or maybe not. It was hard to tell. The mist had devoured everything, leaving our senses groping in the fog. We were all floundering in a giant bowl of semolina.

As I approached the gathering on the beach, individual forms became more distinct and at five yards I could recognise everyone. About ten people stood in a semi-circle around the boat which seemed almost colourless.

George Jarvis was there, it was his boat and he had found the body. Three of his mates were there too. They had plodded along the beach with him to check the boats after the storm. A couple of fishermen's wives had also arrived and they stood with Molly making all sorts of exclamation noises and jabbering their pants off about who it might be and how he managed to get there. Mum stood alone, away from the huddle, staring down at the body and shifting awkwardly from one foot to another. Her face was fixed, a deep ridge furrowing between her curled brow, her eyes tiny and piercing as she focused on my father.

The body had not moved. It looked colder, stiffer and quite, quite dead. A frozen carcass, crumpled up against the side of the boat. Brittle like a china doll with its mouth still gaping. His hair was not ruffled by the wind, it lay flat against the skull. The mist did not settle on his shrivelled yellow skin. There was nothing there. Just an empty shell.

Ron, George Jarvis' son, was there, with his bicycle. He stood away from the crowd, staring down at the body, holding onto both handlebars. He was a tall, stocky boy with very square features and a low brow that sloped down his forehead and landed in a clump of bushy eyebrows. His head was a mass of spiky black hair and cocked to one side as he stared and stared.

I always liked Ron. He was a gentle boy who kept himself to himself, always standing away from the crowd, his eyes lowered, his faithful bike at his side. Some people thought he was thick (idiot) too, but not I. Ron was sensitive: he had his own special affinity with the world. He was a genuine human animal; not thick, but bright and intelligent. That's why he spent so long staring at my father.

George Jarvis straightened his poncho and yawned. The lifeboat had been called out that night and he hadn't managed to catch more than a couple of hours' sleep. 'If the police don't get here quick, we'll all end up like him, froze to death,' he said grumpily.

'I wouldn't mind if we knew who it was,' said one of the wives.

'What difference does that make?'

'Well at least you'd know who you were hanging around for.'

'You'd be here anyway.'

'Not necessarily.'

'Don't make me laugh.'

Suddenly, I heard the sound of brisk footsteps crunching over the beach behind me. Turning, I saw the bulky figure of Miss Stiff-finger materialise at ten, five, two yards. She stopped beside me, put a hand on my shoulder and then strode forward to look at the body.

I was the only child in the village that Miss Stiff-finger liked. In the summer I used to hang around her garden and ask questions about the weeds she ferociously plucked from the soil. She spent hours out there on her hands and knees, peering at her precious flowers through a monocle which dangled from her neck like a pendant. When she lifted the monocle, her eye grew through the glass, the pupil expanded, tiny red veins zig-zagged across the stained, yellow eyeball. I always watched. I always asked questions. And she liked to answer.

She treated me like an adult, or so I thought. She made no allowances for me as a child – I was expected to remember everything she told me. In fact, she took it upon herself to instruct me in what she felt was lacking in my upbringing: manners, gardening, politics, literature, geography, history, the world and everything about it. She was the perfect father.

'Of course it would have to be my boat,' George Jarvis grumbled as Miss Stiff-finger put the monocle to her eye and bent down to examine the corpse.

'Well, it's got to be somebody's,' she snapped, then looked up and around at the mournful gathering. 'Dead!' she pronounced. 'Most definitely dead.'

A vision of my father hanging from a meat hook in one of Miss Stiff-finger's shop windows passed through my mind. Another carcass, I thought.

I looked over at Mum, who was staring down at him, my father. 'Just another bastard' she always said, even though she had loved him once. But he had let her down. And now he had let himself down too.

'What do you reckon it was?' George asked, stroking his bristly chin, still staring at the corpse and then at the boat, looking at each in turn, as though he were watching a tennis match.

'Exposure of course.' Miss Stiff-finger pulled back from the body. 'There's no doubt about it. Who could stand a night out here dressed like that?'

'Oh. So you reckon he's been here all night, do you?' Arthur Matheson, one of the fishermen, chipped in.

'If not longer.'

George scratched his face again. His eyes were screwed up and wrinkled. Like most of the fishermen, he was very superstitious and didn't like the idea of finding a body against his boat at all. It was a bad omen. He sighed deeply and shook his head. 'I don't know,' he drawled. 'Who in his right mind would sit out here on a night like that?'

'Maybe he wasn't in his right mind.'

George shook his head again, clicked and slowly trudged round to the other side of the boat to pull back the tarpaulin that had been loosened by the storm.

Then, suddenly, Mum blurted out, 'I know him. I know who it is.'

At first no one said anything. And then the fishermen's wives looked at each other as though they'd known all along, pursed their lips and nodded. 'Might have guessed,' I heard them mumbling.

Miss Stiff-finger turned sharply and stared at my mother, her hands on her hips as she demanded an explanation. Of course she should have guessed too. She was exasperated by the dreadful types Mum was always picking up. And now, here was another. And a carcass to boot. She really had gone too far.

Mum didn't say anything. She was not going to volunteer any more information until the police came. So she stood still, quite solidly and quite stubbornly, ignoring everyone.

The two wives decided to leave. 'Oh well, she makes her bed, let her lie on it,' I heard them mumble as they trudged off. 'Might have guessed, can't think why it didn't occur to me before. Obvious really, in't it?'

Miss Stiff-finger was also irritated by Mum's silence. 'I suppose someone has called the police.'

'Oh yes,' Arthur Matheson drawled. 'Ages ago, from the coastguards'.'

'Well then. You'll just have to wait for them to come.' Miss Stiff-finger stared at my father again. 'If you ask me, it's the drink,' she said. And with that she turned and briskly walked away.

Once Miss Stiff-finger had left, the remainder of the gathering felt abandoned. They had become bored with looking at an empty shell of a man and began to break away from the boat and trudge back up the beach, blurred shadows moving through the mist. 'Nothing we can do now,' they grumbled. 'No point just standing there, is there? Not gonna bring him back.'

'Stand there much longer and we'll end up the same.'

My mother and George Jarvis stayed with the body. I stayed too. I walked over to Mum and put my hand in her coat pocket, clutching her cold gloveless fingers. She needed me. That dead man was the link that had brought us together in the first place. We had to be there for him, to see him on his way.

'Do you think our father suffered?' I asked Mum one day, as we walked along the road back from the village. I always called him 'our father'; he seemed old and decrepit enough to be her father too.

'Sometimes you have to,' she replied. 'Just to be sure you're ready to move on.'

'Move on where?'

'To the next stage. The next part of the journey.'

It was a beautiful, clear sunny day. The icy January air was quite still, warmed by the sun which had set like custard in the cloudless, pale blue sky. It could have been summer. The sun breathed life into the naked hedgerows that had been stripped by the long winter months. Stretched out behind them lay acres of deep brown soil, ploughed into furrows that curled up and down the land, backwards and forwards, hefty soil ridges from which life would soon emerge. And around the fields, lining their borders, was a labyrinth of tiny streams and dykes that sprang from the marshy fenland.

I didn't know what Mum was talking about. The journey! What journey? All I was worried about was the journey back from the village. My hand had almost frozen to the handle of the frayed string bag. It weighed me down so much, I was walking lop-sided. I swapped hands and hopped, skipped and jumped to catch up with her again. She was striding along, a basket in one hand, a carrier bag in the other, perfectly balanced for once, her face lifted towards the sky, a picture of serenity.

'What journey?'

'*The* journey.'

I stamped my foot on the ground. 'Mum!'

She looked down at me and smiled Two large dimples appeared in her cheeks. I called them 'belly buttons'. I loved her when she was fat; she was more of a mum. I loved her dimples.

'*Our* journey,' she finally replied, having pondered on her answer. 'Yes, our journey.'

And the lecture began.

'Who knows where it begins or ends, our journey. But during it, in every life, we have lessons to learn. All of us. Perhaps that was your father's lesson.'

'Not to end up like that.'

She shrugged her shoulders. 'Who knows? Why not? None of us know what God's got in store. Sometimes it has to be like that, because of us. It's us. Our fault. We just don't want to learn.'

'Well I don't think it's fair,' I said grumpily. 'To put our father through all that. To make him die like that.'

'That's the thing,' said Mum calmly, 'it's not for us to say what's right or wrong. Things just are, that's all. If we don't know where we've come from and we don't know where we're going, how can we say what's right or wrong, what should be and what shouldn't? We've no perspective.'

'I don't care,' I grumbled, mumbled, confused and angry. 'I still think it's horrid. And why do we have to live in that horrible caravan when everyone else has got a house? It's not fair. They all laugh.'

'Huh!' Mum laughed and, swinging the shopping round

in the air, began to stride forward taking great paces with her stumpy, knee-less legs. She marched like a Russian soldier. 'Who cares about that?' she said. 'Forget it. The reason for life, is to live. And that's it.'

I didn't answer. It was better to keep quiet when she was in one of these moods. She needed another adult to talk to. But none of the women in the village were interested in the meaning of life. They were only concerned with the price of washing powder or margarine, or in organising jumble sales. 'They've got brains, but they don't know how to flex them,' Mum used to say.

My mother was a vicar's daughter and grew up in a small village near Poole in Dorset. My grandmother had been a practical and aloof woman who concerned herself more with the running of her husband's parish than with her family. My grandfather, on the other hand, was a small frail man who died at fifty because he didn't belong in this world. It upset him. The violence and pollution and corruption. It was too much for him. And when he finally saw these evils through the thinly guised fabric of his own order, he slowly began to deteriorate. His faith in God, a good and loving God, never faltered. But his faith in mankind did. Slowly disintegrating, it crumbled away from his heart and meandered down through his intestines until it died in his colon, a cancerous and consuming growth that had almost completely eaten through his body.

When he died, Mum left the vicarage. It wasn't that she and my grandmother didn't get on; they were just different. Her father had adored her, encouraged her independence, her free spirit. He spent hours with her in his study, philosophising, theologising, reading the Bible. And when he died, nothing was the same again. It couldn't be. Not even the Bible.

'Everything was changing then, you see,' said Mum as

we walked along the coast road. 'With the Sixties on their way, liberation was the name of the game. So it wasn't difficult for me to leave Poole. When I arrived in Portsmouth I found a squat and moved in, straight away, just like that, with seven others. Unfortunately one of them was your father.'

'Was he handsome?'

'Well, in a ragged sort of way. I thought he was. I was mad about him. But then I was ready to be mad about anyone, that's how it was you see.'

'I see.'

'You don't.' Mum grinned and nudged me and we strode on.

As we turned the corner and the sea came into view, two massive USAF helicopters clattered over our heads, their whirling blades sending the tops of the pine trees into a mad frenzy. They were flying so low we could see the pilots in the cockpits and read the numbers on the choppers' stretched steel bellies. Mum and I screwed up our faces and threw our heads back to watch the two iron monsters pass over. We saw them all the time but never got used to them. No one did.

About six miles from Saltingford was a large American air force base which had been in operation since the war and remained, we were told, for our own protection. Within the perimeters of the base, the United States Air Force had created its own mini-America. Typical American 'lookalike' streets had been built. One-storey houses – bungalows – set in immaculately kept back-yards – gardens. Children of all ages skidded about the sidewalks – pavements – on their bikes. Wives gently cruised down the road in their huge beige station wagons – estate cars – which were stuffed with brown carrier bags from the commissary, their general grocery store that brought them a slice of America in the form of peanut butter and pre-packed waffles. There were schools, gyms, restaurants, bars, shops, cinemas, everything the average American could ever want. Every home comfort was provided. Men were everywhere. All government issue. All the same. Same hairdresser, same outfitter, same teacher, mentality, physique even. They walked separately, in pairs or in groups. They wore dark green fatigues, heavy black boots, caps with long peaks, moustaches, short back and sides and pimples around their necks. It was just as we saw it on the television.

In the past, Mum had had her brushes with the base. Margaret was the result of one of them. During the days of free love and Vietnam, no one wanted to miss out. Everyone wanted everything. And they got it. It was fine for a while but then I think Mum began to get frightened. She didn't know what was happening any more. Didn't know who she was, what she wanted, where she was going. 'Freedom of choice isn't always such a good thing,' she told me later. 'Too much moral choice creates a very unstable society. It's best left to the eccentrics. They know how to deal with it.'

This was the first day I had seen Mum in good spirits since my father's death. She almost skipped along the road, her bulky figure clad only in a black skirt, T-shirt and a purple cardigan that was stretched down over her buttocks. On her feet she wore pumps, black of course, and socks that were meant to coordinate with the cardigan but which clashed terribly. My mother had the worst clothes sense in the world. Clothes meant nothing to her, probably because she barely ever wore anything. I never knew how she kept warm; she was dressed for summer in the middle of January.

Since my father died and Mum had dived into one of her depressions, she had added several layers to her stocky figure. She fed the pain with anything she could get her hands on; sometimes it was food, sometimes booze. Sometimes she would lie on the bench with one arm wrapped around her legs and the other cosseting a bottle of vodka. During these periods she was mute. Deaf, dumb and blind, not only to our needs, but to her own as well.

This was when I had to take over. I took charge of the shopping and cooking and Margaret did the cleaning, under supervision. Occasionally Mum was up to making out a shopping list, although I usually decided what we should eat.

'You might as well put that lot back,' I'd say to Margaret when she plonked her basket on the counter at V.G. Stores.

She didn't say anything. She stamped her foot on the ground and pouted.

'What's the matter? You want your supper in a nose bag?'

'No.' Margaret stamped again. 'Why? It's not fair.' She screwed up her chubby face and blew out her cheeks. 'Mum always lets me.'

'Yes, because she eats it, that's why. We're not going to live off ice cream and cakes all week. And anyway, you're going on a diet. Look at you. You look like that flower pot in Miss Stiff-finger's garden.'

'I don't.'

'You do,' Vera's mother suddenly piped in. She was standing behind the counter and sighed pitifully when she saw Margaret and me wander into the shop on our own. 'I know exactly the one your sister means. There's nothing worse than a fat child. Thank God you don't wear glasses too.'

Suddenly, Margaret swung around and, tensing all the muscles in her face, she glared at Vera's mother, long and hard, piercingly, making the woman feel quite uncomfortable.

Don't you do that to me,' the woman snapped shakily. 'There's nothing worse than an impudent child.'

'What about a "fat" child?' Margaret sneered.

'Leave the basket right here, right now, and wait outside. Go on. Off you go.'

Margaret stuck out a long, fleshy tongue and then shuffled out of the shop.

This staring trick of Margaret's was her latest ploy to put people off their guard. She did it to Mum once but got a whack round the ear so never tried again. She had done it at school to the teacher, once to Father Armitage who wouldn't let her buy a biology book in a church jumble sale, and now to Vera's mother.

'What do you look at them like that for?' I asked as we walked home.

'Like what?' Margaret had salvaged an ice cream from her basket.

'You know. The way you did. In the shop.'

'I don't know. They get on my nerves.'

I turned to Margaret and grinned. She licked her ice cream and when she saw me smiling, began to smile too. And giggle and laugh all the way back to the caravan.

* * *

One day during half term when Margaret and I were sitting in the caravan bored because it was too wet and miserable to go outside, we heard a great deal of cursing and crashing outside the door. It was Mum hauling her green shopping trolley up the steps. Once inside, she began to empty it, pulling out bags of sliced, rubbery white bread, packets of butter, margarine, ham, eggs and cheese. Margaret and I stood watching as she delved deeper and deeper into the trolley like a greedy child diving into its Christmas stocking. 'I've got a plan,' she finally said as she added yet another packet of butter to the mountain of food that was already sitting on the sideboard. 'We can all join in. Keep you two out of trouble.'

Off to work we went making piles and piles of sandwiches, Margaret and I scraping away the top layer of butter and spreading it on the bread. 'Not too much,' Mum said as her mind spun into the heady spheres of profit margins. She was in charge of the fillings, carefully laying a slice of ham on every other piece of bread and cutting off anything that was overhanging the crust. The off-cuts were then added to a small pile which would grow until it was large enough to fill a sandwich of its own. This pleased Mum; this she considered to be pure profit.

On we went, ploughing through bag upon bag of rubbery white bread; spreading, sprinkling, patting, cutting, slicing, chopping. From ham to egg, egg to cheese, ham and egg, ham and cheese, egg and cheese. Margaret and I were covered in butter. Great globules were tangled in our hair, smeared across our faces and grubby hands that had been given only a very token rub under the tap.

I then progressed from buttering to slicing the tomatoes, and every time Mum turned her back Margaret reached out, grabbed a sliver of pink ham and shoved it into her mouth.

'Mum! Margaret keeps eating the ham,' I yelled.

'Stop it, will you.' Mum turned around and whacked Margaret on the back of the legs with a wooden spoon.

Margaret wailed, made a face at me, and we all carried on as before, chattering away, thrilled at the prospect of actually selling these things. The very idea of people paying money to eat our sandwiches was quite beyond Margaret and me. Mum, however, was convinced she had hit on a goldmine of an idea and was already planning a chain of shops that would span the country.

About four miles up the coast from Saltingford lay a massive lump of concrete that had taken over four years to build and was finally open for the business of electricity in 1966. With the power station came a trail of hideous pylons, great lumbering giants with three pairs of arms, that trampled across the countryside towards Ipswich.

No one had wanted the power station. But who would? Especially when plans for its construction were announced so soon after Windscale. Nuclear power was such an unknown quantity. We were all frightened of it. Local lobbying groups were formed: some anti-nuclear, some protesting at the ecological damage it would do to the coastline and some infuriated at having such a monstrosity dumped on their doorstep. Miss Stiff-finger led one of the anti-nuclear groups and spent a great deal of her time wandering around outside the power station with a banner. Sometimes she even clipped through the fences and daubed anti-nuclear slogans on the reactor walls. Of course, no one took any notice of the protesters. The plant was built anyway.

Those for and against the nuclear reactor fell loosely into age groups. The older generation couldn't bear the thought of it (more for aesthetic reasons than any other), and the young saw it as a necessary evil that was easier to accept than fight. Before the power station, there were only two options of work available to the people of Saltingford: the fish market in the nearby town of Rexham, and the iron foundry which brought an uncharacteristic slice of the industrial north to East Anglia. Local manpower was used whenever possible at the power station, and despite the radiation risks, of which everyone was fully aware, situations never stayed vacant for long. The CEGB paid their workers well.

The power station, Mum decided, was where we would make our first 'pitch'. So early the next morning the three of us trudged up to the High Street and waited for the bus that rumbled around the villages, picking up workers and taking them to the plant. The bus stopped at the end of Mead Close, where some of the more senior members of the staff from the plant now lived.

It took almost forty minutes to get to the power station and despite the lengthy journey, the bus didn't warm up at all. We could see our breath as we sat huffing and puffing away. At first it had been fun; we were smoking cigarettes. But then Margaret and I got bored and we huddled up against each other, kicking the seat as our legs were jolted by the movement of the bus.

When the power station came into view, we began to pass small trails of people making their way on foot along the muddy wet verges of the road. Mum prodded me and said, 'That's our market.'

I looked out of the window. But it was so spattered with mud and filth I could hardly see a thing. I turned to Mum and nodded encouragingly.

Mum was sitting in a seat on the other side of the aisle from Margaret and me. Her eyes were everywhere, her mind alert, not missing a trick. On her lap sat a contraption she had spent half the night putting together. Made out of cardboard and string, it was like an ice cream tray usherettes use in cinemas. Hers was full of sandwiches, piled up, sorted into fillings and neatly arranged. She looked very proud.'Now then, what we've got to do is find out where they all go in,' she said, looking round her excitedly. 'We're bound to sell a few before the shift begins. I bet someone's come to work without eating his breakfast.'

'I expect they all go in through the entrance Mum,' I said, beginning to sense an uneasy feeling in my stomach. It wasn't the first time I'd been roped in to one of her fiascos. And it usually took her weeks to recover, not only in her head but financially too. I wondered how the DHSS would wear this story.

'Well of course they do. The thing is, we've got to get inside.' Mum whispered the last few words as though we were plotting our entrance to Alcatraz.

'They won't let us in. Why should they? They don't know who we are.'

'Well we've got to *find* a way, haven't we?' she said, gritting her teeth. She loved it. She loved it until she realised that there was no way the porters were going to let us through the main gates. So she positioned herself by the entrance and proudly displayed her wares to the throngs of plant workers who were beginning to wander through. Most people gave her a wide berth; some laughed, some ignored her completely. And when the last of them had dribbled by, she decided that we should walk down to the beach and wait there until lunchtime.

'They've got a canteen,' I said as we stumbled over the stony dunes.

Mum didn't reply. A thunderous look was fixed to her face as she leant forward to cradle the sandwich tray, protecting it from the wind.

I looked at Margaret, who pursed her lips and grumpily kicked at a stone. She was cold. I was cold. Neither of us dared say anything. Mum was on the verge of her own nuclear explosion.

Lunchtime came and went a non-event.

At three o'clock, one of the porters appeared from the gate house. 'Doesn't look like you're going to have much luck today, does it?' he said. 'Most of us eat at the canteen, you know. Otherwise we bring our own lunch.'

Mum looked up and stared at him, her dark eyes so forlorn, I forgot I couldn't feel my fingers and just wanted to comfort her.

'Here, look, got any ham?' The porter stuck his hand into his trouser pocket and pulled out a handful of change.

'It's all right,' said Mum. 'You don't have to do that.'

'No, go on. I need something for tea.'

Mum looked down at the piles of soggy white sandwiches which had congealed into thick grey lumps. She pulled out a ham and handed it to the porter in her bare hands. 'You can have it,' she said. 'You might as well, I'm only going to throw them away.'

'Come on, fair's fair,' said the porter. And he handed her two bob.

The porter disappeared back into the gate house and the three of us began to funeral march down to the end of the drive to wait for the bus. Mum, her head hanging so low her neck had disappeared, shuffled along almost in tears. And when we began to hear loud sniffing noises behind us, Margaret began to snigger. I elbowed her in the arm and she cried out. Then I stamped on her foot.

Suddenly, Mum stopped right in the middle of the drive and, in a wave of fury, wrenched the sandwich tray from her neck and hurled it into the air. Rounds of ham and tomato, cheese and pickle, ham, egg, egg and cheese went flying into the neat row of conifers that lined the road, the pasty white bread sticking to the branches, slices of tomato pierced by their gleaming young needles. 'Come on,' Mum barked. 'I've had enough of this fucking place. Damn right they should shut it down, bastards that work here. Glow worms. Shit heads. They earn enough and they're still too bloody tight to fork out for a poxy sandwich. Well I don't care, I really don't. I couldn't give a shit.' She threw her arms up in the air and began to stride along the drive, leaving the sandwiches stuck to the trees like Christmas decorations. 'See how they cling to their money,' she ranted, taking a swig from her bottle every few steps. 'That's what happens when you've got it. You become a slave to it. You're better off without, I can tell you. Then you've got nothing to lose. And you can't worry about losing what you haven't got, can you?' Comforted by this, Mum proceeded to tell us about the poor widow who gave the temple her last farthing. It was usual. This story always popped up after a catastrophe.

Already standing at the bus stop was Ron Jarvis's sister, Sharon. She was almost seventeen and had been working at the plant canteen for over six months. She was thrilled when the power station finally opened after so many years of muddy construction and handed in her notice at the foundry straight away. There was nothing there for her. And the power station wasn't a lot better, except that with it came new man-power, and that had to be good news.

Sharon was a real girl of the Sixties; she didn't think twice about nuclear power, nuclear bombs, Vietnam or Hiroshima.

She took it all on board. As far as she was concerned, if it didn't directly affect her, she didn't care.

'You're not going to work at that nuclear place,' George snapped when she announced she was leaving the factory.

'I am.'

'Oh no you're not.'

'You can't stop me.'

'I'd put a bomb under the bloody place if I could.' George picked at the piece of shrivelled pork belly that was sitting on his plate and then looked up and pointed his knife at Sharon. 'That place'll be the death of us all, let me tell you. I don't need to put a bomb under it, it's one already. And let me tell you something else: since that place opened, people aren't buying the fish. They can see the radiation goin' out into the sea, and the fish feedin' from it.'

'That's not radiation Dad,' said Ron, who had been sitting quietly eating his tea. 'It's only the water that keeps the system cool. It's not radioactive. It don't touch nothing.' Then he shut up again. Ron never said much at mealtimes. They were usually dominated by his father and sister bickering at each other. And his mother could never sit down for more than two minutes at a time; up and down, up and down. She had left the table ten minutes ago and he could hear her vacuuming upstairs.

'Listen to mister know-it-all,' sneered Sharon.

Ron blushed and looked down at his pork belly.

George was oblivious to what was going on between his son and daughter.

'That's what they say,' he said. 'Of course they'd say that. And even if it's true, it puts people off. You ask down at the market, sales are down over fifteen per cent.'

'Oh bollocks. In six months' time everyone will have forgot it even exists,' said Sharon throwing her knife and fork on the plate and standing up, noisily scraping her chair back. 'That was disgustin'.'

'Ungrateful cow,' George mumbled. He couldn't stand her

or his wife. He often spent more time down at the caravan with us than with his real family.

'Anyway,' said Sharon, before she made her grand exit. 'You fishermen won't suffer. We all know you're getting paid off.'

George turned red and slammed down his knife. But it was too late, she was gone.

To Sharon, clothes, money and Jimmy, her American boyfriend, were important. She was proud to be the first girl in Saltingford to wobble down the High Street in stilettos and a mini skirt. And she revelled in parading Jimmy through the village, dangling on his arm, for all her friends to see. She loved Americans. She loved their brash ways and good looks, she adored their money and sense of fun. All the time was party time and on Saturday night a special bus (called 'the cattle truck') was laid on to take all the local girls to the dance at the base.

Every girl in Saltingford saw an American as her passport out of the village. The aim was to bag one and marry him as soon as possible. Sharon already had her technique down to a fine art; she knew exactly how long to keep them hanging on. She didn't care if they called her a prick teaser, they always went back for more. Jimmy was mad about her; he knew what she was after, but every time he started to get disillusioned she let him go just a little bit further. He couldn't say no. It was driving him mad.

I thought Sharon was absolutely marvellous and had a huge crush on her. Standing at the bus stop, she ignored all three of us. Then Margaret made matters worse by showing me up and picking her nose. I kicked her again.

When the bus came, I dragged Margaret out of the window seat so that I could sit and stare at Sharon who was filing her nails three rows in front of me. I couldn't see much. Only her thick, dark hair which was cut in a very straight line below her shoulders. When she turned her head, I could see her face. Her long pointed nose and thin sallow cheeks covered in pale, cement-like powder. She wasn't attractive in a pretty or beautiful or stunning way, but she certainly had something. I couldn't take my eyes off her. And when the bus finally trundled into the dimly lit streets of Saltingford and pulled up to a jerky halt, we five remaining passengers had fallen asleep. The bus driver levered himself out of his seat and holding the small of his back with both hands shouted, 'Wakey, wakey. It's the end of the line.' I wiped my eyes and looked over at Sharon, who was fast asleep with her head resting against the cold bus window, her mouth wide open and a stream of dribble running down her chin. I was most disappointed. Disappointed that Sharon should need to sleep, let alone dribble.

* * *

Every week Mum would take Margaret and me along an overgrown bridle path that wound its way round the fields to Molly Johnson's cottage. The purpose of the trip was a bath. And every other Sunday a hairwash. We didn't have a bathroom in the caravan, only a sink and a toilet which flushed by manually pumping water into the cistern. Mum was always screaming at us for leaving our 'doings' in there.

Molly Johnson was the mean, witch-like creature who had dragged my mother along to see my dead father. She liked to think of herself as a saintly character who wouldn't even do her washing on a Sunday. However, such virtue soon went to pot when contested by two shillings. She couldn't take her little rats' eyes off the shiny coin which Mum brandished before her, tempting her away from her wishy-washy morals. 'Satan incarnate,' I had heard her call my mother when they fell out on the beach one freezing cold day while Molly's fishing rod waggled in the wind as she hoped to catch a free meal or two. Some say she ate fried seaweed with it. And tried to sell cuttlefish to tourists. The woman was obsessed with money.

Molly's cottage sat behind a row of fields, halfway up a slope which wasn't steep enough to be a hill but raised the cottage so that it could be seen from the beach. The cottage was a tumbledown affair. The exterior walls were covered by grey plaster and looked like mud. No one would have put it past Molly Johnson to have built it of earth had it not already been made like that several centuries ago. The roof was a mass of chipped and broken tiles held together by thick green moss. Every time we stood under the porch, waiting for Molly to limp over and open the door, we expected to be buried by a landslide of tiles – anything could have set them off. And then there was the garden. The garden had no boundaries at all. It was an area of pale worn grass that had a couple of paths stamped through it and which merged with the surrounding fields. The farmer who owned the land didn't seem to mind. Molly had a scrawny old white goat that wandered around at its leisure, pulling up tufts of stale dry grass. I could never understand why it stayed. It was never tied up and always looked so sad and unhealthy, mooching around in its motley coat that was covered in burrs. It didn't even have a name.

Mum had made an arrangement with Molly. She would pay her two shillings per bath and this would include the extra hot water needed for the hair wash every other week. Sometimes, when Mum was on one of her benders, she would forget about the bath and Molly Johnson would come storming over to the caravan demanding her money because she had kept the bath free for us and could have let it go to someone else had she known we weren't going to turn up. 'Don't be so fuckin' stupid,' Mum sneered, certainly not too pissed to be taken in by that one. And then she slammed the door in the old woman's face.

Despite the hatred that existed between Mum and Molly, Molly still could not resist the two shillings and she grudgingly took us back when Mum sobered up. Of course Mum would never remember anything about the incident and always thought Molly most ungracious. But as the months since my father's death passed and Mum started to lay off the booze, our trips to the cottage became more regular and we made our family pilgrimage every Sunday morning, towels and soap in hand.

One day, when we arrived at the cottage, it became apparent that something was on Molly's mind. Her shrewd little mouth was twitching when she opened the door, her nobbly old fingers flitting nervously around with each other. 'Come you in,' she said, almost smiling, trying to be welcoming in a rather sickening sort of way. Mum looked down at me, raised her eyebrows and we all traipsed into the cottage, wondering what was coming next. Molly took her place by the fire and looked down into the empty black grate. 'Right then,' she said, having obviously rehearsed this speech. 'Well I've been thinking. . .' Mum nudged me and I nudged her back, smirking. 'Yes, I've been thinking,' said Molly again, beginning to fumble with her apron strings which she decided to untie in order to remove the apron and appear more business-like. 'You see . . . well now . . . well, you know the price of hot water's going up and the electric in't the cheapest form of heating by any means. Well, we don't have a choice here do we? If they brought the gas down, I'd have it. Anyway, from now on, I think, every other week, that half a crown would be fairer, for a hair wash.'

None of us replied. We all stared at Molly, who stood by the fireplace looking very uncomfortable. A strand of long grey hair suddenly dropped out of her bun and collapsed around her shoulders. 'You see,' she said, unable to bear the silence any longer, 'there are three of you and that means three heads to wash and three heads take a lot of water. Last time there was no hot water left for me. I couldn't even wash up. Had to wait for the tank to heat up again and that takes an age.'

'Well. What do you think girls?' said Mum. She knew this would irritate Molly. Molly hated children.

Margaret and I shrugged our shoulders and then looked smugly at Molly, who was infuriated that we should be consulted in such a matter. She gritted her dentures and glared at us.

I shrugged my shoulders. 'Don't see why not. It sounds reasonable enough to me.'

'All right,' Mum sighed. 'Why not? But that's starting from next week.'

'Very well,' Molly replied, thinking herself most generous.

So it was settled. Mum, Margaret and I wandered off to the bathroom, leaving Molly standing by the fireplace gurgling with delight at her success. She had expected a battle, but the whole thing had proceeded smoothly and reached a most satisfactory conclusion. She resolved to open a tin of pilchards that evening in celebration.

With three outside walls, the bathroom was always freezing, even in summer. It was on the ground floor and faced north, jutting out of the back of the cottage. There was one tiny frosted glass window which was covered with a thick layer of muck and barely let any light into the room at all, so we always ended up trying to put on each other's clothes. Light may not have managed to enter the dingy bathroom, but the smell of the goat did. Just outside the window was its shelter, which was a sort of kennel on stilts. Even when the goat was roaming around the other end of the garden, even when we closed the window, the smell still overpowered us and Margaret and I made burbling noises with our lips every time we entered the bathroom. We reckoned the walls were impregnated with that smell.

The two shillings that Mum paid to Molly only covered the price of one bathful of water. And Molly had drawn a line around the bath underneath the overflow to mark how far we could fill it. 'Of course, you needn't fill it that full if you don't want to,' she said. 'Not everyone likes a deep bath.'

Although Mum was more or less off the booze by this time, she was still gorging herself with food and I could measure her size by her baths. I sat on the edge watching her wallow like a hippo in the murky water. The white blubber loved it, floating in the water, rippling against the chipped enamel sides, thick sheets of stodgy pasta. She could have just floated away. A look of sheer bliss spread across her face as she lay there.

It was a peaceful scene. I sat on the edge of the bath watching my mother's contented face through the cold, steamy air. Margaret was sitting on the floor, looking through a book that was upside down and back to front. Of the three of us, she was the only one still fully dressed. I was in my vest and pants and sat shivering with a towel over my shoulders, hoping Mum wouldn't fall asleep as she often did.

Suddenly the greasy features of Ron Jarvis appeared through the open flap of the window. I spied him first and yelped in horror when I saw his gawking eyes drill into my mother, devouring her, in his clumsy adolescent way.

At first Mum thought she was dreaming. And then a look of terror began to pass over her face and she started to flap around in the bath like a helpless cow, unable to get up or lever herself out of view. She had become so huge that she was stuck in the tub, totally impeded by her size.

It was a pathetic sight, and one that Ron Jarvis was obviously enjoying. So I went to the window and, grabbing hold of the handle, cracked the glass down hard on his head.

Once I had squeezed Ron out of the bathroom like a blackhead, I turned round and saw Mum standing behind me. Her great blubbery, rubbery body was shivering and shaking like a pink jelly and she clung to a towel barely big enough to cover her bosoms that hung down like a pair of half-winded balloons. She couldn't speak. Her eyes stared ahead, fixed to the window, her face paralysed. I was shocked to see her shocked. Mum had never been known for her modesty. She was quite used to baring her all to the local fishermen when she was pissed out of her head, everyone knew that. But this was different.

During this episode, Margaret sat quite calmly on the floor, resting a book on her knees and pretending to read it. I bent down and snatched it out of her hands. 'Back to front and upside down,' I said, looking at her. She didn't answer me. She shrugged her shoulders and pulled the book back onto her knees again.

I was sure Margaret had something to do with this episode. After all, how else could Ron have known that we would be there? He could easily have been faced with the hollow frame of Molly Johnson.

That week, Mum and Margaret had had a terrible row. As usual it was about what Margaret was going to wear. She had become particularly attached to a pale blue pinafore dress that tied around the waist. Having been worn for well over a week, the dress was filthy and Mum told her to take it off.

She wouldn't. She would not. She stamped and banged and yelled and jumped and in the end rushed into the bedroom screaming her head off.

'I will not be spoken to like that,' said Mum, her voice shaking with anger. She levered herself out of her chair and marched into the bedroom where she grabbed Margaret's arm and, shaking her, forced her to take off the dress.

'No!' With all her theatrical powers, Margaret opened her mouth and yelled.

In the end, Mum got so furious she ripped the dress off and rolled it up in her hand like a duster, leaving Margaret howling on the bed in her vest and pants, beside herself with fury.

Ron Jarvis was about thirteen at the time and hopelessly lost in puberty. His face had sprouted a cabbage patch of ugly white spots that were caressed here and there by a few smooth strands of wispy dark hair. His hair was always greasy, parted by a thick scalpy line that ran along the side of his head. Like all boys of his age, he was awkward and unfamiliar with his changing body. He had shot up to almost six foot in the past year, his hands were turning into huge fleshy shovels and his shoulders filling out into thick blocks of muscle.

Ron lived in the shadow of his sister, Sharon. And with a mother like Lily Jarvis, he was grateful for any attention he could get, particularly if it was female.

Lily Jarvis charred for Father Armitage. She was a compulsive cleaner, and when she wasn't frantically dusting the worn banisters of the Rectory, she was flying around their council house scrubbing down shelves and grumbling about the filth in the place. Ron barely saw his mother. She left sandwiches out for him and his father in the morning (she had already disappeared off to work) and in the evening only just found time to bang a plate of sausages on the table before clearing off upstairs to polish the windows. Lily was a sour and bitter person who never stopped moaning about one thing or the other: the weather, the post, her bad leg, sore throat, bad ears, bad eyes, whatever. And she had never liked men. George, her husband, had treated her well, but she didn't know how to respond. If a man was kind to her, she saw him as weak. She pushed her husband further and further away until he ended up spending all his time with us or at the King's Head.

The only person Lily ever spoke to was Sharon. While she swept the yard she warned her daughter of the marriage trap, of men and their 'ways'. And Sharon listened, pensively smoking a cigarette, leaning against the grey wall of the house. She didn't need to be warned, she'd learned by her mother's example years ago and had no intention of ending up on her knees, scrubbing other people's floors. She'd rather end up on her back and at least make a decent living. Sharon liked men well enough, as long as they could be of use to her. She drove Jimmy crazy. She knew Lily loved to watch him panting on the end of her lead.

* * *

'What's this, your wedding den?' I asked Margaret one day when I strolled over to the wartime pill-box sunk into the beach by the caravan.

'You can't come in.' Margaret stood by the entrance and put her arms out to stop me from entering.

'What do I want to go into that stinking hole for? It stinks in there. Tramps live in there. They piss all over it.'

'They don't.'

'They do.' I bent down and peered through the narrow door into the dark, concrete chamber. Ron was in there, picking up all the soggy wrappers, fag packets and used condoms that were floating in the putrid water. 'Oh my God!' I exclaimed. 'That's disgusting. I see you've given Ron the best job, as usual.'

'I'm standing guard.'

'Guarding what? Who do you think wants to go in there?' I could see that Ron had turned his back to me, probably ashamed to be seen doing such a menial job for a girl five years his junior. I could never see what he saw in Margaret; he was worth ten of her.

Margaret used to tell him about girls. I knew, I'd heard her spouting forth on the caravan steps (as though she knew anything about the variety he was interested in at her age). 'You see girls aren't interested in fishing,' I heard her say. 'They like to do more interesting things. Like going to the pictures to see a film. Or going to cafes for cakes. Unless they're trying to lose weight. A lot of girls like to lose weight.

They go on diets.'

I shook my head at Ron and began to walk back to the caravan.

'Rosie,' Margaret called out.

'What?'

'When it's nice and cleaned up in there . . .'

'You mean when Ron's disinfected the place.'

'Yes. When it's clean, you can join our club if you like.'

'What, the Stinker's Seven?'

I walked off up the beach, leaving Margaret standing there, probably sticking out her tongue, giving me one of her glares.

A few rays of spring sunlight managed to emerge through the puffy sky that had clouded over since the morning when a clear blue spread was criss-crossed by the exhausts of the American jets as they thundered over. We all swore at them as they crashed through the sky making the air crackle and half deafening us. Even Ron's uncle stormed out of his bungalow with a broom in his hand. He shook it at the planes and then hurled it into the hedge like a spear before disappearing back into the house in a fury.

We never saw him for another two months and the broom stayed right where it landed, stuck in the belly of the hedge.

* * *

School was a bugger. And with the beginning of the new term came two new lots of people to keep our eyes peeled and tongues wagging.

The first to arrive was Lucy Grantham, spoilt brat and only child of Jean and Peter. She was a tall, skinny girl with a bush of wiry red hair and a pale white face that was covered in freckles.

The family moved into Summer's Hill Cottage in Swingate Lane a couple of weeks before the beginning of the autumn term. And although the cottage was small in comparison to its neighbouring properties, it was a dream house to the Granthams. They had moved from a modern, three-bedroomed box that lay on the outskirts of Ipswich. The cottage was slightly set back from the lane and surrounded by a very prickly hedge that blossomed the most lavish spread of purple flowers in the spring. A crop of lush green grass had sprung up from the lawn and thick clumps of flowers set the garden aglow. Once installed, it was a delight for Mr and Mrs Grantham to stroll around their grounds, breathing in the mellow evening air and listening to the crickets chirping away.

Mr Grantham was far too fat. He was only forty-five and had already had a minor heart attack, a warning the doctors had said. A few months before moving to Saltingford he had allowed a thick auburn beard to sprout from his face and this made him look fatter than ever. He looked like an ant-eater with his bristly growth and huge nose protruding from it. And I have never seen such enormous nostrils, vast cavernous things full of curly brown hairs. 'That man's got a beard up his nose too,' I told Mum after I bumped into him at V.G. Stores one day.

Owning a house like Summer's Hill was Peter Grantham's dream. After years of saving their measly teachers' salaries, he and Jean could finally afford to move out of town. They had always hated suburbia. Hated the brick box they had lived in for most of their married life, stuck in a row which was a row between rows, in a suburb of a suburb, a faceless urban desert. Peter called their old house a 'unit', especially in the past few years when they had seen their contemporaries move to larger and more prestigious properties. Once, the 'unit' had suited their wishy-washy socialist ideals. But as time passed they became disillusioned and tired. Tired of fighting. And so they gave it all up and replaced their socialist dream with a capitalist dream, and still weren't happy – until they moved to Summer's Hill.

The other new arrival in the village was also a teacher.

One day she appeared on her black boneshaker of a bicycle, emerging from the sunset with a backpack strapped to her shoulders and a small, battered suitcase fastened to the bike. No one, except Mrs Crabtree the headmistress, knew from whence this creature came. But when she padlocked her bike to the rotten fence that surrounded the Rectory, many saw and all talked.

Father Armitage considered himself far too busy to take a lodger into the Rectory even though he had seven spare bedrooms and never did anything anyway. Everything was done for him. His house was kept by Lily Jarvis, and a committee looked after the church, undertaking everything from organising jumble sales to preparing the dusting rotas and arranging the flowers. All Armitage did was to scrawl out laboriously boring sermons that no mind could follow for more than a minute without wandering. He did, occasionally, conduct the odd confirmation class, but confirmations were rare in Saltingford, most of us didn't even know what the word meant.

What persuaded Father Armitage to take a lodger was the money. The Rectory cost a fortune to keep up and there was no reason why he couldn't hide a person in one of the wings. Addicted as he was to thrillers, his poor vicar's salary meant he had to take what he was offered to support his habit. Although they both vehemently disapproved of each other's lifestyle, he and Miss Stiff-finger did at least share one thing in common. After a while, however, they had exhausted their supply of books (exchanged via jumble sale), and reached a stalemate. There was nothing left to read. Father Armitage was lucky to find a tatty old romantic novel in the 'book box' these days.

The next morning, Lily Jarvis was furious to find the new teacher sitting in 'her' kitchen at the Rectory, munching away at a piece of toast and marmalade as though she owned the place. Of course Father Armitage had said nothing to her, even though she assumed she was to 'do' for this creature too. She had heard of the teacher's arrival the previous day in the Stores, but couldn't believe that she was staying at the Rectory. No one would stay at the Rectory unless she was consulted.

The Goat, which is the name we gave the teacher, sat in the kitchen sullenly staring out of the window into the small vegetable garden which was partially drowned by a large shadow cast by an old red brick wall. The wall was covered in ivy and played host to a spindly honeysuckle that weaved its way around the dusty, crumbling crevices. She had ignored Lily's brusque manner; she was used to it. Very few people took kindly to her, especially women, who could never make her out and tended to feel uneasy around her. It was her appearance: it put people off, she knew. She had never taken any care over it and didn't see why she should.

The Goat's real name was Miss Browning, but we called her the Goat because of the wispy grey beard that leaked from her chin. This was matched by a long straggly mane of hair that slithered down her back like a slimy rug. She had a nervous tic and when she was agitated her thin lips began to twitch; 'ants in 'er pants, nits in 'er lips,' we whispered.

The extraordinary thing about this woman was that she was barely thirty-five. Her smooth white skin revealed barely a blemish. She always wore a green parka jacket which was covered in bird shit, a black hat she pulled down over her head and a pair of green wellingtons. She looked like a troll lumbering through the village, frightening children wherever she went. No one would ever guess that she was a *she*, and a teacher to boot.

So, why did she come?

When Lily Jarvis started to vacuum right outside the kitchen door, the Goat picked up her coffee and left for her bedroom. The two women ignored each other in passing.

The Goat had already unpacked her few belongings and placed them on a glass shelf above the chipped white china sink. They did nothing to warm the chilly room which faced north and remained cold and gloomy even in the summer. She pulled out an old dark blue jumper from the pile of clothes that was sitting on the chair by the window and then collapsed on her bed with Silas Marner; he had already managed to keep her up until three o'clock the previous morning.

Lying there, she rested her head in her palms and looked around the bare whitewashed walls. The long, narrow bed had wheels on it and that morning she had woken to find herself in the middle of the room, having propelled herself across the cold linoleum floor in her sleep. She must have been dreaming; mad, frenzied dreams she still couldn't recall.

The school was in the village, behind the church hall. It was a tiny building with only two classrooms: one for the younger children from four to eight, and one for the big children from eight to eleven. At eleven we sat the dreaded eleven plus; this determined whether or not we were worthy of a decent education at 'the grammar' or if needlework down at the secondary mod. might not provide a better start in life. Mrs Crabtree was by far the most popular teacher and one of the few people in the village that Mum respected; she was a gentle, homely woman whose natural generosity and gift for teaching was not marred by ambition. She took the little ones. We all missed her terribly when we moved up into the 'big' class. That class had seen a succession of teachers who never seemed to stay long. Consequently our class tended to be unruly and disruptive and nearly everyone ended up failing their eleven plus, much to Mrs Crabtree's horror. Naturally, as head, she had to take some responsibility. It didn't help matters when the Education Committee threatened to close the school down: with its twenty-three pupils it simply wasn't economically viable.

When Lucy Grantham found me crawling around the brambles of their hedge, she climbed in too and we immediately became friends.

We made ourselves an earthy den, an igloo, inside the dusty branches of the hedge and sat there scratching shapes in the dry mud, chattering away. Her long skinny legs and unruly bundle of red hair fascinated me. I'd never seen anyone quite so ginger, or so freckly, or so lanky before.

'Ssssh,' she hissed. We crouched down and allowed our stares to follow a pair of corduroy legs as they flapped past us into the drive of Summer's Hill.

It was the Goat. She had been invited to tea by Lucy's parents. They had never met before, but Jean had heard of her arrival and decided to pop an invitation through the Rectory door anyway. Now, confronted by this straggly, tramp-like creature, she was shocked.

Sensing Jean's uneasiness, the Goat started to stammer and suddenly strode uninvited through the door into the sitting room in an almost catatonic fashion. She stopped in the middle of the room, looked around and elected a wooden chair by the window to sit on.

Then she sat, quite still, and waited for tea.

'The most extraordinary woman,' said Jean Grantham in the kitchen.

'Why? What's the matter with her?'

'Look for yourself.'

Peter slightly opened the serving hatch to peek at the visitor. As soon as the door was an inch ajar his eyes met those of the Goat, who was staring back at him in a most indignant way. Peter coughed, embarrassed, and then opened the doors fully and said, 'Hello there. Tea will be served in just a few minutes.' Then he shut both doors and turned to his wife, who was spooning Earl Grey into the teapot, grinning.

'What do we do with her?' said Peter, panicking.

'I don't know.'

Once tea was under way, Lucy and I skulked across the black patio and crouched underneath the sitting room window, our hands clamped over our mouths as we stifled our giggles.

The Goat was sitting bolt upright in her chair, looking most uncomfortable. The Granthams were obviously the very breed of teacher she despised. Pseudo-intellectuals that hated themselves for their own mediocrity yet lacked the conviction to be anything else. Their house epitomised the type: it was overflowing with tatty, second-hand comfort and had been furnished by half the junk shops in Suffolk. The sitting room was dark and womb-like, furnished by an odd collection of scruffy armchairs and a sofa that was submerged beneath a shower of cushions.

Possessions meant nothing to the Goat. As far as she was concerned materialism fell into the same category as religion: she saw both as traps set to control society. Religion created law and order by instilling fear, guilt and the threat of divine retribution. If man didn't punish you, God would. Control.

Material greed could only be fed by money, work, debts, work, worry, work, spending, work. Work, work, work. Control.

She, on the other hand, had nothing. She, the Goat, practised what she preached. Talk was cheap. And it meant absolutely nothing. Action counted and if she couldn't live her principles, she might as well be like everyone else and be done with it in comfort.

Lucy and I quickly established our friendship. We were almost exactly the same age and our different backgrounds sustained our curiosity in each other for some months. We made our home in the hedge at Summer's Hill, turning it back and forth from a shop to a kitchen or the doctor's surgery.

The cottage roof was another favourite haunt. We spent hours rummaging through an endless supply of dusty magazines and clothes, triumphantly brandishing battered cordless irons and old television aerials in the dark, musty air. Once we beat a hasty retreat when a piercing squeal followed by the flutter of wings broke the silence. Lucy screamed and lolloped backwards to the trap-door like a crab. I stayed cool, froze, told her not to be so wet and moved only when the bat had decided to hang itself up for the afternoon again.

Secretly, I knew Mum was glad that Lucy and I were friends. Although she had more or less rendered herself 'classless', she still considered the Granthams more our 'sort' and was pleased to see me naturally gravitating towards them.

Jean Grantham was pleased too. She kept Lucy on a long lead, allowing her to do what she wanted 'within reason' and as long as she did her homework and our noise didn't disturb her.

Of course, Margaret would never leave Lucy and me alone. She used to poke her podgy face through the branches of our den, so we'd throw a bowl of mud at her and run off squealing. She followed us everywhere, always stomping along behind us, somewhere in the distance. When I wasn't around, she had to be nasty to Lucy at school. Twice Lucy had found live bait wriggling around in her sandwiches and once a dead mouse in her pencil case.

* * *

One hot day, the following summer, I was sitting alone on the caravan steps reading and picking at the burnt skin that had curled up on the end of my nose like a dead leaf.

No one was around. Lucy had disappeared to Cornwall for two weeks with her parents, Mum was at the jumble sale in the village and Margaret had wandered off, presumably with Ron.

I read anything I could get my hands on. Between them, Mum and Miss Stiff-finger were guiding my literary progress. Mum would carefully select a book for me from the library van that trundles around the villages bringing literature to the sticks, and Miss Stiff-finger would spend hours browsing through her own bookshelves, fingering the hard spines of each work before moving on. Martha, 'the friend', ignored me. She was usually buried in a piece of furniture, her huge bottom protruding into the air as she clambered around the floor, sanding and polishing away.

The beach was deserted. The sun shone through the clear sky which was only streaked by occasional wispy strands of cotton wool. It was one of the hottest days we had had that year and even the sea breeze failed to penetrate the wave of heat that washed over us. Sweat was seeping through my pores, oozing out of my body in a blanket, drenching my T-shirt and my new green shorts. I pushed my hair away from my face and tied it up into a pony tail. Then I lay back on the caravan steps, closed my eyes and listened to the rhythmic lull of the waves as they gently tumbled into the shore, washing over the multi-coloured quilt of tiny, tiny pebbles.

The Martello Tower sat beside me, a great hulking thing that had refused to budge all these years. Margaret and I had a library of stories set in that tower. It was a fortress of its own secrets that lurked within the dark, acrid space enclosed by walls over six feet deep. For us, the tower created an endless nightmare of warlocks and witches, ghosts and evil spirits, bats, rats and other ghastly souls that sent us into terrified giggles of delight.

There had been reports that a pop star was going to buy the Martello Tower but none of us had seen him. Not even Sharon, who suddenly developed a liking for walks on the beach and was frequently sighted wobbling along the shingle in her stilettos and made up to the nines.

Because the caravan was so sheltered, its site turned into a heat trap during the summer. It was too hot for me, so I left *David Copperfield* and decided to take a walk over to the saltings and see if the seals were out.

Miss Stiff-finger was in the garden fervently stabbing at the stony soil of her flower beds with a rusty old trowel.

She was wearing a dark green apron and a huge pair of green gardening gloves.

'Hello Rosie,' she said when she heard me crunch by. I waved, climbed onto the gate and began to swing backwards and forwards. 'You'll break it,' she sang in a tone specially reserved for me. She never spoke to anyone else like that. She barked at them. 'What have you been up to?' she asked, sitting back on her stool and shielding her eyes from the sun.

'Not a lot. Reading.'

'Well, you could do worse. Have you finished *David Copperfield*?'

'No.'

'Well when you have, I've found something else for you. *Pride and Prejudice*.'

I grunted and, without thinking, climbed back onto the gate again.

'Rosie!'

In the corner of the garden was a pile of banners that said: SAY NO TO NUCLEAR POWER. WINDSCALE – HOW OFTEN BEFORE WE LEARN. NO NUKE'S THE ONLY NUKE. Miss Stiff-finger was preparing an extravaganza of a demonstration at the power station to mark the tenth anniversary of Windscale. The arrival of the Goat and the Granthams had initially been a source of great excitement for her; new teachers had to be new socialists and extra support for the anti-nuclear lobby. However, so far they had been a disappointment; neither party showed the slightest interest.

Miss Stiff-finger nodded at the pile. 'Want to do some painting?'

I shook my head.

Hurt, she began to stab her flower bed again. 'Suit yourself. It's your future. So what are you going to do with yourself instead? Laze about all day, I suppose.'

I shrugged my shoulders. 'Maybe. I'm just relaxing.'

'Relaxing! At your age! You're only ten. I've never heard

anything so ridiculous.'

'Ten and three-quarters,' I snapped. The heat was making me irritable and I had no patience for Miss Stiff-finger's sergeant-major ways. I didn't see why I couldn't relax. Everybody else did. I scowled at her for a moment, watching as she put the monocle to her eye and examined a plant she'd ripped from the soil. 'Darn,' she mumbled. And then realising I was still there, added, 'Run along then. I'm not going to entertain you, I'm sure.'

Annoyed, I jumped off the gate and began to trudge over the beach towards the saltings.

The saltings were a secret place where Mum and I wandered together, she ranting about her 'journey' and I patiently listening. They lay between the beach and the coast road where tiny estuaries of murky brown water flowed between the mud banks that glistened even in the most subdued light. The saltings were the result of a natural reclamation of land; they had been transformed from stony shingle banks to fertile land out of which there curved long, arm-like peninsulas stretching over a hundred yards into the water. Now that the land was turning from stone to soil, it celebrated its fertility with a wash of silvery mauve sea lavender. Sometimes alone, sometimes with Mum, I wandered out to the end of the saltings and stood by the mouth of the river watching hordes of birds circle the shores, swooping and diving, pulling wriggling fat worms from the mud. With the lavender (which Mum had been known to try and sell like a gypsy), I picked long sheaths of sandy grass from the wild, overgrown verges and made arrangements so that we had colour in the caravan all year round.

The seals were there, sprawled out on the mud banks, basking in the sun, their long whiskers twitching, their huge, globular eyes shut. They spent most of their time patrolling the coastline looking for food. When the sun came out, they would gracefully glide through the mouth of the river and haul their huge cumbersome bodies onto the banks, flapping their clipped flippers which always seemed so ineffectual on land.

I lay down and stretched out on the spring lavender, breathing in its delicious musty scent and absorbing the sun through every pore of my body.

An hour or so later I was woken by voices. I sat up and squinted at the mud-flats below. A hundred yards away was the Goat, propped up against the bank, canoodling with Miss Stiff-finger's friend, Martha.

I was so shocked I didn't know what to do.

The Goat had spent that whole year standing at our blackboard, smelling. She scrawled words across it with her smooth, lifeless hands. These hands never changed colour, they never tanned in the summer nor paled in the winter. They were always white, like reptiles' hands. And now I could see those hands clambering across Martha's curvaceous contours.

I had never guessed. Never guessed that the Goat was 'like that'. Never guessed that she was like anything. She had always seemed so asexual. A neuter. Like a tadpole.

Martha was no beauty. All that traipsing around antique fairs had done nothing for her figure, which was portly and rounded, bulging beneath the tight stretch trousers she insisted on squeezing into. She was a bright, bubbly character who always wore bright, bubbly make-up that was glued to her face like a mask. When she moved in with Miss Stiff-finger there had been a huge rumpus in the village. Everyone pretended that nothing was going on, they were so embarrassed they could hardly speak. But of course they did manage a few words, gossip all the time, between friends. They just never said *the word.*

The Goat and Martha were so engrossed in each other that neither saw me cautiously lever myself off the ground and scramble away across the lavender.

'I've got a secret,' Margaret hissed.

When Miss Stiff-finger saw Margaret, she pursed her lips and looked in the other direction. She didn't like Margaret at all, not since she had seen her catapulting birds with stones round the back of the cottages.

I was swinging on the gate again. 'Well, what is it?' I turned to her, annoyed at having my tête-à-tête with Miss Stiff-finger interrupted.

'Wouldn't you like to know.' Margaret was evidently pleased with herself. She pulled out the skirt of her blue gingham dress and danced around the gravel, a huge beam lighting up her face that had already been turned pink by the sun.

'Liar,' I growled and turned back to Miss Stiff-finger.

'Why *did* your finger get stiff?' Margaret suddenly called over the gate.

I nudged her hard. She ignored me. She knew Miss Stiff-finger disliked her. She had started to taunt her too. She didn't seem to be afraid of anyone any more.

'I think you know that story,' Miss Stiff-finger snapped without bothering to look up. She was snipping at the edges of the grass with a long pair of shears.

'I've forgotten,' Margaret whined.

'Shut up,' I hissed. 'You know what happened. It got cut off at the shop.'

Margaret clapped her hand over her mouth and went into peals of laughter, bending over and stamping her chubby little bare foot on the stones.

'Well it's not that funny,' I scowled.

'I think it is.' And then her face went serious again. 'I've got a secret,' she said.

I stared at her, totally infuriated by her behaviour.

'Miss Stiff-finger, why don't you go down to the saltings? The seals are out.'

Miss Stiff-finger looked up and stretched her back, then

squinted in our direction. 'What?'

'Why don't you go down to the saltings? The seals are out. Lying on the banks. Two of them, together.'

I turned and stared at Margaret, hardly able to believe what I was hearing. Miss Stiff-finger looked at me and then at her. Her mind, I could see, was racing, confused, sifting, suspicious.

Margaret stood absolutely still, staring back at Miss Stiff-finger without blinking. 'The seals are out,' she said again. And then she suddenly took fright, let out a tiny squeal and scampered off to the pill-box where she hid all night until Mum went and dragged her out.

The next day, The Goat packed up her rucksack and disappeared as mysteriously as she had appeared. And, alas, after eight years of marriage, Martha too decided to leave. It took her longer to make the move, a couple of months, but as far as she was concerned their relationship had been going off for a couple of years. As far as Miss Stiff-finger was concerned, there was nothing wrong at all. Everything was as it had always been.

'I think you're better off without her,' I said as I wandered around the house helping her decide who would have what. 'She couldn't make a commitment to a paper bag.'

Miss Stiff-finger did not seem comforted.

And I would never be comforted either, not by Margaret, despite all her attempts. I would never forgive her for doing that to poor Miss Stiff-finger.

At school, the Goat was replaced once, and then again. We all grew upwards and, in some areas, outwards too. Wiry pubic hair began to sprout from our young white skin. I hated mine and tried to cut it off. But it insisted on growing back again and finally I gave up and let it do what it had to.

Lessons failed to hold our attention. New games, when we were chased and kissed by the boys, did. They provoked all sorts of stirrings in us. Kiss chase was as thrilling as it was repulsive. And when we crammed into the bike shed, we girls fell over each other for just a peek at a flaccid white willy that waggled in the dark.

Lucy did the honours for the girls. It didn't seem to bother her at all letting the boys stare greedily at her as she stood with her knickers down to her knees. In fact, I think she quite enjoyed it. We were all fascinated by her bush of fiery red pubic hair, and when anyone commented on the colour she always haughtily replied, 'Yes, and with collar and cuffs to match.' We all thought it terribly grown up.

After a while, the Granthams began to have mixed feelings about the friendship between Lucy and me. At first it hadn't bothered them: they were pleased to see her settling into the village and making friends so easily. But then they started to have their doubts. The dreaded eleven plus loomed and Lucy's career plans changed from teaching to being an air hostess and then an actress, probably like Tara King in the Avengers. They didn't understand her change in behaviour. She had always been an easy- going child, then suddenly she turned surly and moody, flying off the handle every five minutes. They were afraid to say anything to her. Fights started: when was she going to do her homework, what time was she going to go to bed, what was she going to wear to school?

When the Granthams discovered that Lucy had failed her eleven plus, they were at a loss for words. It never occurred to them that she could. They simply assumed she would go straight to 'the grammar' where they already knew three quarters of the staff, including the head. It was of no consolation that nobody in our class passed the wretched exam – they hadn't expected any of us to, except Lucy, of course.

A double blow was dealt. Of course it was out of the question that Lucy should go to the secondary mod., so Jean and Peter had to scrape the barrel and find the funds to put her in a private school. They never forgave her for forcing them to send her to a school that was the very antithesis of their principles and, of course, the painful part was that they had to pay for it too.

Lucy, on the other hand, was thrilled at the prospect of going away to school, and as soon as she learnt of her new future she stopped coming down to the caravan to see me. I pretended not to care. Mum had told me all about fair-weather friends who came and went like everybody else. Instead I watched Lucy parading down the High Street in her new uniform, her nose protruding upwards, almost knocking her boater off her head. That didn't mean much either, Mum had said.

As for the rest of us, we continued our education at the secondary modern in much the same vein as we had started it. All in all, most of us had a schooling that was a total non-starter. But so was Lucy's, and they'd paid for her education in more ways than one. At least I'd only let myself down, and maybe not even that.

PART TWO

One hot July day while Margaret and I were sitting on the battered sea wall, our tanned faces tilted towards the shimmering sun, my sister announced that she was pregnant.

I didn't say much. 'So whose is it?' I finally asked.

'Dwight's.'

'Should have guessed.'

'Then why did you ask? Anyway, probably. It's probably his.'

'What's that supposed to mean?'

'Probably. That it's probably his.'

'Well who else's could it be?'

'Oh, I don't know.'

Margaret leaned back on her elbows and turned her face to the sun. The tan disguised her sickly, anaemic look. She was still plain, plainer than ever. And fat. 'It's his, anyway. I know it is,' she said after a few more moments' contemplation.

'Well you'll soon find out. When it's born.'

Dwight was a black American G.I. who lived in Molly Johnson's cottage with two compatriots from the base.

Molly had died three years ago, of meanness. So obsessed did she become with her money that towards the end she barely fed herself. She sat by the cold, empty fireplace huddled up in blankets, refusing to light a fire when an extra cover would do. And the tragedy of it was that stacked underneath a loose tile in the kitchen was a pile of ten pound notes she had saved for a rainy day or 'just in case'.'Just in case' never came and Molly was found sitting in front of her empty black fireplace like a marble statue. She had been dead over a week and no one had known.

The pregnancy wasn't suiting Margaret at all. As she developed into a teenager she had grown even larger. Her face changed only by the most artificial means, yet with all the make-up in the world she still remained plain and unmemorable. Her thin brown hair was shapeless and dull and as her face puffed out, her small brown eyes disappeared further and further into her brow. How she had managed to get pregnant, no one knew. Dwight must have been desperate. Or drunk. Or stoned. Or everything.

When Margaret left school at fifteen, she announced that she wanted to work on the base so that she could be nearer her 'true countrymen'. As she grew older she clung with even greater tenacity to the heritage of her father and claimed that she would not be happy until she too was in America, with an American. She managed to find a job working at the checkout of the base commissary, and after a year or so was promoted to the position of assistant manager. Mum and I almost fell over in surprise and she, of course, became unbearably haughty. For a time she assumed a new air of responsibility. But it didn't last. As soon as she found herself pregnant she relaxed, convinced that she, at least, had managed to secure her ticket out of Saltingford.

'What are you going to do when you have it?' I asked.

Margaret shrugged her shoulders and grumpily kicked her heel against the wall. 'Dunno. Get married I s'pose.'

I raised my eyebrows and stared at her. 'Will you stay on at the commissary?'

Margaret shrugged her shoulders again. 'Depends, don't it? On Dwight. Depends where he gets posted.'

'What about Ron?' I asked.

'What about him?' Margaret snapped annoyed. 'I told you I'm not interested in him.'

For some reason, Ron had still not let go of his fixation for Margaret. His push-bike had grown into a motor-cycle and he now worked as a fitter at the power station. Yet in spite of all these changes he was still living at home and still spending most of his spare time hanging around the caravan, waiting for Margaret to make an appearance. He had recently joined the lifeboat crew which was now captained by his father, George, and had hoped that this might win Margaret's admiration. Every boy wanted to join the lifeboat. It sorted the Saltingford men from the Saltingford boys.

Margaret still wasn't interested. She wanted Dwight. But Dwight didn't want her. He could have any girl he fancied.

'Where's the security in marriage, when you're trapping him into it?' I said. 'That won't make you happy. Or him.'

'I'm not trapping him.'

'You are. He's your ticket out, that's all. Well it won't work. You'll never find security in anyone else until you've found it in yourself.'

'Oh shut up. You sound just like Mum. Thinking you're so fuckin' clever.' Angrily Margaret shuffled off the edge of the wall and landed on the shingle with a thud. 'I'm going in,' she growled and began to laboriously plod across to the beach towards the new hut where we had moved after the caravan roof was blown off one tempestuous night.

Tiny granules of salt lay on my lips, deposited by the light blustery wind that wafted across the beach, warmed by the sun which radiated through the cloudless sky. The breeze dived between the masts of the boats and nagged at the dry fern that sprouted from the rough wasteland. I pulled up my feet and lay full length along the wall; my eyes closed, my body stretched out beneath the sun. How I loved to bathe in the tranquillity of such a day when I could be at one with nature and lose myself in the elements as they caressed me, aroused me, sexually. Naturally sexually. Stroked by the tentacles of the wind, penetrated by the rays of the sun, my skin was alive. Rhythmically, my chest rose and sank in unison with the waves as they rolled onto the shore.

Clothes annoyed me. Sometimes Mum and I would wander along the beach and when we reached a point past the fishermen's limit, strip off and lie down in the water. We loved the touch of the waves as they crept up the inside of our legs, licking at our sweaty flesh. Sometimes I watched Mum lying there, her eyes closed as she lost herself in the sensation of the water.

One day, after lying on the shore for twenty minutes or so, we pulled ourselves up from the sand and wandered over to the earthy cliff that fringed the beach. When we reached the top of the cliff we rolled over a grassy ridge and onto a flat plateau of land. Twelve black missiles confronted us, pointing east, their bodies shimmering in the sun like erect penises. Apart from several layers of fencing there was nothing and no one to protect them. Mum and I looked at each other in horror. Horror at seeing them unguarded and horror at seeing them there at all, in Saltingford of all places.

We turned away and went to sit on the edge of the cliff, where we thoughtlessly kicked the sandy soil and watched it tumble down onto the beach, disintegrating as it fell. Below us were two or three battered boats that had been scuttled in the sand and left to die. 'Boats burial ground,' Mum mumbled, nodding at them. 'Poor things.'

'Poor things,' I echoed and turned back to look at the missiles again. I could hardly believe they were there.

A little later, after a prolonged period of pensive silence, Mum said, 'You know Rosie, perhaps you should think of going farther afield. There's nothing for you here. You've got a good brain. You could do so much more with your life.'

'And what about you?'

'I can look after myself. I know I make a pig's ear of it sometimes, but if left to my own devices, I'm sure I'd be all right.'

I was quiet for a moment, and aimlessly tugged at tufts of wiry brown grass. 'Margaret won't stick around any longer than she has to.'

'Oh Margaret.' Mum flapped her hand in the air dismissing

her. 'Margaret's a pain in the arse. If anyone should stay, it should be her. She hasn't got the brains to do anything else. Whereas you have.'

'I don't know. Maybe.' And then I was quiet for a good deal longer. Mum was right, I knew. I did have a good brain. But what would I do with it? I'd never been ambitious. A career always sounded more trouble than it was worth. The fish market, where I had been working since I left school, hadn't much to offer. But it was better than the foundry, the power station or the base. At least it was a happy place to work. We all had a good laugh behind our stinking, wet tables as we scrubbed and gouged and slit and sliced, recounting one story, one joke, one anecdote after the other. And it was healthy too, with plenty of fresh air and, of course, as much fish as you could stomach.

That had been only the year before.

Since then, Mum had retreated into her shell even more. She had grown fatter and her 'well' periods in between the drinking and eating binges became shorter and shorter. When I wasn't working, I would make a special effort for her: cook her lunch, help her bath and wash her hair, choose clean clothes and generally mother her as though she were an invalid rather than a forty-three-year-old woman who might otherwise have been in her prime. Margaret pulled her down. The two of them were at each other's throats all the time; they both had the same faults they denied in themselves and found totally intolerable in each other. How one or both of them were still alive I don't know. Sometimes I could hear them screaming at each other as I walked back from work along the coast road. The fish wives had nothing on them.

After the caravan had blown its top, we moved into the glorified beach hut which we called 'the pen'. The pen sat on the wasteland at the head of the beach, the last of a row of three huts that was sandwiched between the Boat House and the cottages. It had two rooms, a small bathroom and a kitchen. After the caravan it was a palace to us. Margaret and I still had to share a double bed (we had salvaged all we could from the wrecked caravan) and Mum had a single bed in the living room which also doubled as a sofa, though it never looked like one. The pen also had a wooden porch and a tiny front terrace where we took our chairs in the summer and sat reading, or eating or staring at the clear blue skies and miles of murky brown sea.

After I had digested the news of Margaret's pregnancy, I rolled off the wall and went back to the pen. An ugly table had just materialised in the front room. It stood on four spindly metal legs and had a torn Formica top that was covered in rings and cigarette burns. Around the table were three upright chairs, all with plastic seats in different colours, plus another with a grey metal frame and canvas seat. They all looked suspiciously like the chairs stacked in the village hall.

Mum had managed to drag an old brown armchair onto the terrace and was sunk into the seat, devouring a romantic novel.

'Where did that lot come from?' I asked, nodding at the table and chairs.

'What's it to you?' Mum replied without looking up.

She hated to be interrupted when she was reading. These romantic novels had become almost addictive to her; she simply couldn't leave them alone. They went everywhere with her: to the table, the loo, the bath, and she even had one propped up in front of her while she did the washing up. Hospital romances were the flavour of this particular month.

'They look bloody awful,' I said. 'You nicked them from the church hall.'

Mum ignored the accusation, which meant it was true. She probably justified it by saying that no one else was using them and it was a crime to leave them to waste. 'Who cares what they look like?' she snapped. 'They work, don't they? You can sit on them, can't you? Eat on the table.'

I didn't answer, but went into the kitchen to put some tea together.

All that booze Mum poured down her had seeped into her brain and turned her sour and bitter, like a demented prune. She was becoming more and more lazy and apathetic. The mad forays, the crazy projects and wild ideas she used to have had been dampened by the drink and then dried up completely. She hadn't tidied up the coast road for months and had stopped listening to her better nature, to everything that was good and free. She was sinking in the quicksand, helpless like a child.

Mum was fed on romantic novels by the library van that came to the village every other week and stopped outside the church hall (she may well have spied the 'spare furniture' while waiting for such a visit). The van was stuffed with books, which were carefully divided into categories to suit all tastes: fiction, non-fiction, romance, history, religion, thrillers etc.

Mum was wading through the romantic section at an alarming rate. She would stumble towards the horrified librarian, her arms overflowing with books that were covered in stained plastic covers.

'Well, it's not normal to take so many out at a time,' he said, shaking his head and looking down at the books which he meticulously stamped with the date.

'I've got the tickets,' Mum snapped, throwing a handful down in front of him; six were hers and six Margaret's – she never used them. I often gave Mum a couple of my tickets too. Four books a fortnight was my limit.

'Well they're not all yours, are they?' the librarian grumbled.

'They're for my daughters. Anyway, I thought it was your job to bring literature to us out in the sticks.'

'Literature, maybe. I'd hardly call that literature.'

'Well it's a start isn't it?' said Mum, dropping her fourteen books into her shopping trolley. 'For us plebs. We're a bit thick out here, you know.'

'Speak for yourself,' said Father Armitage, who was browsing through the 'thriller' section behind her, also struggling to find something he hadn't read.

Later on that day, I sat and watched Mum sitting outside on the terrace in the filthy old armchair slurping the rest of her tea and the final part of the novel.

It occurred to me that she must be lonely, stuck out in the middle of nowhere with her two daughters. She needed a man, she needed looking after. Wherever her 'journeys' took her, she was still a basic creature that needed a mate. Margaret and I were always nagging her to find someone, but our reasons were more selfish than selfless, we really wanted to get her off our hands. When we suggested a new man, she said she'd finished with them years ago. That wasn't true either, we knew. But what chance did she have of finding someone? Of someone wanting her? She had let herself go to such a degree that no one would go anywhere near her. 'Anyway, I reckon I've healed up by now,' she would say. 'It's so long since I've had one, I wouldn't know what to do with it any more.'

As Mum sat outside, the sun slowly started to set behind us and a slight wind ruffled the pages of the novel. Margaret then appeared from behind the pen. She had been up to Molly's cottage again, in search of Dwight. As usual, he wasn't in. He was never in, according to his friends up there. 'You eat like a pig,' she grunted as she passed Mum who was stuffing a complete piece of fruit cake into her mouth.

Unable to make an immediate reply, Mum sat like a dumpling with ants in its pants almost exploding with fury and beginning to choke. Quickly, she chomped through her cake, forcing it down her gullet, her face puce, her eyes bulging as she gulped and grunted to get rid of it. Nobody could make her see red like Margaret. 'What's it to you?' she finally screamed, sending a torrent of wet sloshy cake through the front door.

'We don't want a shower thank you very much,' said Margaret, sitting down in the living room to watch the television.

'Stuck up bloody cow,' Mum growled. She always said that when she didn't know what else to say. It was her stock answer.

'Only because I tell the truth,' said Margaret, hauling herself out of her chair and changing the channel. 'And no one likes the truth.'

'And least of all you. Listen to a few home truths of your own and see how you like it.'

'Oh yeah.'

'Yes. Like what a little bitch you are.'

'Well that doesn't say bugger all, does it?'

'Unlike you, I've got some thought for other people's feelings.'

'Oh yeah. Whose feelings do you have to worry about? Seeing as no one will have you.'

Furious, Mum slammed down her book and, craning her neck around the front door, glared at Margaret. 'I've had offers, you know,' she shouted. 'Don't think no one's ever asked, because they have.'

'Offers. I bet you've only had offers for one thing.'

'Bitch.'

'Boring.' Margaret began to snore loudly.

'You're one to talk. Doesn't look like you turned much down.'

'Hardly the same thing. Dwight's still with me. Your lot pissed off once they had their way.'

'Still with you, is he? Where is he then?'

'At work. And if you were anywhere near half decent, I'd have a father now. I'm not surprised he pissed off. Look at you. Who would want that? We could all be living in the

States now if it wasn't for you.'

'No one's stopping you from going. Though whether or not you'll get that Dwight to take you is another matter. And that kid won't make any difference either, I can tell you that. Poor thing. A pawn in your sick game to get some unsuspecting bugger to marry you. Well Dwight won't. I can tell you that. I've seen it all before and nothing ever changes. Not like that, at any rate.'

'How do you know? You don't know bugger all.'

'I know about men. And if they don't want to marry you they won't. They always find a way out. If Dwight wanted you, he'd have asked you by now. Don't think a bun in the oven's going to push a ring on your finger. All you'll be left with is the baby.'

'If you knew anything about men, you'd have one by now.'

'That's *why* I haven't got one. I know too much about them. Better off without.'

'Very convenient.'

'I'm telling you. You see that boy as a ticket out of here. He'll let you down.'

'Well I'm getting out anyway, whatever happens. Fuckin' hole. Where you can live and die without batting an eyelid.'

'No one's stopping you.'

'That's just what you want, isn't it? To be left here with your precious little Rosie to look after you. To shovel cake down your gob and wipe your bum till the day you die. You're only forty-three and you look like a fat old bag.'

Margaret's insults didn't seem to perturb Mum any more. She turned away and settled back into her armchair, a serene, almost smug look on her face. Determined to get the last word, she picked up her book and quietly uttered, 'It will be interesting though, to see whether he marries you.' So quietly that Margaret did not hear.

* * *

'Rosie!'

I stopped and looked down at a young woman who was lying on the mound beneath the Martello Tower, resting on her elbows and squinting in my direction.

'Lucy! What are you doing here?'

'Just lying around.' Lucy grinned. 'How are you?' she asked shyly and then patted the grass next to her. 'Come and sit down.'

Lucy had retained the worst of her adolescence. Her body had filled out and her face was blemished by clusters of white spots congregating mainly around her chin. Her frizzy red hair was wilder than ever and pulled away from her forehead by a flowery headband.

To begin with our conversation was stilted and self-conscious. Yet after ten minutes or so, we warmed to each other and started to see the tremendous gap between the paths we had chosen, or had been forced to take, during the past ten years. 'I'm afraid that while you were slogging at your A levels, I was learning all about sex, drugs and rock 'n' roll at the fish market,' I said, slightly superciliously. Lucy's account of her years away at school had irritated me. I didn't see why she and not I should have been given a chance. I was far brighter than her, that was common knowledge. So why did she end up taking A levels whilst I ended up slitting cod bellies?

'I had my fair share of that too,' Lucy smiled. 'That's why I failed everything. That's why I went to drama school, which is where I wanted to go anyway.'

'Well at least you've got what you wanted. Look at me. I work at the fish market. Hardly the pinnacle of success, is it?'

'You could do a lot more. I don't know why you don't.'

'Oh I'm all right. What could I do anyway?'

'I'm sure you could go further than the fish market.'

'How? Where? It's all right for you. You've got the right accent.'

'It's cultivated. One of the few benefits of drama school.'

'It's more than that, you know perfectly well.'

Lucy shrugged her shoulders. 'Well it hasn't got me very far if that's any consolation. Right now I'm living in a squat without a job or a penny to my name.'

I was glad to hear life was not so easy for Lucy. Evidently I was happier than she. She did look miserable. Probably spinning around some bottomless pit of a life. Confused and lost. Seeking solace from the world in Saltingford.

'But I'll be all right. I know I'll be successful.'

I grunted and remembered that time on the cliff with Mum when she suggested I look further afield. What would I learn in Saltingford? I was so sheltered from the world, I knew nothing. How could I know what I wanted when I had no idea what was available, what I could have?

'I hear your sister had a baby,' said Lucy, breaking the silence.

'Yes. He's six months now. Adorable. I can't leave him alone for a second.'

'Do you want children?'

'Oh yes. Don't you?'

'I don't know. Maybe later. When I'm rich and famous. Then I can afford to bring one up on my own. Who's the father?'

'An American.'

'Of course.'

'He's gone back to the States now.'

'That's convenient. For him, I mean. I suppose Margaret's upset she didn't go with him.'

'Yes and no. I don't think she ever really believed she would.'

'The only one who's made it is Sharon Jarvis. I hear she's holed up on some base in Ohio. Personally I couldn't think of anything worse. Have you been to the States?'

'No.'

'Well, I have and everyone says Ohio is a sheep's arse.'

Everything about Lucy was 'London'. So different to us, the way she spoke, her dress, how she held herself, walked and even lay. She was neurotic, yet carefree. Up-tight, yet relaxed. A mess, yet she had the world at her finger-tips. Life for Lucy was not dull. It was fraught with problems, gushing with trouble, overflowing with difficulties. And exciting.

* * *

The dismembered bodies of a hundred flies lay scattered across the window ledge. A wing here, a body there, a head somewhere else. Decomposing. Brittle. Waiting to turn to dust.

'Needs a clean of course,' said Lucy as she leant back against the wall and watched me stare at the insect cemetery. 'Two of the kids used to sleep in here.' She nodded at the floor boards, which were splattered with white paint and water marks. 'Not much of a room for a child really,' she added and then looked back at me and grinned.

'It's fine.' I smiled, and lifted the filthy net curtain to look out at the frowning afternoon sky that was turning darker by the minute. It had to be all right. The room. The flat. It all had to be all right. Otherwise it meant going back to Saltingford, and I'd already passed the point of no return. 'Two cocks in a pit,' I said abruptly.

'What?'

'Margaret and Mum. That's what they've turned into.'

'Oh. Well, you don't have to worry about them any more, do you? Stay for as long as you want. For as long as you can put up with it.'

'It's fine,' I repeated.

'For a slum. Which is basically what it is. They're going to pull the building down soon. The whole thing. That's why all the other floors are empty. Everyone's gone except us and a few other old things they hope will die before they have to re-house them. They know I'm here. There used to be five of us, imagine that. But the others left six months ago and now it's just me. Technically I'm a squatter. Does that bother you?'

'No.'

Lucy pulled her dressing gown around her and shuffled over to the window like an old woman. Standing beside me, she peered out through the speckled grey glass as though she expected the view to have changed. 'That's Borden Towers over there,' she said, nodding at a clump of high rise blocks that towered into the sky like concrete weeds. 'Most of the people from here have been moved over there. They called them the "slats". You know, instead of flats. Terrible place. No one wants to live there. They'll all fall down eventually. Then what? I don't know. Perhaps they'll all be dead and they won't have to bother about moving them anywhere else.'

London Lucy was different to Saltingford Lucy. In London she seemed weighed down by the heavy polluted air of the city. In Saltingford, I found her glib and superficial. She skimmed across the surface of major, minor events. Nothing seemed to really affect or touch her. She was an odd creature I didn't really understand. Or perhaps I did. Perhaps I looked for hidden depths that didn't exist.

'Do you mind if I leave you to sort out your things,' she said. 'I've got to get ready for work.'

I looked up surprised. 'You are working?'

'Only in the bistro down the road, waitressing. Unfortunately.'

'Oh.'

Lucy shrugged her shoulders. 'Well, what can you do? A girl's got to earn her crust. Frankly I think I'm better off on the dole but every time I sign on I get a job with someone who has to pay me above the counter. So what can you do? Fuck all.' Lucy grumpily answered her own question and looked down at her tatty old dressing-gown and pale blue slippers, one with pom-pom, the other without. At four o'clock in the afternoon she was still not dressed.

After Lucy had left, I lay down on the bed and rested my head against the cool, whitewashed wall. Absentmindedly picking at a dry patch of mud that was embedded in the mattress, I looked around the bare dingy room and for a second wished I were back in the pen; squalid it may have been but it was familiar. Safe. This room was bare and cold, containing only a single piece of furniture. The bed. And a dusty yellow lightbulb that dangled on a frayed cord from the ceiling.

Since the baby had arrived, the tension between Mum and Margaret had mounted to such a degree that life around them had become quite unbearable. The situation was made worse when Margaret turned up at Molly's cottage one day and learnt that Dwight had been posted back to the States, and had left the previous day. We all suffered her disappointment and felt sorry for her at first. Yet as she became more disagreeable and abusive, our pity turned sour. She was meant to go back to the commissary, but she seemed to forget all about it. Instead she turned her anger inside, neglecting herself and the baby and communicating through a series of grunts that sometimes crescendoed into the most terrifying shrieks and bellows. Mum and I hoped it was no more than a bad case of post-natal depression and that she would eventually snap out of it. But after six months she was worse, and after nine months utterly intolerable. Mum couldn't cope with it any more and hit the bottle again.

The baby, Dwight Junior, suffered. When Margaret heard that his father had left, the first thing she did was to change his name to Toby. She blamed and resented the baby, starving him of love and affection whilst possessively keeping him from Mum and me. He slept in a drawer and was only fed and changed when his screaming became so unbearable she had to move.

One evening, while we were sitting around watching the television, Toby began to wail in the room next door. Both Mum and I, who had been forbidden to touch him, looked at Margaret, who completely ignored the noise. Instead, she heaved herself out of the chair and turned up the volume of the television. Five minutes later, he was still howling. 'Margaret, Toby's crying,' I said. She pulled herself up from the chair and turned the volume up even louder. 'Margaret,' I yelled infuriated, 'your baby's crying.' And with that I stood up myself and marched into the bedroom.

'Leave him alone,' Margaret screamed, leaping out of the chair and pushing past me to get to Toby first. 'He's my baby.'

'Then do something about him.'

'No. He's all right. I'll do it when he's ready. He's my baby and I'll look after him.'

I couldn't stand it. I pushed past her and strode forward to the drawer. Just before I reached him, Margaret lunged out and pulled me back by the hair, almost yanking it from its roots, until she had me near the floor. 'He's my baby,' she screamed. 'Now leave him alone.'

'You should go,' said Mum later, when Margaret had gone to bed. She bent down and lifted her bottle of vodka. 'I've got my escape, but what about you? There's nothing here for you Rosie. Go. Go and don't feel guilty.'

I woke up a couple of hours later with a dead hand. I had fallen asleep with my head weighing down on my wrist. I shook my arm and stretched out on the grubby mattress; a thin cloud of dust rose into the air. The room was dark. Lucy must have looked in and flicked the light switch, leaving the door ajar to let a thin slither of light creep in from the hall.

I lay quite still and listened to London noises.

It was the first time I had heard London noises, the first time I had visited London. And as I lay there on that bed, listening to the trains that clattered along the tracks, the planes that incessantly hummed over us, and the voices, some shouting some gossiping, I thought how calmly I had greeted the city that afternoon. It should have been a terrifying ordeal. Yet somehow, instinctively, I had known what to do. I'd seen it on television a hundred times.

My bed lay directly underneath the window, so I could pull back the net curtain from where I lay. By this time, the silvery November sky had grown dark and illuminated the orange street lamps in sequence, as though it were passing each one in turn. Outside my bedroom window was a long and partially enclosed balcony which stretched the complete length of the block. The stairs in each block led to balconies on every floor, which in turn led to seventy-eight front doors. Below the balcony was a field and south of the field were dozens of railway tracks which slithered into Liverpool Street Station. Tube trains, express trains, goods trains and single engines crashed by, taking thousands of faceless commuters back to the suburbs. Lighted windows flashed in the darkness. Kaleidoscopes, shaken not stirred, a slice of commuting life.

There was life below the tracks too, where empty dark arches had been converted to garages and storage areas for any commodity, legal or illegal, animate or inanimate. Space was at a premium, never left to waste. Lots Way fringed the arches and was lined by cabs that sat in the gutter like big black beetles. The drivers were taking their break, tea and toast in a broken down Portakabin that had suddenly materialised from nowhere. No one remembered seeing it arrive. Sam, the owner, said it had always been there. Everyone knew it hadn't.

Had my room been on the other side of the building, I would have seen Mrs George plodding down Riggs Road with her big bag of shopping that said Riteprice on the side. Mrs

George always took a frayed dark blue nylon bag out with her because she resented having to pay for carrier bags that turned her into a walking advertisement. On this day she had not expected to do any shopping, she had stepped out simply for a browse and a breath of air. However, as often happened, she suddenly found herself inside the huge discounted food warehouse scanning the shelves for a packet of digestive biscuits and ending up with a complete bagful of groceries she didn't need. At the checkout, she virtually cleared out her purse and then spent the walk back to Riggs Road wondering how she had managed to spend the whole week's housekeeping in two days and how to ask Mr George for more money when times were so hard.

Like Riggs Road, Mrs George was preparing for another hard winter. And having lived in the old tenement block for more than thirty years, she felt a degree of empathy with the great ominous building that stretched along the entire length of the road, its structure crumbling and roof collapsing into itself. Like her, the road would suffer this winter as it had suffered the others before it. New holes would appear, existing holes grow bigger and those that had been filled would re-open like old wounds.

The tenement block we lived in completely dominated one side of Riggs Road. It was a huge Victorian hulk that had always been a slum to one degree or another. Rows of these buildings had been erected to house the soaring urban population in the mid-nineteenth century. They were lined up, one against the other, dark and overcrowded. Facing our block, on the other side of Riggs Road, was a scrap yard, a menagerie of rusty old cars that lay precariously heaped up on top of each other, enclosed in a corrugated iron wall which seemed to hold the whole lot together.

At the bottom of Riggs Road was Riggs Senior, a massive red brick school built in 1897. Surrounding the school was a tall wall, topped by fragments of broken glass. The alley which ran between the scrapyard and the school had been re-named Tin Pan Alley. And then, as those who had baptised it grew up, the name changed again to Groper's Lane.

One day our block in Riggs Road would metamorphose into desirable residences for the middle classes. Negotiations between the council and private speculators were already under way and it was only a matter of time before demolition would begin. The middle classes had already infiltrated the area, sending property prices sky-high, pushing the locals right out of the market. Mrs George saw it all around her; everything was changing, right before her very nose. Posh private schools were opening all over the place. Smart restaurants suddenly evolved out of laundries, pawn shops and greengrocers. And a delicatessen had just opened round the corner; it was full of lovely looking meat and cheeses she couldn't even pronounce the names of and certainly wouldn't dare to ask the price of. Of course, Mrs George had seen all sorts pass through the area but these double-barrelled types were the worst because they never knew the real value of money.

Everyone was moving to the East End, changing the tone of the place, and making it middle-class and smart. So much so that it wouldn't be fashionable to move there much longer – it would be too middle-class. Prices shot up. Locals were squeezed out, or grew out with their newly acquired wealth. The whole city was swapping areas, and that would continue until everyone ended up with what they had left in the first place. The whole area was disintegrating; it could no longer be the dream of the bourgeois or home to those born there. Fantasy and reality were becoming confused, leaving a fragmented and conflicting community that no one felt a part of.

Mrs George turned into the dark uninviting entrance that led to flats 36 – 48. Her shopping weighed her down as she began the long, lopsided haul up the dark stairwell. Everything was wet and damp; the walls through which the heavy November air perspired, the steps that led to each vacant floor, the wooden planks that had been nailed across the broken window panes, the sodden paper bags that disintegrated in the corners of each landing, the cigarette packets that were swept along the gutters outside, clogging the drains, a mushy mess, papier maché that never dried.

Heaving like a great cow, Mrs George struggled up the final flight of stairs which was lit by a dusty yellow light bulb. There had never been adequate lighting in the common parts of the block. Bulbs often fused in the damp or were broken by the drunks who found shelter in the dark corners of the landings. All temporary visitors to Riggs Road left some memento of their visit. Empty cider bottles rolled around the concrete steps, pushed by a draught that swept through the building. A sickly combination of urine and disinfectant made it almost impossible to breathe. The council barely bothered with the block any more. There had been a caretaker, a short stumpy fellow with a club foot they called Lurch. But he had been moved over to the 'slats' and only returned to Riggs Road every few weeks to throw a bucket of milky coloured water down the steps. Repairs were always put at the bottom of the council workers' list.

Mrs George always wore a mauve coat and black platform boots with square toes that caused sniggering at bus stops. The shadow of her large bulky figure grew as she turned left at the top of the stairs and plodded along the balcony towards her flat, which was next door to ours. She and Lucy never talked. Mrs George had tried to make the effort a couple of times, but Lucy hadn't been in the mood so she gave up and wrote off her neighbour as stuck-up and stand-offish.

Lucy dismissed Mrs George as an old bag the first time she saw her and never bothered to give her a second thought.

When I emerged from my cell, I found Lucy in the living room dressed in a pair of jeans and white shirt, ready for work. She was lying on a balding old white plastic sofa with her feet up, grunting into the telephone which was clamped between her shoulder and jaw. When she saw me, she beckoned me in and gestured towards a red and white striped deck chair which was allocated as 'my' chair. I sat down.

When Lucy mouthed 'coffee' to me, I immediately realised my role and dutifully hauled myself out of the deck chair and disappeared into the kitchen.

Outside, gentle rain pattered against the window, tap tap tapping on the glass. It wanted to come in. The night was not as black as Saltingford; it was quite light, for night. A very soft glow lingered above the city, growing fainter and fainter until it disappeared into the black sky above. Somewhere out there I could see that it got very dark, but nowhere near us, darkness fell a very long way away.

When I turned on the kitchen light I found a battered old kettle sitting on a gas stove that was covered by a thick layer of slimy brown grease. The sink, a huge enamel thing covered in chips and cracks, was full of dirty plates and cups, knives and forks and ashtrays, ash, food and a pair of dirty knickers somewhere at the bottom of it all. To fill the kettle, I had to move some of the debris onto a wooden draining board which had long ridges full of scummy water. 'Have you ever thought of lending this draining board to the local hospital?' I called out to Lucy, hearing her shuffle into the kitchen after me. 'They could grow cultures on it.'

Lucy ignored me. 'The coffee's in the cupboard,' she said, leaning against the stove and watching me suspiciously.

'O.K.' I nodded at an old enamel bath that was standing along the wall, covered by a door. Memories of Molly Johnson flooded my mind. 'Does it work underneath that lot?'

'S'pose so. I've never really tried. Getting it going looked such a hassle I found it easier to go round to friends. And cheaper.'

'Do you mind if I try?'

'Do. If you can.' Lucy slid her hands into the pockets of her tight jeans and took a deep breath. 'God knows what you'll find under that door though. I've never dared look.'

The cupboard containing the coffee was splattered in black, damp patches. It reeked of mildew. As I reached in, I sent a saucer of left-over cat food rolling across the bare floorboards.

'The cat came with the flat,' Lucy groaned. 'Bloody thing. It won't go away. God knows where it is now. Every time I think it's found another home it turns up here again. God knows why. I never feed it.' She looked down at the saucer, which was coated by a crusty ridge of dry cat food in which there was embedded a hefty sprinkling of maggots' eggs. 'Shit. Bloody thing. It's filthy. And I'm sure it's got worms. It looks like a mangy skeleton.'

Lucy picked up the saucer and threw it into the sink with the dishes, knickers and scummy water. 'I'll do that lot later,' she said, taking a final drag from her cigarette and dropping it into the water too.

The cigarette sizzled and gave up the ghost. I wondered if germs could survive in that sink.

Every time Mr George climbed the stairs to the third floor, they seemed steeper and longer and more in number. These days there was never much in his briefcase and he certainly wasn't carrying any extra weight himself, so he couldn't understand why they were becoming such an effort to climb. Perhaps it was the onset of old age, or the passing of middle age, even though he was only fifty-six.

When he reached the balcony, he wandered over to the railing and clung onto it for a few moments, catching his breath and staring at the 'slats' and the hundreds of tiny square boxes stacked up against the granite sky like the windows of fruit machines.

The slight figure of Mr George cut a silhouette of a younger man. His smooth, grey face gave him fewer years. He took pride in his thin, black moustache, there wasn't a white hair in it. And his hair was still smarmed back with Brylcreem; it gave him the continental look, the gigolo look of a travelling salesman. There had been a time when he had tried to live up to his looks, when he'd been known as the office letch and couldn't keep his eyes off a pretty girl. Of course, he'd never done anything. It was all harmless fun. A bit of slap and tickle. Winks and innuendoes. And then he'd be back to his wife. If the truth be known, he wasn't a highly sexed man at all.

These days, however, Mr George had lost the glint in his eye. The reflection of those massive concrete hulks clouded his vision and lowered his spirits to the empty, rat-infested flats on the ground floor of Riggs Road. It had been over a year since the council had been trying to move the Georges out of their flat and into the 'slats'. They were expected to give up their home of thirty years at the drop of a hat, the signing of a name, the stroke of a pencil, the allocation of a number. 'Unfit for human habitation,' the council worker had spouted like a parrot.

'It's perfectly fit,' Mr George had replied, wringing his hairless hands and then nervously turning the silver signet ring he wore on his little finger. 'Fit as a fiddle,' he added. 'In fact, it's the fittest flat in the whole building.'

The council worker looked at him condescendingly and said, 'Well we can't knock down the block and leave just your place standing, can we?'

'I don't see why you have to knock anything down at all.'

'Unfit for habitation.'

'You've already said that.'

The council worker looked down at his flip chart.

'Number 47. That's you isn't it?'

'Oh I see, it's reduced to this, is it? Numbers.'

'You are number 47.'

'No I'm not. George is my name . . . '

' . . . Well look George . . .'

' . . . Not my first name.'

'Well look, number 47 is your flat, isn't it?'

'Yes.'

'And George is your name.'

'Yes.'

'So, we have a nice new flat waiting for you. All the mod cons. Lifts. Central heating. Proper bathrooms. I can tell you, it'll be paradise after this place.'

'Oh for God's sake.' Mr George suddenly took the council worker by the arm and dragged him over to his front door. 'Look,' he hissed. 'This is my home. We've been here for thirty years. We've built a bathroom. And a kitchen. Brand new. Fully tiled. Fully heated. With chrome mixer taps, a double sink and one of them French bidets in the bathroom. It cost a bloody fortune.'

'All that's waiting for you in Borden Towers. All that and more.'

'Not a French bidet.'

'You can't stay here for that.' The council worker fished a cigarette out of the packet that was peeking from the breast pocket of his jacket and contemplatively tapped it against the back of his hand. 'Look, I know it's tough, but you can't stay here for the sake of a French bidet.'

'It cost a fortune.'

'Twelve years ago. It's hardly brand-new. If you'd just had it done I might understand. But it's dated already.'

Mr George pulled away from the council worker and stared sulkily down at the field.

'We'll let you stay here as long as we can, but you'd better get used to the idea of leaving this place. You're going to have to go.' The council worker looked at Mr George, who was gloomily staring over the balcony at a scraggy mongrel shitting on the grass directly below him. He shrugged his shoulders and added, 'Not to worry. You'll like it over there once you've got settled in. No one likes change. It's fear of the unknown.'

Later that night, when his wife was ostensibly down the bingo hall, Mr George sat back in his chair and relaxed for a moment, enjoying the comfort the gas fire provided within the security of his home. The telly was on. He liked the telly. He found that comforting too. He didn't like to be on his own much. A year ago he would have gone down to the pub and met a few of his friends if his wife went out, but of course he couldn't afford to do that now. He felt isolated and frightened. Nervous like a child. It was ridiculous for a man of his age. He'd never batted an eyelid before at the drunks and vagrants that rolled around the stairwells and streets outside, but now they had become a threat to him. Who knew what they might do? Especially with all the other flats empty and boarded up. He and his wife were virtually alone in the building. Alone when they had previously been surrounded by almost a hundred families. Everything seemed to be breaking down around him. A light blanket of perspiration began to cover Mr George's forehead, he clutched the arm of his chair and looked around at all his worldly possessions: the pink Draylon sofa, a teak sideboard with glass doors displaying their best crockery and six coloured glasses, a set of carved giraffes on the mantelpiece, a patterned carpet and matching curtains. All this was theirs. It had taken a lifetime to gather and now Mr George felt that it was going to be taken away.

After Lucy had left for the restaurant, I wandered around the flat for a while, opening drawers, peering into cupboards and restlessly throwing myself onto the sofa, where I attempted to watch television. Five minutes later I was up again, rummaging through my suitcase, wondering where I was going to put everything. Seeing that there was no furniture except a bed in my room, I threw everything back in the case and, feeling tired and grumpy, went to bed.

A pale light shone through the window from the balcony outside and I could hear the muffled noises from the television next door. It was all vaguely reassuring on my first night in the big city. A little later, the television was switched off, leaving a gap in the night that was soon filled by a man shouting in the distance as he stumbled out of the pub. The last trains home rumbled by less and less frequently, followed by the steady clatter, clatter of the heavy goods trucks trundling over the arches.

The night became darker, more still and more quiet. Sounds were different and distant: cars churning along the wet streets, police sirens wailing, voices shouting or murmuring, planes and trains. No waves. I missed the steady pulse of the sea: it had always lulled me into a trance that eventually turned to sleep. Here I could not sleep. So I lay in bed and savoured the delicious smell of freedom and solitude.

Lucy turned up at about two o'clock in the morning, crashing along the corridor and finally banging on my bedroom window. She was so drunk she couldn't get the key in the door.

'Sorry,' she said, staggering past me and taking a dive onto her bed, 'my key doesn't seem to be working.'

'I'm sure it would have worked eventually,' I snapped, annoyed at being woken when I had just managed to drop off to sleep.

'Oh don't be like that.'

I wandered into Lucy's room, which may well have not seen daylight for several weeks. Thick turquoise curtains were pulled across the window and the air was heavy and warm. Clothes were strewn everywhere and a collection of coffee cups and overflowing ashtrays was scattered across the floor. I had always thought of Lucy as a healthy individual, perhaps because she was tanned and rested when I saw her in Saltingford. In London she looked a sickly product of urban living.

'I feel awful,' she groaned, lying flat out on her bed with her face buried in a pillow.

'Do you want some coffee?'

'No. Nothing.' She rolled over, squinted and lifted her arm to shade her eyes from the glare of the overhead light. 'Oh God, turn it off will you,' she mumbled.

I turned off the light and stood by the doorway in my long nightshirt, my arms folded, staring down at her and wondering what to do. Her body was inert, her limbs outstretched as though she had landed there from a great height. Her make-up had run and black smudges surrounded her eyes, contrasting with her pale, white face. 'You look like a vampire,' I said.

'Thanks,' she groaned, then, 'I think I'm going to be sick.' Suddenly her body kick-started into action and she rolled off her bed and charged head-first to the loo. All sorts of vomiting and retching noises emanated from it for at least the next ten minutes.

Home from home, I thought and went into the kitchen to make a pot of tea.

You snore,' I said to Lucy the next morning when she eventually shuffled into the living room looking like death.

'I don't.'

'You do. I could hear you in my room.'

'It was probably next door. He snores. Or she does. Now she looks the type that would snore. You should see them; he's lost his job and she washes up at the Star of India.'

'How do you know?' I asked, feeling sorry for the poor neighbours. Sometimes Lucy was so heartless, she didn't seem to care about anything.

'Because I've seen her there, through the back, behind the bar, in her great big blue housecoat.' Lucy puffed up her cheeks and walked across the room like a gorilla. Then she groaned again and clutched her head.

'Serves you right. For being cruel.' I said. I lowered myself from the sofa and puffed up the cushions. 'There you are, lie down. You look terrible.'

'I feel it,' Lucy collapsed on the sofa and stabbed her hand around the floor for the newspaper I had bought that morning. When she saw what it was, she threw it down and groaned. '*The Times*. What's wrong with the *News of the Screws*?'

'It's not out today.'

'I can't read *The Times*. I can't even read the instructions on the back of the cornflakes packet. What is to become of me!' Lucy wailed dramatically.

The Times had never been my paper either. Usually I skimmed over the tits and bums at the fish market and that was it. I hadn't a clue what was going on. Now, as I had decided to participate in the world, I wanted to find out what was really happening. 'I thought I'd better educate myself,' I said. 'Now I'm in London. Maybe I'll join some radical movement or go on a march.'

'Oh God.'

'Greenpeace springs to mind.'

'Well that's not very London.' Lucy was groping around on the table behind her for a cigarette.

'True.' I shrugged my shoulders. 'Oh well, something's bound to come up sooner or later.'

I put on the kettle to make more tea and then returned to the living room. Lucy had fallen asleep again, her head resting on the cushions, her mouth partially open. She still hadn't washed her face or bothered to take her make-up off. Most of it was probably impregnated into her pillow by now.

'It's raining again,' I said, looking out of the window and across the shining slate roof of the school. It seemed as though the sun had swallowed itself never to re-emerge from the hazy grey clouds that lined the sky. Everything looked bleak and dismal, or brown. It was comforting to be indoors, in the warm, with Lucy dozing on the sofa.

When I returned with a cup of tea, she had come to again and was lounging across the sofa with her arm suspended in the air in a catatonic position. In the hand that was attached to the frozen arm, she held a cigarette from which a spiral of blue smoke juddered unevenly upwards. She had the shakes.

'Do you always come home from work like that?' I asked, putting the tea down on the floor beside her.

'No. We went out. To the Blue Baboon. It's a club.' Lucy leaned over the side of the sofa, picked up the mug and took a noisy sip of tea. 'Actually, I met a man.'

'Oh?' I raised my eyebrows.

'Yes. He brought me home, I think.' She crumpled her eyebrows and tried to recall the previous night. 'Yes, he did bring me back,' she confirmed. 'But he didn't want to come in. God knows why. God knows why he brought me back if he didn't want to come in. I hate men like that. They get on my nerves.'

'Oh? Why?'

'Well, you don't know what to do with them, do you? I mean, what do you do with them? Give them a cup of cocoa and turn on the telly?' Lucy stopped and pensively took a drag from her cigarette. 'Oh God!' she spluttered. 'I can't even smoke! What a state!' And she threw the cigarette into the mug of tea where it died with a hiss. 'Well, maybe he'll call,' she added, yawning. And then she went completely limp, as though someone had pulled out the plug and drained her of energy.

As time passed, Lucy and I worked out a routine that suited us both. She very quickly got used to me being around and soon began to treat me like a maid. She saw herself as a Doctor Dolittle figure, teaching the bumpkin her manners. When her snooty friends came round, she struggled to hold herself back from giving me orders.

'What do you do, Rosie?' her friends would ask.

'Nothing.'

Blank faces abounded. One girl nodded thoughtfully and said, 'How interesting.' She was very drunk.

I said, 'Lucy's the career girl amongst us.'

Lucy blushed and, for a while, stopped giving me orders.

Sometimes, when her agent wouldn't call her back and when she didn't get recalled for one rehearsal after another, Lucy would plunge into a hideous depression. I had to call the bistro and inform them that she was sick while she hibernated beneath her duvet and became lost in her own world of fame, fortune and leading ladies. The curtains were drawn, the sheets were stinking, around the bed was a wash of overflowing ashtrays, beer cans and coffee cups. A major drama was playing under the covers. But I had to be sympathetic. She was utterly miserable. Sometimes I used to sit on the edge of the bed and brush out her wiry red hair, spending hours untangling the knots and gently scolding her, like a mother.

Men, or their absence, also sent Lucy plummeting into the throes of depression. She usually liked to keep several on the boil so that if one left her she could bring in a reserve. Misery fell when she had exhausted her supply and was left with no one but herself. As far as she was concerned, the quality of life was directly proportional to the man – or men – in it. The more attention she was paid, the happier she was, and the better she was. Better woman. Better lover. Better friend. Better actress. Better all round.

What Lucy couldn't tolerate was if I had a man and she didn't. If this happened, she stormed around the flat slamming doors and snapping at me like a spoilt child. 'You kept me awake half the night, fucking,' she moaned in the morning.

'You keep the whole of London awake,' I replied, 'with your fake orgasms.'

'They're not.'

'Well I've never heard anyone make a row like that before.'

'You've heard the whole world screwing I suppose.'

'No. But I've only ever heard a noise like that at the pictures.'

'At the "pictures". No one says that any more.' Lucy sneered and sloped off, closing the dispute there and then.

* * *

Once I had settled into the area, I began to run out of money and decided to pay the DHSS a visit.

When I walked into the hazy smoke-filled waiting room, the first person I saw was Mr George. I couldn't have missed him sitting there in his worn suit and tie, immaculately groomed yet quite vacant in himself. He was quite a different breed from the rest of the crowd who slouched over chairs, sprawling, coughing, rolling up cigarettes and spluttering. Some looking filthy, some smelling. Mr George, on the other hand, sat quite still as though he were putting himself through an endurance test, his hands resting on the black briefcase which sat on his lap.

Mr George was hating every minute of his wait in that filthy room. For a start he could hardly breathe: the air was so thick with cigarette smoke it had turned the walls yellow. There was no proper ventilation, only a couple of windows that were so high up, no one could reach them. The air circulated only when the outside door was opened to let in an icy blast of wind that swept round the room. What really irked Mr George was that once again he had turned into a number. There was no receptionist to take his name or note down his business, just a machine on the wall that issued numbered tickets. He was number 56 and had to wait until it was bellowed out through a plastic speaker nailed above the door.

'Number 49' crackled the voice. We all glanced down at our tickets. We knew it wasn't our number, but we looked all the same.

A man wearing an odd pair of trainers pulled himself out of his chair and lolloped on to the swing door. Behind it ran a corridor that was sectioned off into cubicles with iron mesh windows to separate the 'haves' from the 'have nots.'

Mr George looked up and checked the clock by his own watch. It was ten minutes fast. Typical, he thought. Typical they should put the clock fast like that. Trying to push us out as soon as they can, as though they're herding a flock of mindless sheep through their bloody system that's so tied up with red tape it's strangled itself. What right did anyone have to complain? Who would listen? Who would care? Everyone could come back another day and wait two, three, four hours. What did it matter? No one had anything better to do. No one had a job.

Working himself up and beginning to fidget on his chair (also screwed to the floor), Mr George began to feel trapped. He was prisoner number 56. Punished for not having a job. Imprisoned with everyone else who was too lazy to work, or too weak, or too ill, or too drunk, or too old. Punished for failing. He had always said it would be a disaster if the accounts department went computerised. No one would ever be able to pick it up. And now look. He would never forgive Mundy for making him redundant, for betraying him after nine years of loyal service.

* * *

Being unable to telephone home and not having received a word from either Mum or Margaret, I began to wonder whether they hadn't murdered each other, cooped up together in that pen like a couple of battery hens. In the end, guilt got the better of me and I sent them a note announcing my return in two days' time for Christmas.

When I arrived the pen was shut up and the curtains drawn. I opened the door and stepped into a cushion of thick warm air. Margaret and Mum were both sitting slumped in their armchairs, staring at the television in a hypnotic trance. Neither of them looked up when I walked in. Neither seemed to realise I had arrived. 'I see nothing's changed,' I said loudly, stammering, furious.

Margaret and Mum turned and stared at me in surprise.

'I told you I was coming. I sent a note. It was inside the Christmas card.'

Both faces were blank. Mum leant over the arm of her chair and shakily poured herself half a tumbler of vodka.

'Oh for God's sake!' I was furious and hurt. Furious with them for being such total lumps and hurt because they'd forgotten I was coming back. They looked like a couple of hags from *Macbeth*. 'It absolutely stinks in here,' I said. 'How you can keep a baby in this mess I don't know!' There was no sign of Toby. 'Where is he anyway?'

'What's it to you?' Margaret growled. She was wearing a blue house coat and a pair of Crimplene trousers that would suit a woman twice her age.

'Rosie!' said Mum. Suddenly a glimmer of recognition swept across her face suggesting that she had only just realised who I was. 'Rosie. You've come back today.'

'Yes, we didn't think you was coming back today,' Margaret barked.

'Didn't you get the card?'

Mum turned to Margaret, shrugged her shoulders and then let out a rather mad, childish giggle. Margaret shook her head as if she hadn't a clue what I was talking about and it was nothing to do with her anyway. 'We thought you was coming another day,' she finally drawled.

I stood by the door staring at them. Something had changed. Mum seemed to have abandoned herself to Margaret and deteriorated into a dithering vegetable. I sensed they didn't want me there at all. Neither of them made the slightest attempt to move.

'I'm glad you're so pleased to see me,' I snapped again.

Mum took a sip from her glass and turned to me. Then she opened her mouth and gave me the most sickly grin I've ever seen. Her teeth were disgusting; black and decayed, they looked like stumps of fossilised wood hanging from her gums.

The pen was a shambles. No one would have believed it was Christmas – there wasn't a card or a piece of tinsel in sight. When we were small Mum had always taken Margaret and me to the forest which lay about two miles inland to gather holly and steal a Christmas tree or two for the big day. And then George Jarvis would come down with a chicken and usually stay and help us eat it before going back up to spend the rest of the day with his real family. I think he preferred to be with us. He had a soft spot for Mum. Yet he was so loyal to Lily. We couldn't think why. She didn't deserve it.

Having got over the shock of my arrival, Margaret managed to haul herself out of her chair and offer me a cup of tea. I followed her into the kitchen. 'Where's Toby?' I asked again, taking advantage of her better mood.

'He's asleep. In my room. He always sleeps in there now.'

I nodded and leant against the wall with my arms folded watching my sister's bulky figure as she crashed around the kitchen, filling the kettle and then plonking it on the stove. 'Looks like things have gone downhill a bit,' I said.

'Everything's fine. You've caught us on one of our off days, that's all.'

'I see. Mum doesn't look too good.'

'I told you, it's an off day, that's all,' Margaret snapped.

Toby suddenly started up next door. Margaret froze for a second and then looked at me, almost frightened. I stared back and slowly levered myself away from the wall. 'I'll go,' I said. She had to let me.

Toby was covered in sore, red pimples that lay in blotchy

patches all over his pale brown skin. Once I had washed and changed him, I sat at the table and held him in my arms, feeding him with his bottle. The television was on again, quieter this time, and when Mum got up from her chair to go to the loo, she wandered over to me and smiled inanely. She ran her podgy hand through my hair and let it slide down to stroke Toby's cheek. She loved us both, I knew. Everything took so long to filter through her soggy brain.

What had happened to her in those few weeks since I had left? All signs of life had drained completely from her face; she was dirty and reeked of alcohol. The dress she wore clung to her like an oilskin, showing every horrendous bulge as she slowly dragged herself along like a great mass of frogspawn.

When Mum saw Toby greedily sucking at his bottle, she put out her arms and tried to take the child from me. I pulled him away, appalled. 'Not like that,' I said. 'Not like that Mum.'

Mum toppled back a little and looked at me inquisitively like a puppet.

'You're drunk Mum. And filthy. Clean up and you can have him when you're sober.'

The next morning, when I struggled out of my homemade bed on the floor (I refused to sleep in Margaret's filthy sheets), Mum was already in the bathroom, running herself a bath. I pushed the door open and stared at her through the steam. 'I can manage,' she said. So I left her alone.

Then the baby woke, so I picked him up and left Margaret in her room with a pillow over her head to block out the world. She hated that baby. He had ruined her life before it had even started.

When Mum finally emerged from the bathroom an hour or so later, she was wearing a bright red kimono that didn't meet around her middle and made her look like a Sumo wrestler.

'You look a bloody joke,' sneered Margaret, who had

managed to struggle out of bed and position herself in front of the telly again. 'I'm sure Rosie isn't interested in seeing what you've got on offer.'

'I'll get you some pants,' I mumbled. It was true, the gap in the kimono could not have revealed a less endearing sight.

It upset me to see Mum deteriorating so. She was in her mid-forties and already seemed to have given up on life. With no hope, there was no future for her. She had just surrendered. I stood behind her and gently combed through the knots in her matted hair, wondering how I could change the situation. But I knew what would happen: I'd build her up and as soon as I left she'd let herself down again. 'Your hair needs a cut,' I said. 'It's full of split ends.'

'I've only just had it done.'

'When?'

'Only just. Can I take the baby now?'

Mum sat in the chair and I slowly lowered Toby into her arms, then stood back and watched her cooing and cuddling him, and holding him so close. A blissful look spread across both their faces until they finally fell asleep in the chair together.

That evening was Christmas Eve and I suggested that as Mum was doing so well with Toby, Margaret and I should wander up to the King's Head for a drink.

Mum was thrilled at the prospect of spending an evening on her own with Toby and stood at the door, jiggling him up and down as she watched us plod across the shingle towards the coast road.

Although she pretended she didn't care, I could tell that Margaret was dying to ask me about London. She had never been there and as her chances of getting to the States seemed more and more remote, she threatened to move to our own metropolis instead. I noticed a curious conflict of envy and bitterness in her. She partly resented me for deserting the flock, yet also held me in awe because I now lived in the city. I was no more a part of Saltingford. I had risen above

Saltingford life. So when I suggested we go to the King's Head that night, she rejected the idea outright at first. And then, as it occurred to her that here was an opportunity to show off 'her sister from London', she changed her mind.

After Margaret had bathed and smeared a generous layer of bright blue glittery shadow across her eyelids, we left. It was a cold night and dark, so dark. I had become accustomed to the street lights in London and found myself stumbling clumsily along the road, unable to see in front of me. 'You drunk already?' said Margaret, grabbing my elbow as my ankle almost doubled up on the edge of a pothole.

'It's this fucking road.'

Plans were being drawn up to extend the King's Head and add a lounge bar for the ladies. The men had grudgingly realised that women were there to stay and pestered Randalls to build a special bar to put them in. However, work had not yet begun and when we arrived, the public bar was oozing with people. I flapped my hand to try and clear the air of cigarette smoke and, grinning at Margaret, began to make my way to the bar.

'Ah! Look who it isn't!' exclaimed George Jarvis, grinning and revealing an uneven set of stained teeth.

'Hi George,' I said, and then turned to Ron, who was standing next to his father. 'Hi Ron. How are you?'

'Oh fine, fine,' said Ron, blushing and looking down at his pint, as he always did.

If Ron had ever been discovered, he would have been stuffed and displayed in the Natural History Museum. He was a modern-day Neanderthal man. His forehead sloped over his skull, levelling out into two ridges of bristly dark hair that overhung his eyes like wire brushes. Everything about him was big, huge. His hands were shovels, his shoulders ox-like. And various reports had also been bandied around concerning the size of his penis; the best I had heard was ten inches long and four inches round. No wonder he had problems finding a girlfriend.

Having said that, Ron was not unattractive. He had beautiful deep brown eyes and a mop of curly black hair that made me want to ruffle it whenever I saw him.

Ron dug his hand deep into the pocket of his black cords. 'What will you girls be drinking?' he asked as soon as he saw Margaret behind me.

'Light ale,' Margaret snapped without even greeting him. Her eyes were fixed on a group of three G.I.s who were drunk and standing by the fireplace, pints in hand, telling each other lewd stories. Her face lit up and she shuffled a few paces back, so she was standing directly in front of them.

I could see Ron was hurt when he saw Margaret's face brighten up as soon as the Americans began to talk to her. Within seconds she turned her back on us and totally ignored us for the rest of the evening. Ron and I discussed London, the power station, Saltingford, school, who was doing what and where they were living. And all the time he watched Margaret. He couldn't take his eyes off her. He tormented himself as he stared at her laughing and chatting, flirting and getting more and more drunk as the G.I.s plied her with booze.

The more Margaret drank, the more she kept disappearing to the loo. The third or fourth time this happened, one of the G.I.s disappeared with her and then returned separately about ten minutes later. Half an hour passed and off she went again, with another G.I. And then later, the third followed her out of the narrow oak door.

Ron couldn't believe his eyes. I tried to steer his attention in another direction, to involve him in the chat and rumpus with all his fishing cronies. But he wouldn't budge. He stopped talking. His mouth fell open. His face became furrowed and wrought, desperate and confused. When the third American disappeared through the door, I saw tears welling in his eyes and he quickly took a huge slurp of his beer to quell them.

The two other men stumbled towards the bar to refill their glasses. They both had cropped hair and moustaches; one was blond, the other darker. Ron stood back to let them pass and then stared down at them, a look of disgust on his face.

'God dammit,' said one, 'I swore I'd never poke an old bitch like that.'

'Hey! It's Christmas!' yelled the other, brandishing his glass into the air and wobbling over, stepping on George's toe.

'Oi! Watch it!' George barked.

The American put his hands up defensively. 'Hey, sorry, sorry; I don't need to fight. I already got rid of *my* aggression tonight. Tonight I'm peaceful man. It's Christmas.'

'Yeah. And he's just stuck a sausage in the mother-fuckin' turkey,' screamed the blond one, and they both doubled up with laughter.

I didn't see the expression on Ron's face. I only felt myself being pushed firmly aside before I heard a tremendous crack and saw the owner of the sausage stumbling backwards, his arms flying everywhere as he grasped for his balance, a trickle of blood running down his face.

'I never had men fight over me like that before,' said Margaret as we walked back. Her face was serene and contented, gently smiling as she contemplated the evening. 'I wish I'd been there,' she added. 'I wish I'd seen it.'

'I don't think you do.'

'Why? I missed out on the good bit.'

'Didn't seem like you missed out on much at all.'

Margaret giggled. 'That's true. Now that is true. You know, I think that Gerry might contact me again. He said he would. I liked him the best.'

* * *

When I returned to London, the first thing I did was to get

a job in a steamy little cafe. The Peach Melba was ninth in a row of partly derelict and partly standing shops in Lots Way. It was owned by a woman called Muriel who lived in the flat upstairs. Muriel was very down-to-earth, working-class and proud of it. She said exactly what she thought and had no bones on her whatsoever. We all envied her enormously. We all wanted her approval. We all wanted to be mothered by her. There was a genuine warmth to Muriel and everyone liked her, even when she spoke her truths, even when they hurt. But she was true to herself and who could not respect that?

No one knew exactly how far Muriel was into her forties, but she certainly never stopped grumbling about giving the best part of her life to a dump like the Peach Melba. We thought she was probably about forty-six, though she always made out she was younger. She was a tall striking woman with a protruding constipated belly. She had deep auburn hair which sat on her head like a hat. I thought it was a wig but never dared ask. As the day wore on, the hair style always began to slowly melt like an ice cream and slither down her neck until it was completely unravelled by the steam and lay lank against her bony shoulders. 'It's like a fuckin' sauna in here,' she would complain several times a day, to no one. Then she would wrench a few strands of hair round to her face, glare at them, and say, 'I don't know why I bother. I really don't.' And let the hair drop in disgust.

The massive steel still gurgled in response. 'Shut up you,' said Muriel. She was always talking to it as it huffed and puffed behind the counter like a steam engine. It was the still that made the cafe so steamy. Not only did it ruin Muriel's hair style but it also made the paint on the walls blister and caused large mouldy patches all over the ceiling. The front window always steamed up; no one could see out and no one could see in. Sometimes Muriel and I sat watching the face of a passer-by as he pressed against the window, straining to see in. We waved and hooted but he could never see us.

Sometimes we would emerge from the cafe to find the weather totally changed since we had arrived. It was always cold inside – the condensation on the walls made the air damp and chilly. It confused the senses: in such a steamy climate I expected to be hot and sweating, yet was always freezing.

It was a relief to be working again. Apart from having no money, I noticed that I was becoming lethargic and slow. I couldn't drag myself out of bed in the morning; there didn't seem to be any point. Visions of ending up like Margaret passed through my mind. She had barely done a day's work in weeks. From assistant manager at the commissary, she was now relegated to potato picking. A lorry would come and collect them in the morning and they'd climb into the back and trundle off, like cattle. But Margaret rarely did that any more. There was always some excuse: the weather, no potatoes, a bad crop, enough labour already. 'You must work,' said Miss Stiff-finger, when I was back in Saltingford. 'It's the only way you'll learn how to get on with people you don't like.' I shrugged my shoulders and grunted; it wasn't exactly my main motive for getting a job.

When Mr George walked into the cafe, he didn't recognise me. He hadn't recognised me at the DHSS either. Yet he passed me several times a week on the stairs. He never looked up, never spoke; his stare was fixed to the cracked concrete stairs that climbed the four floors.

Muriel nudged me when he walked in. 'That one,' she said. 'That's a right one.' And then she shouted 'Afternoon' as though he were deaf, or a geriatric, or half-witted. 'Cup of tea?' she added in the same tone, once Mr George had edged behind one of the yellow Formica tables at the back. Muriel nudged me again and hissed, 'He always sits there, so no one can see him from outside.'

Mr George managed a watery smile and took yesterday's newspaper out of his tatty black briefcase. He knew Muriel talked to him as if he were demented, but he was grateful even for that. Grateful that someone should recognise him.

That he should be thought worthy of a conversation at all.

Round the back, Muriel hissed, 'That one got the sack months ago and he still hasn't told his wife. Every day he gets up, puts on those clothes and marches off as though he's going to work.' Muriel stabbed viciously at a tray of sausages. 'Shame really. Poor bugger.'

'His wife must know,' I said, having decided not to mention that Mr George and I were neighbours. Muriel was bound to blurt it out and embarrass him.

'How could she know?'

'People just know, don't they? She's probably trying to save his pride.'

'Well he's got plenty of that,' said Muriel, picking up the tray of sausages and slamming it under the grill. She had been married herself at one time. It didn't last long. We weren't quite sure why they broke up; she said it was because her husband never gave her enough sex; we suspected he had gone off with someone else.

'Had lunch, have you?' Muriel shouted as she went to the counter and lifted a huge enamel teapot from which she poured a cup of ready-made, milky tea.

'Yes thank you.'

'Well you could have eaten it here you know. You can always have it here, providing we've got room. I don't mind.'

'Thank you,' said Mr George with as much dignity as he could muster.

When Muriel plonked the tea down in front of him, she raised her eyebrows inquisitively. 'Well?' she asked.

Shamefully, like a child, Mr George looked down and slowly shook his head while he stroked his moustache.

'You've got to tell her you know,' said Muriel, who believed in coming clean about everything. 'It's not a crime.'

'I know. Something still might come up though.' For a moment Mr George tried to look bright and optimistic, but it didn't last. His face quickly dropped again.

'Stop kidding yourself. At least let yourself off the hook

and give up this bloody charade. What a load of bollocks it all is.'

Tears suddenly started to well in Mr George's eyes. He felt as though he were being told off like a naughty child yet he was powerless to make the situation better. Why should he have to tell his wife he was unemployed? Unemployable it seemed. She depended on him and looked to him as the provider. She respected him for it and for all that he stood for as a man. It wasn't right that a man should not be given the right to work. There was something fundamentally wrong with society and he felt the victim of it all.

'Come on.' Muriel rubbed his shoulder as she rested her arse on the table and watched him sinking his head into his hands and rubbing his sore, red eyes. 'It'll be O.K. Everything will work out. It always does.'

Mr George shook his head and bit his lip. He wanted to explode, to let out all the anger that had been welling up inside him over the past months. Yet he couldn't.

Muriel sighed, shook her head and shuffled back into the kitchen. 'Poor bastard,' she said. 'Now, what about fish pie for tomorrow's "special"?'

* * *

The next few months brought a lot of changes, not only to my life in London but also to Saltingford, where things were improving gradually.

One evening, Margaret managed to drag herself away from the television and stumble over the grass to the public phone box. She called me to say Ron had asked her to marry him.

'Well? Are you accepting?'

'S'pose so.'

'You don't sound very excited about it.'

'Not exactly what I was hoping for, is it?' she grumbled.

'What do you expect?' I said, beginning to raise my voice. 'Frankly I think you're lucky to have Ron.'

'Why? Do you fancy him?'

"No. But . . . well, you know.' I didn't want to push Margaret too much. I knew if I did she'd back off. 'Anyway, it's worth considering,' I said.

'S'pose so,' Margaret drawled again in her thick Suffolk accent which was becoming more and more noticeable to me the longer I stayed away.

Then there was a long silence, during which all I could hear was heavy breathing.

'Got a cold?'

'No. Got the telly on?'

'Yes.'

'What's on?'

'Not a lot.'

'Oh.'

'It's worth considering,' I said again. 'Ron's all right, isn't he?'

'S'pose so. Anyway, I'm going now. Bye.'

Totally unused to using a phone, Margaret abruptly hung up, leaving me stranded on the other end. I had wanted to ask how Mum and Toby were. I'd been back a couple of times and things were looking much better. Margaret seemed to have given up Toby altogether and was glad to leave him in Mum's hands. This worked perfectly. It gave Mum some purpose to her life whilst leaving Margaret free to watch as much television as she wanted.

In London, Lucy continued the round of rehearsals, readings and heated conversations with her agent that usually ended up with one of them slamming the phone down. One day, she was asked to go along and audition for a new soap. Two weeks later she was recalled. And then again. Until, finally, she was offered the minor part of an obstreperous daughter (very fitting, I thought).

She was thrilled. I was thrilled. Of course it wasn't

Shakespeare, but it was fame and a steady income. To celebrate, she spent her whole week's tips on two bottles of champagne and we both got as pissed as rats in a sewer. It was wonderful.

Of course, as soon as rehearsals started, Lucy became far more exuberant. She told the bistro where to go for starters. And then one evening she flew through the front door, slammed it behind her and leant against it, breathing heavily. 'Oh God, I think I'm going to come,' she said, bending her head down and trying to catch her breath.

I was en route from the kitchen – where I had just taken a bath – to my bedroom and stood in the hall with a towel wrapped around my head staring at her.

'You won't believe it,' she said, flapping her hand at me breathlessly. 'You won't believe it.'

'What?'

'I've just experienced the second coming. And he's right outside the door.' She slammed the palms of her hands against the door and mouthed 'Outside the door.'

'Oh God. Lucy!' I left her in the hallway and began to unravel the towel in my room.

She followed me in and scrambled across my bed so she could position herself by the window. A few minutes later, she said, 'Shit. He must have gone.'

'I've never known anyone make such a drama out of nothing.'

'That wasn't nothing.' She let the curtain fall and flopped onto the bed, her eyes wild and burning with passion. 'That was Samuel.'

'Oh, you've spoken to him already then?'

'Of course. I couldn't let him get away. He was sent to me. How often do you meet someone like that in a dump like this?'

'He was here?'

'Yes. He's an architect, redesigning the block. Converting them to desirable residences for the middle classes, my dear.'

Lucy's big break at work was completely overshadowed by this new man. She had to force herself to go along to rehearsals, and whenever she wasn't needed, she spent her time hovering around the block, scrambling over disused staircases and peering through boarded-up windows. Meanwhile, Muriel and I began to take it in turns to open the cafe in the morning; there was always a steady stream of cab drivers and workmen who came in for tea and toast or a full breakfast from seven o'clock onwards. What a treat it was for Muriel to lie in bed every other day. It was worth paying my wages just for that. After all, she hadn't busted a gut for the past fifteen years to drag herself out of bed at the crack of dawn and then work all day like a dog. It was high time she indulged herself and started to enjoy life, rather than slave her way through it.

I liked working at the Peach Melba. Gradually I got to know who owned or leased the other shops in the row. A couple of them, including the Post Office, were owned by Indian families who always managed to get the rough end of everyone's gall. Sometimes when I walked along the parade, I could see the women peeking from behind a curtain in the flats upstairs. They were terrified to walk the street. Everyone seemed to hate them, just for existing: the blacks, the whites. They were everybody's scapegoat.

One evening, while I was walking the short distance home from the Peach Melba, I almost tripped over a man who was lying crumpled up on the pavement holding his belly and choking. I bent down and tried to help him, turning his head so he could breathe properly. His eye was gashed, drowning in blood which was still pouring from the wound and seeping into his turban, turning it a deep crimson red. 'No. No. No,' he protested when he saw me and he put out his hand to gently push me away.

'It's all right. I'll help you,' I said.

Suddenly a group of young Indians materialised from nowhere. 'We'll take him now,' they said, surrounding the man and picking him off the pavement. In a second they had disappeared. Only the blood on the pavement was left in evidence that anything had happened at all.

I wasn't to blame, I knew. But I still couldn't help feeling guilty, for being white.

Five shops down was the Post Office, owned by Raman Patel and various members of his multi-faceted family. I popped in here almost every day, either to buy a newspaper, cigarettes for Muriel or stamps so I could send Mum five or ten pounds every week.

Mornings were busy in the Post Office. Often when Raman trudged downstairs from his small flat above the shop, there was already a queue of up to twenty people waiting outside, impatient to cash their Giro cheques and claim their pensions. All he seemed to do was dole out money, counting it with his long bony fingers, picking change from the rows of coins he lined up on the counter behind the metal grill.

Raman's wife, Hemma, looked after the shop in the morning when the Post Office was at its busiest. In the afternoon, she went to help out at her brother's launderette while old Uncle Dadu slowly climbed onto the stool behind the counter and laboriously ploughed his way through the afternoon's business. He was too old to cope with the morning queue.

The shop side of the business was where Raman hoped to make his money. In the centre of the cracked linoleum floor was a large stand with three shelves on either side and a card display at the end. Goods had been carefully laid out, in no particular order. Stationery sat with tins of soup, condensed milk and hairgrips. Tampons, dustbin liners, shoe cleaning accessories and biscuits were on the middle shelf. And on the bottom shelf were a few tatty, out of date magazines which Raman had marked down in price with a thick black felt pen. Along with the magazines were various ketchups and sauces, washing-up liquid and an assortment of other cleaning materials. A dreary selection of birthday and special occasion cards adorned the end of the stand which was, in effect, the centrepiece of the whole display.

Hemma was dusting the shelves when I left. She was always dusting the shelves and keeping a very close eye on the Post Office queue, especially the part of it that wore large coats with deep pockets. Stock had a habit of disappearing. Only a week ago Raman had caught two boys nicking one of the new lever-action bottle openers. But when he grabbed the boy's arm, the boy spat in his face while the other pulled a knife and told him to 'fuck off back to Bombay'. Neither of them had been much more than fifteen. But what could Raman do? The shop window had had three bricks and a saucepan through it already. They had had to invest in an expensive iron grille just to protect their property.

When I emerged from the Post Office, the sky had turned a darker grey and a sheet of rain was beginning to fall, obscuring the 'slats' and the railway lines with a semi-transparent layer of cloud. I began to run towards the Peach Melba, and when I crashed through the filthy glass door the first person I saw was Lucy.

'Your friend's 'ere,' said Muriel sourly. She didn't like Lucy much, especially since she had started to rehearse her new part and become even more arrogant and full of herself. I preferred Lucy when she was depressed. At least she was quiet and showed some degree of humility. As a possible rising starlet, she was unbearable.

'Rosie,' said Lucy. 'Look, look; I've got something to show you.' She frantically waved a sheet of paper in the air and then eagerly put it down and started poring over it again.

'Why aren't you at rehearsals?'

'They don't need me today. I'm not in any of the scenes,' she replied hurriedly. 'Look Rosie, I'm going to buy a flat round here. I've found the perfect place. Second floor, two bedrooms, sitting room k and b.' Lucy thrust a photocopy of an estate agent's details into my hand and sat staring at me, waiting for the sign of approval. Before I had even had time to read it she snatched it away from me again and said, 'And look – communal garden and parking space.'

'But you don't have a car.'

'Well I will have, won't I? I'm not going to spend the rest of my life on the buses. I've made an appointment for this afternoon. We're going round there.'

I grunted, finding it hard to muster any enthusiasm.

'Well don't worry,' she added. 'You'll live there too. I'm not throwing you out.'

I grunted again, feeling slightly better.

Between rehearsals and wandering around Riggs Road hoping to bump into Samuel, Lucy had an annoying habit of hanging around the Peach Melba. She couldn't stand being alone, and if none of her friends were available, she'd come and pester Muriel and me. Lucy saw the cafe as an extension of our living room. Because I worked there, she thought it perfectly within her rights to wander in when she wanted. She was most put out when I said I'd have to charge her for two cups of coffee and the day's 'special'. She expected to be fed and watered too.

Partly because I didn't want to encourage Lucy to hang around and partly because I was busy, I left her to her own devices. Usually she hovered around the tables making airy conversation with whoever was about. If the cafe was empty, she impatiently flipped through a couple of women's magazines, annoyed that I wasn't paying her any attention and waiting for me to finish so I could go and talk to her. That day, while I was in the kitchen finishing off the liver and bacon special, Lucy suddenly appeared around the door.

'Oi you,' Muriel bellowed, a fag balanced precariously on the edge of her bottom lip.

'Oh shut up,' said Lucy, annoyed that Muriel should bellow at her when she obviously had something vitally important to tell us. 'Look, you'll never guess who's just walked in and sat down at table four.'

'Who?' Muriel grunted, plunging her red hands into a sink

of soapy washing-up water and then shaking them dry.

'Him. Samuel,' she mouthed like a goldfish.

'Oh Christ.' Muriel pushed past Lucy and, without even bothering to look for the man, went to the still and pressed down the tap.

'Miserable old bitch,' said Lucy. 'Look. Come on. You can serve him if you get there first.'

'Muriel can serve him,' I answered, annoyed that Lucy should expect me to leave my post for one of her whims.

'Come on,' she whined, 'I swear you won't be disappointed.'

'I'll look later.'

'You've turned into a right fucking bore, haven't you. Frankly I don't know why you didn't stay in Saltingford with those other bloody bumpkins.'

I glared at Lucy, then wiped my hands on a greasy white rag and followed her into the cafe where she sidled against the counter and nodded towards a man sitting by himself on table four. 'There,' she hissed.

'Well it couldn't be anyone else, could it?' I whispered. 'There's no one else here.'

He was a long, thin string of a man with thick blond hair and a strong chiselled jaw. He was about thirty-two, and looked as though he'd been put together by a girl's magazine. 'He's straight out of *Jackie*,' I said.

'He's not.'

'He is.'

'Well so what? He's gorgeous. Go and serve him. Go on. Go and ask him what he wants.'

I looked at Lucy in a long-suffering way and, wiping my livery hands on my apron, marched over to him. Just as I reached the table, Muriel barked out, 'It's self-service here. Unless you want anything hot.'

I blushed and retreated. The man didn't seem to notice. He looked up and asked for a menu. 'Rosie,' Muriel snapped. 'The gentleman wants a menu.'

'I'm not a skivvy,' I snapped at Muriel when she marched into the kitchen. I was furious at having been shown up like that. Lucy had retreated into the corner in a fit of giggles.

'Only staff are allowed in the kitchen,' Muriel barked at her.

And that was that.

Half an hour later Lucy disappeared with the man, Samuel, to view the flat. 'I thought I was meant to be moving in there with you,' I complained, hurt at being left out so instantly.

'He's an expert,' Lucy hissed, as though I should have known better. And she pranced off, almost hanging onto his arm.

An hour later, she sailed through the door with her arms in the air like a flamenco dancer, clicking her fingers and swirling her hips at Bill, one of the cabbies, provocatively.

'Oh Christ, she's back,' said Muriel. 'Look, I've just about had enough of that one, she's a bleedin' nuisance.'

'I don't know what to say. You tell her.'

'She's your friend.'

'Now's not the time,' I said and wandered over to table five with tea and toast.

'Guess what,' said Lucy, dancing over to the counter. She picked up a Danish pastry, took a huge bite from it and then put it back on the pile.

'Look you,' Muriel snapped angrily, 'you can pay for that.'

'Fine. How much is it?'

'Thirty pee.'

'O.K. I'll pay you tomorrow.'

'I won't forget.'

Lucy had already forgotten about the pastry. 'Guess what,' she sang again. 'He's asked me out. For dinner. Tomorrow. And I'm going.' She let her arms drop down for a moment and looked for our reaction. There was none. 'Well don't sound so bloody pleased, will you,' she said sulkily.

'Fine. Great. Wonderful,' I replied flatly, still peeved at

having been left out of the flat-hunting visit.

'You're jealous.'

'Oh don't be so bloody childish Lucy,' I snapped. 'I don't even fancy him.'

Lucy shrugged her shoulders and then, deciding to totally ignore Muriel and me, she started her flamenco dance again. Swirling across the cracked lino floor, twisting around the tables, repeating to herself almost word for word everything Samuel had said. Prattling away to herself, she went on for at least fifteen minutes and once she was tired of dancing, she stopped and stood by the window, staring dreamily out at the rain; a frame on celluloid, a scene from some old Hollywood movie.

'Why don't you give it a break?' Muriel shouted to Lucy. 'You're drivin' us all fuckin' mad. He's not Prince Charles you know.'

'Oh leave 'er be,' said Bill as he rolled up a cigarette and ran his thick, beige tongue along the edge of the paper. 'Nothing wrong with it. Makes a change to see someone happy round here.'

'Thank you Bill,' said Lucy theatrically. She knew quite a few of our customers by now and couldn't resist telling them her stories of simple, everyday television folk. They loved it and she loved to tell. Both Muriel and I were dreading the time when the series went on the air. We hoped her head would be so big she wouldn't be able to get through the cafe door.

'I've got to do something about my boobs,' said Lucy, following me back into the kitchen. She leant against the greasy tiled wall and folded her arms, positioning herself for a chat.

'Look Lucy . . . ' I started, dumping a pile of dirty dishes into the sink.

'They look like melons. Look.'

Lucy pulled her jumper tightly down over her breasts. They did look like melons.

'They're too big. I can't stand big tits. No one's got big tits any more. Women just aren't built like that now. You haven't got big tits.'

'Well I'm not the same shape as you, am I? I'm thinner than you.'

'Oh. So you do think I'm fat, I knew you did.'

'I didn't say you were fat. I just said I was thinner than you. I've got a different build, that's all. You're more. . . voluptuous.'

'Fat you mean. Well I am. Look at this.' Lucy lifted up her skirt and wobbled her large white thighs, then she grabbed a great lump of flesh and shook it. 'Look at that. There's so many craters in that thigh they could do a moon landing on it and never know the difference.'

'Don't be so ridiculous.'

'It's true.'

'How was the flat?'

'Fine. I'm having it.'

I groaned. 'Look Lucy, I'm sorry but you know Muriel doesn't like you in the kitchen. You'll get me sacked.'

'You can get another job. She's such a miserable old cow anyway.'

'That's not the point. I don't want another job.'

'It's about time you did a bit more with yourself, stretched yourself a bit further than this dump.'

I didn't reply, just glared at Lucy who shrugged her shoulders and, feeling deflated, slouched back into the cafe and sat by Bill, who quickly reassured her that she had great tits, a lovely arse and the best bod in the business.

* * *

Lucy immediately fell in love with Samuel. Within a week she was spending every night at his flat and within a fortnight she'd virtually moved in. Things kept disappearing from Riggs Road, first of all her make-up, then shampoo and bubble bath and then records, books and even the hearth rug, which left me with a matted bald patch in the middle of the carpet.

She was obsessed with him. Nothing else existed. It was impossible to talk about anything because every subject somehow led back to Samuel. This is the sort of thing that used to happen.

Muriel and I were sitting at the table enjoying a quiet cup of tea after the lunch time rush. Mr George was sitting at his usual table, lurking in the shadows at the back of the cafe. All was very peaceful and quiet; only the still gurgled away like a great rumbling tummy, letting off steam every now and again. Suddenly Lucy wafted in. Muriel groaned. Mr George sank further back into the shadows. 'Hi Lucy,' I said.

'Just passing,' said Lucy out of breath. 'God it's disgusting out there. I swear we'll end up like Venice one day. Going to work by submarine, waterlogged and flapping around like a horde of drowned rats.' She pulled a chair out and sat down. Then glanced at Mr George, knew who he was, but chose to ignore him. He always ignored her. 'Thought I'd just pop in to say hello,' she said, wrestling with her soaking coat.

'You're dripping on my floor,' said Muriel curtly.

'Sorry,' Lucy leaned forwards and glared at Muriel. 'Sorry if it's raining. It's not my fault, is it? What do you want me to do? Hang my coat up on a lamppost in the street?'

Muriel did not answer. She pursed her lips and took a cigarette from the battered box that was sitting on the table, then snapped off the filter and stuck the rest of it into her mouth. She sat back and stared at Lucy, the unlit cigarette hanging out of her mouth.

'Do you want a light?' Lucy asked flippantly.

'No thank you.'

'Oh. I see. Saving money perhaps.'

Muriel stood up and noiselessly pushed her chair under

the table. 'I'll be down a bit later,' she said and disappeared through the door in the wall to her flat upstairs.

'I don't know how you can work for a bitch like that,' said Lucy airily. Then she sat back in her chair, looked around the cafe as though she expected some change to have taken place, and lit a cigarette herself. She inhaled deeply and then dramatically blew smoke into the air.

This was during the early days of Samuel. 'Thank God he lives somewhere decent,' she said. 'Imagine if they found out where I was living when the show goes out.'

'Who?'

'Everyone of course. I can give them Samuel's address now.'

'You've only been with him a few weeks.'

Lucy dismissed this point with a wave of the hand. 'Of course, in a year's time we might not be so ashamed to live in Riggs Road. Samuel showed me the plans for the block, really quite spectacular. He's terribly clever you know.'

I looked over to Mr George, who was sitting with his back against the wall, staring at Lucy.

'Samuel re-designed the whole lot from scratch. He used to work for the council so he's had experience of these places.' Then she turned around to Mr George and shouted, 'You see, you'll be able to buy your flat in a year or so. It should be quite nice by then.'

A sour look spread across Mr George's face. His moustache twitched and his hand trembled as he grabbed his coat and clumsily made his way out of the cafe, knocking into the tables and chairs as he went.

Lucy raised her eyebrows. 'What's the matter with him then?' She was obsessed.

Samuel lived in a street of large Victorian terraced houses not far from Riggs Road. This street, like so many others in the area, had been the subject of extensive renovation and was made up of the usual jigsaw of estate agents' boards which were either wired to the black wrought iron railings or hung precariously from balconies. Some of the houses had been divided into flats and had front doors with up to eight bells and eight names beside them. And then some of the houses had been left as houses: many tarted up, others allowed to decay. Neglected properties blemished the street every few doors: boarded windows, graffiti smeared across walls and bald patches of mud as front gardens. They wouldn't stay like that for long. These houses were snapped up by anyone who could or couldn't afford them.

Samuel lived in a house. When he opened the front door, he was wearing an apron that preached the virtues of real ale. 'Rosie!' he exclaimed, as though I was totally unexpected. 'Come in, come in.' And then he gave me a kiss, took my hand and pulled me into the sitting room.

Lucy appeared from the kitchen, also wearing an apron, with tits on. 'Rosie!' she chirped, rushing over to greet and kiss me as though she hadn't seen me for months. 'How are you?'

'Fine,' I mumbled awkwardly, taken aback at having been greeted so enthusiastically, firstly by someone I had barely met and secondly by my flat mate.

'Sam's cooking,' said Lucy, grinning at her love, 'but I've promised to make the salad, so I'll just leave you two to it for a moment.'

Leaving Samuel and me together was obviously part of Lucy's plan for us to get to know each other quickly. We both stood there feeling uncomfortable and finally Samuel suggested I take off my coat. I took it off, and he hung it up.

'I'll just see how the spaghetti's doing,' he said when he came back from the hallway. Then he disappeared into the kitchen.

The room was painted white. It had a large bay window and a high ceiling under which there ran a blue cornice.

Polished wooden floorboards were covered with various oriental rugs and the walls were blotted by a selection of nondescript paintings. 'Don't ask me what they're all about,' said Lucy, coming in with a bottle of wine and a couple of glasses. 'They don't mean anything to me.'

'Me neither.'

'Blots of paint spattered on a canvas; that's what it looks like to me.'

'What is it?' I asked, cocking my head and trying to make sense of a series of red streaks that were smeared across the picture.

'Huh. God knows. Sam says it's the apocalypse. I say the painter's girlfriend's got the curse.'

'It's the apocalypse,' Samuel interjected, taking the wine from Lucy and pouring a glass for me.

'Of course. I should have known. What else could it possibly be?' Lucy replied. 'A glass for me too please.'

'Coming.' Samuel handed her a glass of wine and then lowered himself downwards, letting his body ooze onto the floor like a string of spaghetti. 'Do you like art?' he asked.

'That's not art,' Lucy snapped.

'Some,' I answered, ignoring her. Samuel ignored her too. He smiled and nodded his head at me understandingly, as though he expected me to suddenly unburden my life story. I didn't know what else to say. 'I don't know anything about it,' I finally said. 'I like what I like. And I don't like what I don't like.'

'Very profound.' Lucy perched herself astride a chair and was pinning back her mass of red hair with a clip she had clamped between her lips.

'Well,' I decided to stumble on, 'I like what I understand. If I don't understand art, like that,' I nodded at the period piece on the wall, 'then how can I like it? It doesn't mean anything to me. Surely it's the job of the artist to communicate. That's what art's all about, isn't it?'

'Yes.' Samuel slowly began to form an answer in his mind

as he stared at the dreadful painting. 'Personally I prefer abstract art. I find it more challenging. Sophisticated.'

'I wouldn't call that sophisticated.'

'A juvenile delinquent could do that,' chirped Lucy.

'Rarefied then.'

'Subjective,' I added. And everyone seemed happy at that.

'Samuel writes,' said Lucy.

'Oh.' Of course Samuel would write.

Later, during dinner, I watched Samuel laboriously wind the spaghetti around his fork, his long head drooping from his neck as he sucked the pasta into his mouth, splattering the front of his shirt with sauce. From a distance he was quite good-looking, but on closer inspection rather nondescript. True, he had the famous square chin, but the rest of his face was a disappointment. His narrow, pointed nose sloped down from a pair of cold, grey eyes and his head was crowned by a thinning mop of sandy hair that was cut very short and receded almost halfway across his skull. He said very little while he ate, though he knew he was being watched by Lucy and me. Like a child he drew attention to himself through his silence. I tried to ignore him but couldn't. Lucy couldn't either.

'You know there's a rapist about,' said Lucy, picking into her salad, which sat in an oily heap on her side plate. 'He's claimed two victims in the past week. I saw it in the paper.'

'Where?'

'Round here. Down alleys. Late at night. Frankly, I think, more fool them if they're going to wander around in the middle of the night. They're asking for it, don't you think?'

'No I don't.'

'I'd be more scared for my life than my virginity,' said Lucy in a very matter-of-fact way.

'Well, if it was only a question of virginity, you wouldn't have much to lose, would you?' I snapped, annoyed.

'We're all capable of rape,' Samuel mumbled. 'It's inherent.'

'In men.'

'In us all.'

'Hardly. Women can't rape men.'

'They can rape his mind.'

'Darling, you sound as though you've been hurt,' cooed Lucy sarcastically. 'I'm talking about physical rape. Anyone's capable of mental rape.'

'Women have a special technique.'

'Oh, he has been hurt.'

'You would say that. You're a man.'

'Men always think they're the bearers of all suffering. The slightest thing and they'd lie down and die like hedgehogs.'

Samuel ignored her. 'Mass rape, of course, can be turned to sport. The nazis did it. So did Cromwell. Personally, I'm amazed it doesn't happen more often. I'm amazed we don't look at why it doesn't happen more often, rather than why it did happen.'

Lucy began to make loud snoring noises. She then dropped her fork on her plate and sat back folding her arms and grinning. 'Don't mention the war.'

Samuel and I looked at each other and raised our eyebrows.

'I'm sick of the war. We never hear the end of it. When will they bury it for good?'

'When people lose interest,' said Samuel. 'When the war generation dies off.'

'An extinct race. Of course, everything is still recorded on film. Twenty million versions of the war. Just in case we could ever forget.'

'We're not meant to forget.'

'No. And we never will, will we?' Lucy stood up and noisily began to scrape the leftovers of the congealed spaghetti onto one plate. Then she stacked them up, and marched into the kitchen leaving Samuel and me alone.

After supper, Lucy was keen to show me round the house. More for her own benefit than mine. She was very proprietorial at Samuel's.

'That was the sitting room,' she said, leading me out of the stripped pine door. The hallway was dark, lit only by a light in a stained glass shade of a very strange shape. Clothes – coats, hats, shoes, scarves, jumpers – newspapers, fluff and dust were everywhere, trailing up the banisters that disappeared into great black darkness on high. 'And that's the loo.' A solitary lavatory sat in what must once have been a cupboard under the stairs. 'The dining room – which we never use.' 'The spare bedroom. Another bedroom. Bathroom. Our bedroom.' Lucy stood holding the door open, staring at me expectantly.

'Nice,' I said.

'Come inside.' She dragged me into the large, cold room which was dominated by a huge brass bed that rested centre stage on the polished wooden floor. It was a very masculine room, with deep red curtains draping onto the floor and architectural plans adorning the walls. It smelt of man. A heap of clothes had been dumped on top of a round mahogany table that sat in one corner, and somewhere in the pile I detected a few of Lucy's things. 'Well,' she asked eagerly, 'what do you think?'

'I think it's very nice.'

'No. About him. What do you think of him?'

'Oh. Well, he's all right.'

'You don't like him.'

'I do. I don't really know him.' I paused and looked round the room. 'I don't know. There's something . . . something about him. Men like him always have rich parents and social consciences.'

'So what's wrong with that?'

'Nothing I suppose.'

'You're such a snob, Rosie. Come here. I want to show you something.' Lucy took my arm and dragged me around the bed; she then opened the drawer to a small mahogany bedside cabinet. 'Look,' she said, handing me a pile of black and white photographs. 'They're all me.'

And there she was. Naked. Tied to the bed. Legs astride. As close as you could get without putting the picture out of focus. Shot from behind, in the foetal position, legs up, cunt out. Somewhere, in every shot, was either a glimmer or the full flowering of Lucy's genitalia. After I had seen the first five or six pictures, I handed them back to her.

'You don't like them?'

'It's not that. I don't like the eye behind it.'

'What do you mean? Samuel's a brilliant photographer. Look at this.' Lucy eagerly shuffled through the pictures and pulled one out of her hanging naked on the wall, like Christ on the cross. 'Look at the light.'

'Was Samuel looking at the light?'

'Yes. Look. It's the composition. You're just looking at it from a sexual angle. There's a lot more to it than that.' Lucy paused and looked at the picture. 'It is erotic. It turned me on like mad posing for them.'

I had barely walked twenty yards along the street when it began to drizzle again. Tiny drops of water appeared out of the black night and slowly dribbled down the back of my collar, gliding over my neck. The temperature had dropped several degrees, so I wrapped my arm around my waist and scuttled along with my head down. Past one in the morning the streets were deserted, the moon obscured by the clouded sky.

I had had to leave, then, on my own. I forgot about the rapist, until I contemplated taking a short cut down Groper's Lane. Lucy thought that girls who were out alone in the early hours 'asked for it'. Was I 'asking for it'? What if you had no choice? What if you were working?

That evening, after dinner, after the guided tour and the

unique insight into Lucy's anatomy, a man called Paul had arrived. With him he brought a portable telephone, two grams of cocaine and the new Supertramp album. We all settled down, the record was placed carefully on the turntable, the cocaine (a proportion of it at least) was neatly chopped and sliced into four lines and the telephone lay on the sofa, dormant.

It transpired that Paul had actually been invited to dinner as well, to make up a foursome. But he had clients to wine and dine and graciously managed to honour us with his presence once he had got rid of them. 'I didn't think I was going to make it at all,' he said. 'At one point I feared the Gaslight might be next on the agenda.'

'What's the Gaslight?' I asked.

Paul looked at me and raised his eyebrows, grinning. He had a nice smile, full of manicured white teeth. 'A club,' he said. Then he looked at Samuel, who was also smiling. 'A drinking club . . . of sorts . . .'

'I see.'

Paul, it seemed, existed almost exclusively on cocaine, black coffee and champagne. He was tall and gaunt with wavy dark hair and black semi-circles under his eyes that looked like bruises. I liked him. I liked his easy-going manner, even though it was laced with a touch of city neurosis.

Having downed several glasses of wine, it didn't take much to convince me that 'cocaine was good for me'. I took the rolled ten pound note and ran it along the line of white powder, snorting it up my nose like an elephant. I sniffed, closed my eyes and let my head drop backwards. Immediately I could feel the effects. Immediately I felt good.

'I've smoked dope,' I said later, when Paul handed me the mirror for my third toot. He had stretched his long, sinewy body out onto the floor next to me and seemed to be taking an item of clothing off every five minutes. First it was the jacket, then the tie, then the shoes and now he was beginning to open his shirt.

'Oh, that stuff's no good,' he said. 'It just makes you want to go to sleep. Now this, this is the high performance drug.' He shook the little white envelope and smiled again. 'Little packets like this have made me a lot of money.' He raised his eyebrows again and put the envelope into his pocket.

'You deal it?'

'Oh no. I indulge. It keeps my performance at a peak, for longer.'

I grinned. He grinned. We all grinned. We all felt absolutely wonderful. Lucid. Clear. Alert. Half-baked ideas that had been mulling around in my mind for years suddenly popped out of my mouth, perfectly formed and presented. I felt confident, bright and in control.

Then, suddenly, I was gripped by a terrible, consuming fear. Fear of nothing. But I had to get out. I had to get away. I had to get home. Anxiety was tugging at me from the inside, pulling me into a vacuum. I was drowning in a prickly guilt that stabbed at my gut, making me want to shit.

That was why I found myself walking home at one a.m. Paul had offered to drive me, but I didn't want him anywhere near me. They had tried to call a cab, but I didn't want to wait. I just ran. Scuttled off into the night.

'Hey babe.' Two black men appeared from a warehouse entrance. 'Hey babe, we'll take you home.'

I didn't know what to do. The street was deserted; a few dim lights spread an eerie glow across the wet road. There were no cars about. Nothing. So I kept my head down and carried on. I knew there was no point in running. If I ran, they'd run after me. And then I thought, should I reply, or should I ignore them? If I replied, they'd take it as a come-on. If I ignored them, they'd take it as a rebuff and think I was insulting their colour. Either way I was at their mercy.

'Hey, come 'ere baby.' The one wearing the multi-coloured tea cosy suddenly stumbled back against a dustbin. He lunged out to grab his friend and break his fall, holding up his can of Special Brew so as not to spill any. Then he yelled 'shit' and disappeared arse first into the black hole of the bin, still holding his beer like the Statue of Liberty brandishing her torch.

As they negotiated the dustbins, the two men forgot all about me and I hurried away. They weren't rapists. But how could I tell? Walking that street at night, every man I met was a potential rapist. It was infuriating to be totally at the mercy of these men, to be so dependent on how they felt. Would I get home safely or not? It was up to them. As though I were at their mercy. Anyone would think they had a right to rape or mug or murder. Had they been given that right? By whom? By women? Or had they taken it?

* * *

Mr George had been looking forward to seeing Muriel all day. He found her a source of comfort and strength. And there was nothing Muriel liked better than to feel she was needed by her customers. A few of her loyal and long-serving regulars – all men of course – had been singled out for the special 'Muriel treatment'. She would listen to their problems, offer advice, comfort them, coddle them, mother them and fuck them. Muriel saw herself as playing a vital role in the lives of all these men. It made her feel better to be of use, she said.

When Mr George arrived outside the steamy cafe window, he didn't see Samuel at table four reading *The Guardian*, with one eye on the paper and the other on me. He slid behind his table, quietly opened his briefcase and took out a copy of *The Mirror*. He'd read half of it the afternoon before but hadn't been able to concentrate for long. These days his concentration only lasted a few minutes before his mind began to wander, usually to sex. It seemed as though his whole body was gradually grinding to a halt, his movements became slow and heavy and his mind seemed to be clouded by a hazy fog. He tried to keep his brain alive by reading some of the quality papers or attempting a crossword, but sometimes he didn't even have the strength to lift the pen.

'Morning,' said Samuel, lowering his paper and peering over at Mr George.

'Morning,' Mr George grunted nervously, then ruffled his paper and let his head drop.

'Morning George,' said Muriel. She always called him George; she didn't realise it was his last name. 'Cup of tea?'

'Please.' Then he looked back at his paper, aware that Samuel was staring at him in an irritatingly nosy way.

'Great cup of tea here,' said Samuel, holding up his cup and grinning at Muriel.

Muriel smiled at him patronisingly and roughly pulled the tap of the still down to re-fill her huge teapot.

Mr George ignored him. He despised people like Samuel, social worker types, sanctimonious do-gooders who never stopped asking questions and always wanted to be taken into your confidence. This one was even worse; this one was instrumental in Mr George's eviction from his home. A home that had become a part of him, that he and his wife had shared their life in. A home he had looked after and cherished. And now, in a sweep of that man's pencil, it was going to be gutted, tarted up and turned into 'desirable residences' for all the snot-bags in London. God he hated them.

That morning, I had retreated into the kitchen to do a stock-take and prepare the 'special' which was Shepherd's Pie. The stock-take had been a spur-of-the-moment decision, made when I saw Samuel's long droopy body wade through the door of the cafe. I wasn't quite sure how to deal with him. Recently he had made several visits to the cafe – alone – and sat behind his newspaper, staring at me. I could feel his wishy-washy eyes following me round the room. 'Any chance of another cup of tea, Rosie?' he'd ask. 'A cup of Rosie Lea.' And then smile. I smiled back, feeling guilty but not sure how else to react. That morning, when I put the tea down in front of him, he said, 'You made quite a hit with Paul the other night, you know. He keeps asking me for your phone number.'

'Oh.'

'To be honest, I'm not so sure I want to give it to him.'

'Oh?' I stammered again.

'Well? Shall I?'

'I don't know. If you want.' And I scuttled back into the kitchen.

Luckily I was still in there when Lucy breezed in on one of her impromptu visits. She had spent the past couple of nights at Riggs Road. Samuel claimed to have work to do, and she was convinced he was bored with her. On this day, she was especially shocked to see Samuel in the cafe because he had known she wasn't working that morning.

She stood by the door, dressed in a smart grey wrap-over mac with her hair pulled up in a bun. She looked quite elegant; her appearance had changed since the series had gone on the air and she had made her debut in the public eye. It seemed inconsistent when she emerged from Riggs Road done up in all her regalia.'It's like a lamb crawling out of a pig-sty,' she said. I could certainly see her point. 'What are you doing here?' she finally asked Samuel.

'I . . . er . . . well I was just on my way round to the flat actually,' Samuel stammered, blushing.

'Then why didn't you ring and say you were coming?' The terror on Lucy's face was pitiful. Her pale green eyes were frozen; her hands quivering as she fiddled with the strap on her handbag.

'I was going to surprise you.' Samuel fumbled with his newspaper and roughly began to fold it up. 'And I didn't know if I'd have time . . . '

'But you've had time to come in here.'

'Yes I know.I wanted a quiet read of the paper first. . . before coming round. Do you want a coffee?'

'No.'

'Tea?'

'No.'

'Well come and sit down then.' Samuel patted the seat beside him, as though he were enticing a child. 'Come on.'

Lucy's bottom lip was trembling. She didn't believe a word he said. Not a word.

'Shit,' Samuel yelled, flopping back into his chair and throwing his arms up. 'All I've done is come in for a cup of tea. Now I find myself being put through the third degree.'

Lucy did not move from the door. 'I'm not putting you through the third degree.'

'That's what it sounds like.'

'I haven't said anything.'

'You don't have to. My God, you really don't have to.'

Samuel pursed his lips together and stared defiantly out of the steamy window. He couldn't see much. Smudgy black cabs dotted along beneath the arches.

'All right,' said Lucy, moving towards him.

'No don't. You know, it's just not on.'

'Well I'm sorry. But what do you expect me to think? I didn't know you were going to be around . . .'

'What did you think?' Samuel snapped.

'I don't know . . .'

'Do you have to think anything at all? Why read a thousand words into an empty book?'

'All right. I'm sorry.' She looked at Samuel with her naughty little girl look and cautiously smiled.

'And I can't stand that look,' he snapped.

'Come on darling,' said Lucy. 'I've said I'm sorry. You know what I'm like.'

Mr George sat at his table and smirked. It was the first time he had smiled for over two weeks.

That evening Lucy got completely drunk. Once again, she

had been relegated to Riggs Road and lay inertly on the sofa, staring into space, swigging Soave from the bottle and rambling on endlessly about Samuel. I sat, bored, in the armchair, vaguely watching television, vaguely listening to her prattle on. 'I'm not surprised you're not happy with him,' I said. 'You spend all your time worrying about breaking up with him.'

'I am happy with him.'

'Doesn't sound like it to me. You never leave him alone.'

'I do. I haven't seen him for four nights.'

'Only because he's booted you out.'

'You've got such a nice way of putting things.'

'Well it's true.' I sighed and turned to the game show that was droning away in the background. I had been bad-tempered ever since Lucy had told me Paul was married. He had phoned me that evening (Samuel must have given him my number after all) and invited me for dinner. He was the only man I had liked since I'd been in London, and a far cry from the abrasive Suffolk boys who had lured me behind the changing lockers at the fish market.

'It doesn't mean to say you can't go out with him,' Lucy had said. I glared at her and screwed up my mouth. 'He won't leave his wife though, I can tell you that. They never do. It's too expensive.' I frowned again. 'Anyway, he and Pat have a great marriage, the perfect marriage, the perfect couple. She's gorgeous and he's loaded. Or rather he's gorgeous and loaded.'

Lucy took a noisy slurp of Soave. 'Sam needs space,' she said, staring up at the ceiling.

'That's because you're stifling him. Honestly Lucy, you've got everything you've ever wanted and all you do is sit around moping about that prick.'

'He's not a prick.'

'Whatever he is, he's not worth getting so morose about. Why don't you go out and do something instead of clinging to him like a limpet? You'll push him away. You're already pushing him away.'

'Oh?' Lucy turned and glared at me.'What makes you say that?'

I shrugged my shoulders. 'Well . . . it's obvious, isn't it?'

'Is it? Not to me it isn't.'

'It's obvious Lucy, because he wants space.'

'Actually, I think he fancies you.'

'Don't be so stupid.'

'I do. How many other times has he been into the Peach Melba on his own?'

'He is allowed to, you know Lucy. He does work around the corner.'

'Ah, so he has been in before?'

'I don't know. Once or twice maybe. I never really notice.'

'What do you mean, you never notice? He's your best friend's boyfriend, you've been to his house for dinner and you don't even notice when he's in the cafe?'

'I don't because I hardly ever speak to him. I'm always busy.'

'He does fancy you.'

'Don't be stupid.' Why did I feel guilty and try and cover up for Samuel? After all, I had nothing to hide. I certainly didn't fancy him. Of course, Lucy wouldn't believe that. Lucy always believed what she wanted, particularly if it was for the worst.

'I don't know what to do,' she said, letting out a hollow sigh. 'I just don't know what to do.'

'Don't do anything. You're making a big deal out of nothing. There's no problem, so why create one?'

Lucy scowled and stretched out on the sofa. She was curled up in her dressing gown with make-up smudged around her eyes, her face looked pale and tired. 'If I let him go, he'll fly away,' she said, throwing her arm into the air and then waving her hand around.

'Then why do you want him?'

'He's probably out with some bitch now.'

'Why should he be? He told you he wanted some time on his own. Why should he lie?'

'Because they always do. Pass that ashtray over, will you? This one's full.'

'You enjoy it, don't you? Lying there like a wallaby. Sunk into the depths of your own morbid thoughts.'

'If he wasn't around I wouldn't have them.'

'You'd have them whoever you were with.' I sat back in the chair and turned to the television – the game show was over at last.

The battered gas fire belted out a stream of heat, filling the room with a soft, drowsy glow. Lucy, I could see, was getting more and more drunk. She was well into the two-litre bottle of wine which was now three-quarters empty (I had had only two glasses). Suddenly a skinny grey cat poked its head round the living room door. It looked at us both and then disappeared again, fast.

'It's that fucking cat,' Lucy screamed, picking up her slipper and hurling it at the door. 'Where did it come from?'

'I don't know.'

'Well how did it get in? There's nothing in the kitchen for it to eat.'

'Only floorboards. It might have acquired a taste for them by now.'

Lucy folded her arms determinedly. 'Well I'm not feeding the fucking thing. It hasn't been back for weeks.'

'How do you know? You haven't been here for weeks.'

'You haven't been feeding it, have you?'

'Well someone's got to. Poor thing. It'll die otherwise.'

'Oh shit Rosie. Let it die, can't you. Why not? What sort of a life does it have anyway?'

'That's not the point.'

'Revolting, disgusting, mangy thing. It's one big tapeworm covered in fur.'

'Take it to the vet then and get it treated. Or put it down.

You can't just leave it to die.'

'Cats are very independent creatures. They can look after themselves.' Lucy hauled one leg and then the other onto the floor, preparing to stand up. 'Shit,' she said when she finally managed to pull herself up into an almost vertical position. 'Shit. I feel sick.'

'Are you O.K.?'

'No. I feel sick.' Suddenly, she lumbered forward, swaying from side to side, knocking into the chair, banging either side of the doorway and finally crashing into the loo. She headed for the big white china basin she had come to know so intimately, pushed up the seat, collapsed into a heap on the floor, and then began. She had to be sick. Once it was out of her system she'd be better, she knew. She knew how to make herself sick: gin, vodka, whisky, white wine, dry white wine, acid white wine, wine vinegar, a pint of it, a pint of acid white wine, drink it down in one, drink it down, your pint of dry, very dry wine. She retched.

A wave of acidic brown fluid surged through her gullet. She hadn't eaten that day, so there wasn't much to throw up.

Gin, vodka, whisky, white wine, dry white wine, a pint of it, drink it down in one, and another, and another, drink it down, go on, throw it down.

She vomited again.

Finally Lucy emerged from the loo looking terminal. Her eyes were watering, her make-up everywhere and her hair sticking out in all directions, held there by sweat. She collapsed back onto the sofa and let out a loud groan. Death seemed inviting. 'Turn the box off will you,' she moaned.

I turned the television down. She must have felt bad. She always had to have something on – the radio, television, record player — some noise. Any noise. She hated silence.

'I just want to be quiet,' she gasped.

'There's some coffee down there,' I said, nodding to the cup I'd put on the floor beside the sofa.

'Thanks.'

Then she fell asleep and never touched it.

I decided to meet Paul for dinner. After all, I didn't want to marry him and it was his problem if he had a wife already. I suggested we meet at the bistro where Lucy used to work.

'Oh for God's sake. Couldn't you do any better than that?' Lucy moaned as she interrogated me when I got home that night. 'Why didn't you get him to take you somewhere decent?'

I grunted. 'I quite liked it . . .'

Lucy clicked, annoyed. 'All right. Then what?'

'Well, nothing really.'

'Obviously, seeing as you're back here already.'

'We talked, that's all. Had a nice dinner.'

'Didn't he ask you back? Didn't he try anything on?'

I paused for a moment, not sure how to answer this. I hadn't formulated what had happened in my own mind yet. 'Well he did, yes. He asked me home actually.'

Lucy reached out for her cigarettes and shook one out of the packet. 'And . . .'

'Well I went . . .'

'And . . .'

'Stop saying "and" like that. It's getting on my nerves.'

'Well . . . and . . .'

'Well I liked him. I thought, well, you know, why not?' I paused for a moment. 'And . . . er . . . well, his wife was there.'

Lucy didn't say anything. She stared at me, smoking, waiting, watching.

'She was going to join in.' I looked at Lucy and shrugged my shoulders.

'Well come on. Did you do it?' Lucy snapped.

'No, of course not. That's why I'm here.'

'Oh you're so boring.'

'I'm not. Why should I? I'd never even met her before.'

'She's gorgeous.'

'So?'

'And so's he.'

I sighed and frowned at Lucy. 'Really Lucy. You would have run a mile.'

'I wouldn't.'

'You would.'

'How do you know? I might have done it with a woman.'

'You might have, you'd like to have, but you haven't.'

'I don't see how you can be so sure.'

'Because you would have told me if you had. You never would have been able to keep something like that to yourself.'

Lucy grunted.

'Honestly, you're so full of bullshit. You should hear yourself sometimes.'

She grunted again and then shrugged her shoulders. 'Oh well; are you seeing him again?'

One evening, when I came in from work, I noticed that the Georges' windows were boarded up. 'What's going on next door?' I asked Lucy, flopping onto the sofa. For some reason she had taken to my deck chair and was sitting in it looking very serene, with a pair of horn-rim glasses on the end of her nose, reading her lines for the next day.

She looked up. 'What?'

'Next door. It's all boarded up.'

'That's what the racket was. It drove me mad. How can I remember a thing with that bloody din going on?'

'Well . . . have they left or what?'

'I don't know.' Lucy wasn't in the least bit interested. She puckered her lips and looked back at the script. 'Can you read Jud?' she asked.

'In a minute. I want to see what's happened next door first.'

'I don't see why you're so worried. If they've moved they've gone to the 'slats', which are infinitely better than this rat-infested hole anyway.'

'You've changed your tune, haven't you?' I said, as I unbuttoned my jacket and threw it on the sofa. 'I suppose it doesn't matter to you any more. Now that you're all right, Jack.'

She looked up at me, screwed up her forehead and let the script drop onto the floor. 'All right then.'

On the balcony, Lucy stood behind me shivering while I examined the boards which had been roughly nailed across the window. 'I wonder why they haven't boarded up the door,' I said.

'Try and open it.'

I cautiously pushed open the letter box and tried to peek inside. 'It's been boarded up from the inside. I can't see anything.' I let the letterbox drop and walked back to the window, cupping my hands to try and see through a gap in the planks. 'It's boarded up on the inside too,' I said. 'Hang on, there's a light on in there. Lucy! I can see a light!'

'They must be in there,' Lucy hissed.

'They are. I'm sure I can see a shadow moving.' We were both whispering.

'Oh my God, Rosie. They've barricaded themselves in.'

PART THREE

Many changes were made during the next few months, both in London and Saltingford.

In London, Lucy bought her flat and we shortly moved around the corner into the smart part of Bethnal Green where they lined their streets with trees, and the interiors of their houses with Laura Ashley wallpaper. Lucy became more unbearable. As her success in the series grew and she became more familiar with fame and fortune, she grew more insecure in her relationship with Samuel. When she was at home she was always grumpy and bad-tempered because he had kicked her out for the night. When she was with him she followed him around like a lap-dog, begging for reassurance and grateful for the smallest pat on the head.

When I first telephoned the council to tell them the Georges had barricaded themselves into their flat, no one seemed bothered. After a week, they sent someone round. And after ten days they began to panic. The last thing they wanted was a couple of corpses and a scandal on their hands. The Georges finally emerged from the flat, pale, vacant and broken. Of course they knew very well that they would never be able to stay in their home and so, eventually, Mr George agreed to come out providing they never referred to him again as a number and always called him 'Mister' George, as was his due. It was the only way he could get out with his dignity intact. When he and his wife did finally teeter over the threshold of their front door, Lucy began to clap. She received a grateful smile from Mrs George, who thought her husband had gone completely mad and was convinced they were both going to die in there. It was the most terrifying ordeal of her life.

After this incident, Mr George was sectioned in the loony bin for three days. Apart from a very painful ingrowing toenail, they couldn't find anything wrong and released him one day early. He spat in their faces and marched off down the drive, swinging his arms like a nutter.

In Saltingford, Margaret married Ron and they moved to the bungalow on the beach which had been timely vacated by the death of Ron's uncle. Nobody went to the wedding, which happened in Ipswich one morning while no one was looking. The marriage was acknowledged in the village by a piss-up in the King's Head, when even Randalls was spotted smirking as a jug of beer was emptied over Ron's head of thick black hair.

Since Margaret had married Ron and moved into the bungalow, things improved greatly for Mum, who was left with Toby. Margaret had decided that this would be best for everyone, particularly her. She had become so lazy she couldn't be bothered to look after anyone, including herself. 'Ron don't want Toby in the bungalow,' she grunted as she packed her things to move out of the pen. 'And I'll have to respect his wishes, as he's to be my husband.'

Mum spluttered. 'Well, no one will ever think Toby is his, will they?'

Margaret ignored her and finished packing. She was thankful to get away from Mum and the baby. Of course, moving a couple of hundred yards over the shingle wasn't what she'd hoped for. But at least it was a start. I knew she couldn't give tuppence for Ron, I could see it in her eyes. Even after she was married she couldn't keep her eyes off those G.I.s. She was obsessed with them. If one of them ever offered her more than a quick poke behind the lavatory wall, she'd be off. As far as she was concerned, Ron offered no more than temporary relief.

One day, Lily Jarvis was found tangled up in the Hoover

at the bottom of Father Armitage's stairs. Father Armitage discovered her and went into a complete panic, rushing down the High Street with his cassock hitched up to his knees and calling out for Doctor Figgs. Of course, it was too late for the doctor so Father Armitage did what he could and stood mumbling over Lily's crumpled body, his hands clasped in prayer while he waited for the appropriate authorities to come and scoop the body off his precious Persian rug.

Ron was sorry not to mourn the death of his mother more, but they had never been close. He was far more concerned about his father, George. Six months ago, the lifeboat had been called out in a storm to find two boys who were lost at sea. They found the small dinghy tossing around in the waves less than half a mile out. As George tried to steer the lifeboat towards them, they were lifted by a tremendous surge of water and thrown against the small sailing boat, sending one of the boys flying into the sea. Shakily George stepped down from the helm and Ron took over. It wasn't the first time an accident like this had happened. Yet for George, it was the last time he wanted to experience it. He had seen too many colleagues, too many friends, too many strangers, drown in that sea. The boy was dead before he even hit the water, and though there was nothing he could have done, George blamed himself for yet another wasted life.

Ron had noticed George changing even before Lily died. Sharon's move to Ohio had upset him to begin with, thrown him into some sort of a male menopause and all the attendant depression that came with it. Ron had invited George to live in the bungalow rather than stay up in the village on his own, but his father vehemently refused. He couldn't stand Margaret. No one could stand her.

'You look pasty,' said Mum when I arrived back for Easter. She always said that.

'You're one to talk.' I always said that. And then I took Toby in one arm and cuddled Mum in the other. She looked a lot better. Better than I'd seen her for years. She'd shed almost two stone, her hair was clean and I even detected mascara on her eyelashes. 'No, you look good,' I said. It wouldn't have been fair to leave her thinking she looked pasty, when she looked wonderful.

'Well, you don't. I don't know what you get up to up there in the smog. What good's it to you? Not a lot I can see.'

'I like it.'

Mum bent over and gently tweaked Toby's nose as I held him in my arms and nuzzled my face against his. He was happy, gurgling and clean. He'd grown; his face was beginning to take shape, to take on some character, beyond the pudgy baby face. And he was sprouting more hair, wiry black curls spiralled out of his head. His whole body wriggled like a worm in a nappy as he grinned and wrestled to get back to the floor. He had passed the age when he was happy to lie like a lump in our arms. Now he wanted to find out what life was all about. What a shame. I liked him as a lump, it was comforting to be needed.

'Give him to me for a minute, I'll put a jumper on him. It's cold today.' Mum stretched out her arms and Toby willingly allowed himself to be passed over and 'jumpered'. Mum obviously had her hand in again. It took her ten seconds to get that jumper on; it took me ages. Then she gave him a huge kiss on the cheek and lowered him to the floor. 'He likes it down there,' she said. 'Just like you. Always sticking your nose into one thing or another. I had to watch you all the time.'

I looked around the pen. It was almost tidy and certainly a lot cleaner than I'd seen it before. An assortment of brightly coloured toys were strewn around the floor, some chewed, some not, some with paint, others without, and I noticed Mum had actually hung a couple of paintings up, one of a nearby castle and the other a sea view.

'They look nice. Where did you get them?'

'Miss Stiff-finger donated them. She said she was having

a turn out and wondered if we wanted them. Look all right, don't they?'

'Fine. It looks a lot better in here.'

'You can sleep on the sofa,' said Mum, nodding at the tatty single bed she used to sleep on. 'Toby and I sleep in the other room now. Look, I found him a cot in the jumble sale.' Mum led me into the bedroom and proudly pointed at the cot, in which there lay a couple of soft white blankets. 'It's better than a drawer. Mind you, he's big enough to have his own bed now.'

I looked down at Toby, who was sprawled across the floor, his eyes fixed intently on a battered old car he was pushing across the hearth rug. 'How's Margaret?' I asked.

'Don't know. Don't see much of her really. God knows what she does with herself all day over there. Same as she did here I suppose. Nothing.'

I grunted and turned back into the main living room, where a large Calor gas heater was blasting out hot air. 'Isn't that thing dangerous, with Toby around?'

'He knows it's hot.'

For a while Mum stood in the bedroom doorway with her arms crossed, watching me as I looked around the pen. She gauged my reaction, waiting for me to find fault, to question, to approve or disapprove.

I never knew what to expect when I went back again. I dreaded finding them in that nightmare situation, slumped in front of the television with Mum drunk, Margaret inanimate and Toby screaming in his drawer.

'It looks lovely Mum,' I said. 'Look, sea lavender.' I went over to a small pottery jug which contained a bunch of the purply blue flowers and bent down to inspect them. 'Let's go to the saltings tomorrow,' I said. 'And take Toby with us.'

'He loves it down there. We watch the seals, don't we?' Straining, Mum lowered herself towards the floor and squatted on her thick white legs. 'You love it down there, don't you darling?' she cooed at Toby, who immediately rewarded her with a huge grin before returning to the pressing matter of his yellow car.

Later, after we'd bathed Toby and put him into his cot, we pulled the bedroom door shut and crept back into the main room. The gas fire churned out a steady flow of heat, and with only one lamp in the corner dimly lighting the room, it was very cosy. Mum and I both collapsed in armchairs and closed our eyes, relaxing to the sound of the waves as they slithered across the shingle outside.

'You must get that hair off your chin,' I said, suddenly noticing that Mum was growing a beard.

'It's all right,' she grumpily replied, not even opening her eyes.

'It looks awful. All you need is a razor.'

'And then it grows back worse. Like stubble.'

'Get some of that cream then. I'll get you some tomorrow, when I go into the village. If I can find it round here.'

'Things do get this far, you know,' Mum snapped. 'Anyone would have thought life stopped at Ipswich.' She crossed her arms and sat pouting, staring straight ahead of her at a blank wall.

'I didn't mean it like that.'

'Oh! How did you mean it then?'

'Just that . . . well . . . just that it's only a small shop in the village. So they're not going to be able to carry much of a stock, are they?'

'Just because you've got some toffed-up life in London, you think everyone else lives like pygmies.'

'I don't. And I don't have a "toffed-up" life.'

'Huh! That's not what it sounds like to me.'

'Well then, you haven't been listening.'

'Huh!' Mum hated London. London was immoral. Not because it was full of filth, drunks, drugs and perverts, but because it was destroying our world. The city was a murderer; it polluted the atmosphere and killed off the plants. The soil was infertile, the air unbreathable. As far as she was concerned, we didn't need a bomb. We were killing ourselves anyway, a long slow suicide. It made her weep when she spoke about it. That's why I didn't talk too much about London. It made her weep.

The next morning I was woken by Toby, who had managed to scramble up onto my bed and was rolling and giggling and squirming all over me. I lifted the eiderdown and made a little hole for him to nestle into. He didn't stay there for long. Within seconds the cover had been thrown back again and he was leaping up and down on my stomach, half winding me.

Ten minutes later, Mum shuffled through and started playing around with the heater, persistently clicking the ignition button and trying to make it spark into action. 'Bloody thing. One day it'll blow us all up,' she grumbled.

'It doesn't look very safe.'

'It's all right.'

Although she doted on Toby, I knew it was a great relief for Mum to have someone else watch him for a while. I stayed with him for the first part of the morning while she enjoyed a walk to the village in search of depilatory cream. Toby and I watched her walking up to the coast road, swinging her arms with her head in the air. She was probably singing, enjoying her freedom. Oh God, it was wonderful to see her happy.

May has always been my favourite time of year. Everything is so raw, so fresh and alive. When Mum came back with a bagful of shopping (she was unsuccessful with the depilatory cream), I decided to wander off for a walk along the beach while she got lunch ready. These days, I could leave her to make our meals. She enjoyed doing it; she insisted on doing it, saying I was back for a break, not to work, and what a real busman's holiday it would be if I was expected to get lunch there as well.

The beach was brown, shimmering in the strong mid-day sun. There was barely a cloud in sight and the air was sharp, turning my cheeks red, pricking them, sharp spiky needles. I didn't care how cold it was. Nothing could beat a clear day in spring.

Already, London seemed a dream. Each breath of the sharp, salty air cleansed my body of the city pollution. Here, I could breathe again. Once I had been suffocated by Saltingford. It had been a prison that drove us all further and further into the cells of our minds. Now, it was a refuge. A return to safety. I only wished I could be sure it would last.

As long as Mum had Toby to look after, she would be fine. I hadn't seen any booze around the pen and hadn't smelt it on her breath for the first time in years. The real problem was Margaret. She had become so unbalanced it was impossible to tell how long she would let Toby stay with Mum. She could change her mind any day, any hour, any minute even. She could even have been setting Mum up by letting her have Toby for a while, so the two could form an attachment, before suddenly separating them. Anything was possible. I shuddered at the thought.

Miss Stiff-finger picked up a huge wicker chair that had gone mouldy sitting in the back shed all winter and took it around to the patio. She then carried out bread, pâté, a small bowl of salad and a butter dish, carefully arranging them all on the white wrought-iron table. Then she sat down, put on her gardening gloves, which she always wore to read the newspaper, and completely disappeared.

'Anyone in?' I called.

Miss Stiff-finger rattled her paper, annoyed at being

interrupted, and peered at me over the top of her pince-nez (the monocle had been abandoned as both eyes were on the blink). 'Rosie!' she said, jolting her head back in surprise.

'I thought you'd drowned, either in the chair or the newspaper.' I opened the gate and slowly walked over the grass to the patio.

'Oh well, this thing. This thing has seen its last summer I think. Look.' Miss Stiff-finger pulled out strands of loose wicker from the arms. 'Frankly, I'm surprised I'm still two feet up. The seat is covered in mould. Look at that; I had to put a cushion down.' She tugged the corner of a dark blue cushion that was peeking out from under her bum. 'Go and get a chair from the kitchen and sit outside in this utterly glorious weather.' She pulled off her gardening gloves and threw them on the ground underneath her. 'Now, of course, it will kill me trying to pick them up again. One has to change one's habits as one gets older, you know. It's most inconvenient. Still, I suppose old age is a privilege many don't enjoy.'

A couple of years short of seventy, Miss Stiff-finger showed signs of having mellowed. She had never been the same since Martha left: it was as though she had taken a piece of Miss Stiff-finger with her. A piece of happiness, a piece of hope, leaving her with the dismal realisation that she was doomed to spend the rest of her life alone. She knew, full well, that it would be impossible to find another partner at her age. Sometimes she wondered if she really wanted one. A companion would have been nice but eventually she grew out of that too. Her cats were company enough; they were independent and didn't answer back. As a strong-willed and selfish person, Miss Stiff-finger grew used to her solitude, devising her own little treats, lunch on the patio being one of them.

'I can't stay for long. Mum's putting lunch together.'

'Well what a relief that is. Thank God she's finally managed to pull herself together, don't you think? Look here, come and sit on the step. I can't stand looking up to people; it strains my neck and the sun's blinding me. Coffee?'

'No thanks.'

'Oh. Why not?'

'I've got to get back.'

'Well, suit yourself. You don't mind if I start my lunch.' She reached over and began to scoop some pâté out of its small earthenware pot. 'I rather like these pots, you know. They look all right, don't they? Don't you think? For keeping bits and pieces in. Knick-knacks and suchlike.'

'Yes. They're useful. We get the larger bowls at work, and then use them for veg.'

Miss Stiff-finger spread the pâté on a chunk of bread and then pushed the whole lot into her mouth. 'Really,' she said, her cheeks bulging as she rolled the food around with her tongue. 'How are things up there? All right?'

'Yes, fine. We've moved. Lucy bought a flat, so we're installed in the posh part of town now.'

Miss Stiff-finger nodded her head slowly, as she digested both her lunch and the news. 'The Grantham girl?'

'Yes.'

'Well, I certainly hope she's got a bit more spunk than her parents. They've been a great disappointment to the lobbying committee. Even Chernobyl hasn't managed to stir them.' She paused for a moment while she prepared another chunk of bread. 'I'm sure someone mentioned they'd seen the daughter on television.'

'They would have. She's an actress. In a soapy sort of serial.'

'Ah. Well then, it is true. I don't watch that much television myself. Do you?'

'Sometimes.'

'Oh dear.'

'Why?'

'Well, your sister.'

'I'm not like that.'

'Oh good.' Miss Stiff-finger picked up the lump of bread and popped it into her mouth. 'Because that's all she does, isn't it?'

I looked blankly through the french windows into Miss Stiff-finger's dark sitting room. 'She used to. I don't think she does now.'

'Ah. Well, I think you'll find she does. Not that it's any of my business. It's just that at night, I can see it flickering through the curtains of that dreary little bungalow down there.'

'Most people watch the box at night.'

'Do they? Oh. Well of course it's not my business.' She stuck her little finger into her mouth and quickly worked it around to the back of her teeth, where she dislodged a gooey lump of bread. 'It's just that the curtains are usually drawn during the day as well, so I assumed she'd be doing the same thing.'

'I don't know,' I moodily replied. 'God knows what she gets up to.'

It was a huge relief to have Ron take Margaret off our hands, though I wondered how he coped with her. I wondered what on earth their relationship could be like. What did they talk about? Did they talk? Did they have sex? What was that like? What was Margaret like in bed? I couldn't imagine either of them getting up to much. All I could see was Margaret slowly wearing Ron down, year by year, decade by decade. I saw him ending up seeking refuge in the pub like his father, George.

Margaret was different to Lily in that she was a lazy lump who never did anything, whereas Lily had always been a manic worker and couldn't last ten seconds without 'doing something'. Both women were the same as far as their utter bossiness and contempt for everyone went.

'Of course Ron has done both you and your mother something of a service by taking Margaret on,' said Miss Stiff-finger hesitantly.

'Poor bastard.'

'I hope he knows what he's let himself in for.'

'He's known her all his life.'

'A third man from the power station has just been diagnosed as having leukaemia. Did you know that?'

'No.'

'He works with Ron, as a fitter.'

'Ron's never said anything.'

'He wouldn't, would he? It's all hushed up. They don't want to cause a stir. They'll lose their jobs.'

Miss Stiff-finger looked very serene considering she had almost been arrested the previous day. Her anti-nuclear group had held a special vigil to mark the anniversary of Chernobyl and Miss Stiff-finger had joined hundreds of others in throwing wreaths into the sea. As she began to walk away from the beach, she spotted a lorry that was used to transport building materials for the third reactor. Moved by the ceremony, she suddenly sprang up into the empty cab of the lorry, released the hand brake and leapt off as it started to rumble forward, building up speed before finally nose-diving into a dune. No one was more surprised by this action than Miss Stiff-finger herself. She received various nods of approval and pats on the back from her fellow supporters and her only disappointment was not to have been arrested. A night in jail was considered one of the highest accolades in the lobbying circuit.

The following day was Easter. Mum and I had been dreading it because Margaret invited the three of us down to the bungalow for lunch. There had to be a catch. I decided to watch who was served with what in case she tried to poison us all.

George Jarvis had also been invited because he and Mum always had a soft spot for each other and we all hoped that, with Lily dead, they might get together. When Margaret and

I were children and we lived in the caravan, he used to turn up with a huge slimy cod or a tub of jellied eels. Sometimes he stayed for a glass of brandy before setting off to spend the evening at the King's Head. He liked Mum. She provided the friendship and understanding Lily had failed to give him.

So the next day Mum wriggled into an orange Crimplene dress and tied a long leather thong around her waist. The dress was hateful, but I knew she was trying her best and told her she looked nice. It pleased her. She smiled and two large dimples were sucked into her chubby white cheeks. The previous night I had actually persuaded her to let me attack her chin with a pair of tweezers. What an improvement! I saw her standing in the bathroom rubbing the palm of her hand around her smooth, hairless chin and nodding in approval. Her hair was clean and tied back into a pony tail. She looked like a child, standing there admiring herself in the mirror. It was the best she'd looked for years and even though we were only plodding over to the bungalow, neither of us could remember the last time she'd been invited out.

Toby was grizzling. He'd been ready for ages and was impatiently crawling around the floor after Mum. Anyone would think he knew where we were going. He whined and cried at the slightest thing, and every time he stumbled into the arm of a chair or slipped on a toy, he let out a long bleating wail.

'Now, now,' said Mum, picking him up and carrying him over to the window where she stood holding him, slowly rocking him backwards and forwards. 'What's all this about, then?' And she'd sway him to and fro as they comforted each other.

Finally, we were all dressed and ready to go. The three of us slowly began to trudge across the beach with Toby in the middle, holding a hand each as he reluctantly allowed himself to be half-lifted across the stones. Mum had never been very steady on shingle, drunk or sober. She kept up the pace and plodded along clutching a red slipper in each hand. She was wearing a pair of black wellington boots for the journey; they didn't do a great deal for the outfit but she didn't have anything else. Boots for outdoors, slippers for indoors. It was all she considered she needed.

Since moving into the bungalow, Ron had made an attempt at clearing the garden, which was strewn with rubbish including rolls of rusty barbed wire his uncle had salvaged from the beaches when they were mined during the war, bits of boat motors, oil drums, soggy cardboard cartons and the old broom which had been slung into the hedge in protest at the American Air Force years ago. As we approached the miserable little dug-out, I saw Margaret peering at our procession from behind the curtain of her bedroom. She stared at us for a while, as though she were wondering what business we had to skirt so close to her territory, and then, as we pushed open the gate, she let the curtain drop and went and sat down on the sofa, waiting for us to ring the bell.

Marriage had not done much for Margaret. She looked worse than ever. Fatter, greasier, paler and shabbier. She hadn't made the slightest attempt to smarten herself up for the lunch; her hair didn't look as though it had been washed for weeks and she was still wearing the same ancient mauve cardigan that was completely stretched out of shape and hung in various lengths around her vast hips. 'Come in then,' she mumbled, sounding irritated at having been disturbed.

Clutching Toby, I stepped into the dark entrance hall. Mum followed.

It was the first time Mum had been down to the bungalow. She had never expected to be invited because Margaret insisted she had only married Ron to get away from the pen. Our mother always seemed oblivious to Margaret's scathing remarks. I often wondered whether she'd cut herself off or if she really didn't care.

All three and a half of us stood in the musty front room

looking around, away from each other, out of the window, at a picture, any focal point. I couldn't admire the bungalow, it was as much of a tip as the pen; filthy, dusty and strewn with crisp bags, biscuit packets, cigarette ash. The curtains were closed and the air stale. The whole room smelt like a very old fart.

Margaret stared at me. She knew what was going through my mind and that there was nothing I could say or do about it. This was her place and I was, in effect, a guest. Instead, I grabbed Toby, who had been totally ignored by his mother, and sat down on the ugliest sofa I've ever seen; turquoise with black plastic arms and four spindly black legs with gilt feet.

'I'll put these on then,' said Mum holding up her slippers and backing up to the wall, where she landed on a chair.

Margaret stood against the kitchen door with her arms folded, staring at Mum struggling with her boots. I was pinned to the sofa by Toby, who had firmly planted himself on my lap with a Postman Pat book. We both watched Mum as she huffed and puffed and finally managed to pull the boots off, one by one, with a great whoosh.

I looked around the room, already annoyed with Margaret. The place was filthy and I couldn't smell anything cooking. 'You were expecting us, weren't you Margaret?' I snapped.

'Oh yes.' And she scuffled off into the kitchen leaving Mum and me to make long-suffering faces at each other.

George Jarvis was sitting on a stool leaning against the soggy wooden bar of the King's Head. Around him were old cronies of fifty years or so, boys and men he had grown up with and come to love. Like himself, some of them had given up on the boats too. Arthur Matheson had arthritis so badly he could barely drive his van any more, and gone were the days when you'd pass him sewing up his nets that were spread over the beach like huge string vests. John Smythe still opened his small wooden hut in the summer and sold fresh fish to the tourists, but sales had dropped off since Chernobyl and all the bad publicity that surrounded the power station.

Because the electricity board had built their rigs on the fishing ground, the fishermen were paid a substantial amount in compensation. This was also intended to cover the fish that were lost when water was sucked from the sea into the massive cooling system of the two reactors. The fish were sifted out and, to prevent any extra loss of revenue to the fishermen, minced up and piped back into the sea. Consequently, there were always flocks of gulls swarming around where the warm water and minced fish were pumped back into the sea.

The CEGB insisted, however, that virtually no radioactive waste went into the sea.

Smythe spluttered in his beer. 'I don't know what they're talking about. You can see it bubbling up at the end of the pipeline, barely a couple of hundred yards out.'

'That's not waste. That's just the water they use to cool the reactor. It makes steam to drive the turbines.'

'That's what they say. They'll kill everything off in the end. Not just the fish, but the soil, the birds, the animals and then . . .' Smythe ran his forefinger across his neck '. . . us.'

'Oh you. You're so bloody morbid,' George snapped. He hated talking about the power station; it was all they ever talked about since the bloody thing had first been built. Why get so upset? It was there to stay. You could protest until you were blue in the face and they wouldn't take the blindest bit of notice. No one would. They never did. Nothing was going to change so they might as well accept it. He was glad not to be on the boats any more. He felt as though his whole livelihood had been contaminated. He didn't want to touch the fish now; they were infected and diseased, polluted from inside to out. These days he had odd jobs gardening and helping Randalls out at the pub two mornings a week. It kept him occupied and he didn't want to do much more than that.

Ron nudged his father. 'Drink up Dad, we've got to get back for lunch soon.'

George grunted and lifted the tankard to his mouth, allowing it to hover for a moment with his chin stuck inside the glass. He had been trying to forget about the lunch. As far as he was concerned it was yet another patronising attempt by Ron to try and 'cheer him up'. What's more, he couldn't stand Margaret. He knew what she was after. He knew she'd be off as soon as she got a better offer. What George couldn't understand was why his son couldn't see that either.

That morning, George had tried to convince himself that it was just another day and dressed in his old blue poncho. But of course it didn't last. Of course he knew it was Sunday, Easter Sunday, and that he was going down to the bungalow. As he stepped out of the door in his everyday clothes, he looked up at the sun, squinted and gave up. What could he do? He had to change. He had to shave. Easter wasn't going to go away.

'That Margaret behavin' 'erself is she?' Arthur Matheson suddenly asked. He was standing beside Ron in his Sunday best, the same brown herring-bone suit and cap he had worn for the past thirty years. Arthur was the only one who still went to church and he always called in to the King's Head after the service.

'She's all right,' said Ron, looking down at his father, who was already scowling at the very mention of his wife's name.

'Well we never see 'er about the village. That's why my missus was wonderin' what she gets up to down there on 'er own all day.'

'She's got plenty to do,' Ron grunted.

'Well, if she hasn't, get 'er pregnant. That always gives them something to think about. That's what I always did with my missus if I thought 'er mind was wandering astray.' Arthur nudged Ron in the ribs sharply and then gave George a wink before grinning at each of the other four men that stood in their usual formation around the bar.

George was not amused. 'Shut yer trap will ya?'

'Huh! hark at that.'

Ron threw down the rest of his pint. He could see that his father was in no mood to go down to the bungalow. His only chance was to get him drunk. 'My round. Come on, finish your glasses. Randalls.'

Randalls was sitting on his stool, leaning against the cold whitewashed wall by the beer taps. Since the lounge bar had been built, he always positioned himself there, so that he could keep an eye on both bars and pull pints of best bitter without having to get off the stool. He rarely said anything to anyone and sat reading a battered copy of *Maritime Warfare*, waiting for everyone to go.

'Five pints and a large Bell's,' said Ron, slamming everyone's glass down on the bar.

Randalls clicked, annoyed, and slowly slid off the edge of the stool to shuffle over to a row of five gummed-up optics that were fixed to the far wall.

'Who's that for?' George Jarvis snapped, knowing perfectly well it was for him.

'Who do you think?'

'There's no point trying to get me drunk.'

'Who said I was?' Ron sank his hand into his pocket and pulled out a pile of coins.

Sitting in a cluster of chairs around the fire in the lounge bar were the Granthams, Lucy and Father Armitage. Sunday lunchtime in the pub was a ritual for Jean and Peter Grantham, who were by now an essential part of village life and had folded very well into the rounds of cocktail parties and jumble sales. Their 'unit' in Ipswich had quickly faded from their memory and it wasn't long before they felt they'd lived in Saltingford all their lives. They were on first-name terms with everyone (except Miss Stiff-finger who no one was on first-name terms with), and after only a short while in the village, had allowed most of their social values to slide into obscurity. At first they felt twinges of guilt for not being more 'active' in local groups, but eventually the twinges went away and they let it all go. There wasn't much room for a social conscience in Saltingford.

Lucy was sitting next to the fire roasting her right thigh and staring at three young 'townies'. Her face was quite blank as she leant forward to watch them. She'd only been back one night and was already bored to death. Saltingford stifled her, even when she returned the conquering film star. Everyone stared at her; children asked for her autograph, adults asked on behalf of their wives, their children, their Aunt Elsie who lived down the lane, anyone would do. But somehow, in Saltingford, it never meant much. Anyone could be a star there. A fisherman who caught a five pound cod was a minor celebrity. So was Mrs Crow who got a mention in the local paper for winning two hundred quid on the premium bonds. And Father Armitage didn't even realise she was famous. She'd been sitting there almost an hour and he hadn't mentioned the series once.

Lucy couldn't stop her mind from drifting back to the events of the previous night, when she had been infuriated by her parents' lack of interest in what she was doing. Of course the series wasn't 'their sort of thing'. Not of any social or cultural significance. She tried to explain, to enlighten them, but they never listened. Or if they listened they never remembered. Basically they just weren't interested. Lucy gave up with the series and moved to the rewards: 'I love the flat. Of course, I could never have bought it on the tips from the bistro.'

'Well, that's something, isn't it?' her father had said, calmly stroking his beard, which had grown so thick and so grey it looked like a dusty old bush.

'And the car.'

'It's a jolly good car,' said Jean, helping herself to the

steaming bowl of stewed lamb that sat in the middle of the table. 'What sort is it?'

'It's a Golf.'

'Oh!'

'German.'

'Oh! We used to have a Beetle years ago. When was that, Peter? When we got married wasn't it? I always rather liked it. We had it for years, didn't we?'

'Always very reliable. Got you from A to B.'

'It was white. Well, of course it didn't stay white for long. And we used to put the roof down. It was wonderful in the summer: we'd put the roof down, you in your carrycot on the back seat, and off we'd go. Off for a picnic in the country.'

Jean picked a carrot out of her stew and popped it into her mouth. She stared ahead, gently smiling, reminiscing. The past always seemed much happier, with life simpler and less cluttered. 'No one wanted much then, did they Peter?' she mumbled dreamily. 'Everyone seems so greedy now.'

'I'm not greedy,' Lucy snapped defensively.

'Oh no, no. I wasn't saying you were. It's just that everyone was happier with their lot, that's all.' She picked another carrot out of the floating mush that lay on her plate and let out a long pensive sigh. 'Just thinking back to the picnics; life was so happy then.'

'It wasn't. You were miserable,' Peter snapped.

'I wasn't.'

'You were. You'd just had the baby and you hated it. Stuck in the house all day, unable to go out to work. It was a terrible time, for both of us.'

Jean did not reply but sat sulking, staring vacantly at her plate.

'It wasn't that bad,' she finally said. 'There were good moments.'

'Not many.'

'I wish you could meet Samuel,' Lucy suddenly chipped

in. She hated it when her parents talked over her. She had expected it to stop when she became a somebody, a respected and recognised person. But nothing changed, least of all them.

'Oh. Who's he?' Jean asked.

'You know who he is. I'm always telling you about him.'

'The architect,' Peter grunted, wiping his bread around his plate to soak up the gravy.

'I wish you wouldn't do that. It makes me feel sick.'

'Don't look then.'

'You did it last week at the Browns'. I could have strangled you.'

'Oh so what? Who cares?'

'It looks awful. That's all.'

'Yes, he's completely redesigned the block of flats I used to live in, you know, in Riggs Road. The whole thing. There's almost a hundred flats there altogether.'

'I thought they were council flats,' her father grunted.

'Well they are. They were. But they're in such a state the council couldn't afford to renovate them, so they flogged them off to a private developer.'

'And where's everyone supposed to live then? What about the people who can't afford to buy their own place? What are they meant to do? Set up home in the gutter?'

'New blocks have been built.'

'That won't last five minutes.'

Lucy blushed and looked over to Jean for help.

But her mother was already beginning to noisily stack the plates. She ignored Lucy and her husband. She was bored with arguing about who was entitled to what. It didn't seem to make any difference whatsoever. All she wanted to do was take what she could get. Trundle into work and do her job until she could give it all up and retire in the garden.

'He used to work for the council,' Lucy added.

'So why isn't he now?' Peter snapped.

'I don't know. He didn't want to, I suppose. He doesn't have to.'

Peter grunted and stood up from the table. He dropped his napkin and, pulling his navy jumper over his pot belly, began to march out of the room.

'Where do you think you're going?' asked Jean curtly.

'To the study.'

'We haven't had any pudding yet.'

'I'll have mine later.' Peter ignored his wife and strode into his study, where he holed himself up for hours on end.

Lucy was quite aware that her parents were virtually independent of each other. In public their lives merged, yet in private, at home, they barely saw each other. The only time they spent together was during the drive into Ipswich every morning, and even then they hardly spoke. There was little animosity between them; they had simply grown apart and wanted to follow their own separate paths. They had both thought autonomy within a marriage would be the perfect solution and, without realising it, had created this very ideal.

Lucy turned and looked at her parents, who were intently listening to Father Armitage. The vicar was as busy as ever, rushing around doing nothing, putting ants in everyone's pants and causing a scene when an answer would do. He always went to the King's Head after the eleven o'clock service and had two ginger wines before returning to the Rectory for lunch. Of course Lily's death had been a terrible shock. It had been he who had found her at the bottom of the stairs, her top set of dentures protruding from her mouth in the strangest way and the wire of the Hoover wound around her bosoms, lifting and separating.

Knowing how dependent Father Armitage had been on Lily, all the old biddies in the village took him under their wing and treated him like a bereaved child. Home-made cakes were deposited on his doorstep, along with quiches, pies and loaves of bread. He received countless offers to have the Rectory cleaned, to join so-and-so for lunch, tea or supper – all of which he accepted. He was pampered like a baby. And it wasn't until the offers began to wear thin that he went as far as putting a postcard in the Post Office window: 'Wanted. Lady to cook and clean the Rectory.'

'Mrs Cook (that really was her name) is a dear soul, of course,' said Father Armitage as he drained his ginger wine from the glass. 'But she really can't cook. And I haven't the heart to tell her. She thinks,' he looked around to check no one was listening, 'she thinks she's a marvellous cook. Well, what can you say? She can't even boil an egg, I swear. Well, I don't. Of course I never swear,' Father Armitage paused – this joke had made the flower arranging class laugh – not the Granthams. 'I swear,' he continued, 'that yesterday she served me a bullet in an egg cup. I almost asked if she found it on the beach.'

Bored, Lucy looked around. The lounge bar had been decked out in a red patterned carpet, red plastic seats, pretend beer barrels and the usual splattering of horse brasses. It could have been anywhere.

Over the counter, she could see Ron in the public bar with his father and the usual crowd of fishermen. She had barely seen him since school. How he had changed. He looked like a huge baboon.

She stood up and slowly wandered around to the public bar, where she tapped Ron on the back and made him jump.

'Hi.'

'Oh . . . er . . . well, now. Hello there.' Ron turned bright red and began to stammer. He knew that all eyes were on him, and saw Arthur Matheson nudge John Smythe, who in turn nudged Ron. Ron turned redder than ever.

'How are you?' Lucy asked, slightly cocking her head to one side and enjoying the stir she was causing. She looked over to George, 'Hello Mr Jarvis,' she said.

George didn't answer. He touched his cap, grunted and continued to stare at her.

'Well, er . . . well now . . . all right I s'pose. And you?' Ron stuck his hands right down into his pockets and, hunching his shoulders, nervously began to jangle the change in his pocket. 'Back from the smog are you?'

'Yes.'

'Rosie's back too, you know.'

'I know. We drove down together.'

'Oh.' Ron looked at Lucy awkwardly. From where he was standing, he could see straight down her cleavage. 'Would you like a drink?'

'No thanks. Not unless they've got a decent bottle of wine in the house. They've only got that shit.' Lucy nodded at a cheap bottle of Spanish plonk that had been gathering dust behind the optics for several years. 'I reckon Randalls brought it back from his travels half a century ago,' she whispered to Ron, making him laugh and then blush even more.

'We've seen you on the telly,' said Ron. 'Margaret always watches it. And if I'm back from work, I see it too. Well, we all do. We all watch it.'

Lucy smiled, trying to affect some degree of humility.

'I see you've got a nice new pair of gates down at Summer's Hill,' George suddenly barked out of the blue.

'Oh have we? Can't say I've noticed really.' Lucy sighed and looked around. Everything and everyone looked so brown and boring. All wearing brown clothes, sitting on brown furniture, drinking brown beer and smoking chewed up old brown pipes.

No one said anything. Lucy stood, allowing herself to be admired as the five men stared at her, clenching their tankards that moved mechanically from the bar to the mouth and back again.

Then, suddenly, John Smythe slammed his mug down on the bar and bellowed, 'Drink up you lot.'

Eyebrows raised. Elbows creaked. Mouths opened. And the beer slid down.

There wasn't much that could put them off their beer. And it wasn't often that Smythe bought a round either.

Twenty minutes later, the Granthams and Father Armitage drained their glasses and left the pub to go home for their

Sunday lunch. Lucy waved her parents off, grinned and announced, 'My round.' She was having a wonderful time. After her third gin and tonic, she accepted the offer of the bar stool from George and nestled in with the crowd; after the fourth she grinned at their filthy jokes and after the fifth she was telling her own.

'Let's have your glasses,' Randalls suddenly bellowed, sliding off his stool and lifting up the bar hatch. He slouched over to the 'townies' table. 'It's time,' he snapped and then picked up the overflowing ashtray and chucked its contents into the fire. 'I'm closing in five minutes,' he growled and then shuffled back to the bar and slammed the latch door shut.

Ten minutes later he'd shooed out the 'townies' and bolted the back door.

'Right then,' said Arthur, licking his lips lecherously. 'This is where the real drinking begins. Come on Randalls. Get 'em in.'

Once again, Lucy drained her glass and sat sucking a large chunk of ice while she waited for it to be re-filled. By this time she was beginning to feel dizzy, the voices around her were muffled and every now and again the row of optics became blurred.

'Ever met Bob Monkhouse?' Arthur asked.

'Never.' Lucy's elbow slid off the edge of the bar and the top part of her body collapsed into her lap. Suddenly she felt terrible. Too terrible to move. She knew that if she stood up, she'd fall over.

'Nicholas Parsons? My wife likes him.'

'Uh uh,' Lucy shook her head and tried to focus on a card of peanuts that was hanging from the wall.

'I thought you were on telly.'

'I am.'

'Well then?'

Finally, at about four thirty in the afternoon, the five men and Lucy rolled out of the King's Head and stood in the outside yard squinting at the sun and looking around, as though they didn't know which foot went first and in which direction to put them. One by one, Arthur Matheson, George Heron and John Smythe stumbled off, leaving Ron, Lucy and George to make their way down towards the beach.

By this time, Lucy was revived. She had had a little sleep on one of the benches by the fire and, when she awoke, decided to accept Ron's invitation to lunch down at the bungalow.

'Oh hello,' said Margaret. smiling inanely when the three finally rolled up on the doorstep. 'Your lunch is ready. Just step this way.'

During the walk from the pub to the beach, Ron sobered up very quickly and began to wonder what Margaret would say when he, his father and one extra arrived two and a half hours late for lunch. Margaret's welcome made him uneasy, and when he followed her into the living room, he saw the burnt and shrivelled carcass of a chicken sitting on the table, awaiting their arrival.

Lucy spluttered with laughter and put her hand to her mouth, like a naughty child.

'Do sit down,' said Margaret, stretching out her arm and ceremoniously gesturing towards the table. 'Whoever you are.' She didn't recognise Lucy.

'I thought you'd like to see Lucy again,' Ron stammered.

Margaret looked at Lucy and realised who she was. 'Oh yes. I've seen you on the telly,' she said. 'Do take a seat. Luncheon is served.' Once again she affected a sweeping bow and then disappeared into the kitchen. Two minutes later she reappeared with a bowl of powdery cauliflower and crumbled potatoes.

The three stared at the table, not quite knowing what to do. George thought he was so pissed he was imagining it all and, hanging on to the back of a chair, stooped over the spread to take a closer look. Still not sure if his senses were deceiving him, he pulled back and grunted. He hadn't noticed Mum.

Mum was slumped in the corner, and in a terrible state. Had Margaret not set a bottle of sherry down beside her as soon as I left the room earlier, she would never have drunk at all. The booze affected her in much the same way as before. Once she started, she wouldn't stop until she passed out. I tried to make her stop, but she became violent and took a swipe at me, so I let her carry on, furious with Margaret who, as usual, played the innocent.

Why did Mum drink? I don't know. Just because of Margaret.

'How adorable.' Lucy had spotted Toby, who was very subdued and sitting on the floor, leaning against my legs and leafing through his book. She went over and crouched down in front of him. 'Hello, you gorgeous little thing.' She looked up at me and smiled. 'Isn't he adorable? It makes me go all broody when I see them like this.' She pinched Toby's cheeks. 'I want one. I do. Really I do.'

Toby looked at Lucy inquisitively and then began to whine and wriggle back to hide behind my legs. Lucy grinned, shrugged her shoulders and then collapsed on a tatty armchair that sat beside the fireplace.

'You can't sit down yet,' said Margaret, who was standing by the door in her favourite position, with her arms folded, 'you haven't had your lunch yet.'

'Oh shut up Margaret,' I snapped.

'Well, it's there. Waiting for you. Pity to waste it.'

'Lucy didn't come for lunch. She came down to see me and . . .'

'Yes?'

'To see me.' Margaret had not touched Toby once that afternoon. When she hadn't shut herself in the kitchen fussing over her miniature chicken, she skirted around the floor, carefully avoiding him. And when the lunch was ready, she came into the living room, switched on the afternoon film and collapsed into a chair. By this time, Mum was well out of it and Toby and I had dropped off on the sofa together.

'You should have come to the pub,' said Lucy, stretching her legs out and ignoring Margaret. 'It was quite good fun actually, wasn't it Ron?'

'We had a few laughs.' Ron was still standing awkwardly by the table, wondering what to do. Suddenly he realised he still had his brown anorak on, so decided to take that off for starters. Then he took off his father's coat. And then he pulled out a chair from the table and set it down next to the sofa. 'Come on Dad, you sit yourself down here,' he said, taking George's arm and leading him to the chair.

'Get off will ya,' said George, roughly pulling his elbow away from Ron, 'I'm not a bloody geriatric.' Breathing loudly and still feeling very much under the influence of nine pints of Tolly Cobbold, George slowly lowered himself into the chair. Then he saw Mum, who was slumped in a corner at the end of the sofa like a sack of turnips. 'What the hell's she doin' with that bottle?' he growled, beginning to stand up again.

'It's all right Dad,' said Ron nervously, putting his hand on his father's shoulder to try and calm him down. 'She's not doing any harm. Just having a quiet drink, that's all.'

'She's drunk.'

'Well . . . so maybe she is. But you're not stone cold sober yourself, are you now?'

'Who gave her that bottle? I can't stand the old bitch when she's drunk.'

'Look. Calm down and have a nice cup of tea. After that, if you want, I'll take you home. You're in no fit state to go anywhere at the moment.'

'What do you think I am? A girl?' George shouted, his worn hands shaking as they clung to the back of the chair. 'I can get 'ome perfectly well on my own. Now if I wanted.'

'Stay for a cup of tea and then see,' said Ron, calmly

holding up his hands to defend himself from the wrath of his father.

George was silent for a moment. A cup of tea might at least sober him up enough to see the road home. 'All right,' he finally assented, sitting down again. 'But I'm only staying for a cup of tea and then I'm off.'

'Right.' Ron turned to Margaret and raised his eyebrows.

'I'm not making it.'

While Ron was crashing around in the kitchen making the tea, Margaret decided to desert her post by the kitchen door and walk over to the empty fireplace, where she positioned herself next to Lucy. 'Who do you know that's famous then?' she asked, as though she expected Lucy to sing for her supper.

'Oh God. Not you too.' Lucy turned to me and raised her eyebrows. 'What's wrong with this lot Rosie?'

Mum piped up. 'What's wrong? I'll tell you what's wrong. The bloody lot of 'em have gone off their fuckin' heads. That's what's wrong. Look at that old bastard over there. Sitting there like the dog's dinner . . .'

'Shut up Mum,' I snapped.

'Oh shut . . . yer . . . shut . . . yer fuck up . . . yerself . . . you,' she garbled and then disappeared back into the quagmire of her head.

'Go on then,' said Margaret, challenging Lucy again.

'Oh God, do I have to?' The boozing session at the pub was beginning to take its toll; Lucy was looking very pale and washed out. 'I feel awful,' she moaned. 'I think I've got a hangover already.' Sitting in that horrible dingy brown room was making her feel worse. More brown. And it smelt of fish.

Lucy sat back in the ugly chair, gripped each arm and closed her eyes. 'Lana Turner. Ava Gardner. Judy Garland. Glenda Jackson. Judi Dench. Ralph Richardson. Laurence Olivier. Steve McQueen. Robert Redford. Humphrey Bogart. Mickey Rourke.'

'Who's Mickey Rourke?'

'A film star.'

'I don't believe you.'

Without bothering to open her eyes, Lucy shrugged her shoulders and then let her head roll sideways on to her shoulder, where she feigned sleep.

Suddenly Mum realised that George was in the room and tried to haul herself out of the sofa. 'Ello George. No one said you'd arrived. Come for your dinner, have you?' she rambled.

George glared at her, disgusted.

'Stop it, Mum,' I snapped, grabbing hold of her flabby arm and pulling her back onto the sofa. She landed like a suet pudding and let out an angry wail before lashing out at me.

'Watch out!' I shouted. 'For Christ's sake. What the hell do you think you're doing?'

She shut up and collapsed back into her corner.

'You're not going to sleep are you?' Margaret said very loudly to Lucy. She gave her a kick on the shin. 'Not going to sleep are you?'

Annoyed, Lucy pulled her head back into an upright position, keeping her eyes closed. 'No,' she muttered.

'I think you're pissed.'

'I was. Now I'm just hung over.'

'Everyone seems pissed round here this afternoon. Except me . . . and Rosie.' And then, as an afterthought, Margaret added, 'And him of course.' She stood leaning against the green-tiled fireplace, staring down at Toby who was, by now, busy scribbling in his book. 'He's my baby, you know,' she said to Lucy.

'Yes, I know.'

'He's staying with his grandmother at the moment, while I settle in here with Ron.' Margaret ignored me and continued. 'Of course, you can understand why one man wouldn't want to bring up the child of another. I can. If the tables were turned I wouldn't fancy it.' Margaret looked down at her bitten nails and then over to Ron who was clumsily laying out the tea things on the table. 'Anyway, things are about to change a bit round here, now that I'm expecting a baby of our own.'

Lucy woke. I looked up. Ron broke a saucer. George and Mum did not hear.

'What?'

'A baby. I'm expecting a baby.'

Ron didn't know what to say. He was as shocked as everyone else. He pulled himself up to his full six feet five inches and slowly began to massage the small of his back, staring at Margaret as he tried to work out whether or not she was bluffing.

Nobody said anything for a moment. Lucy was too hung over to be moved by the announcement, both George and Mum missed it, and so that left Ron and me. We both looked at Margaret, yet said nothing.

'What's Bruce Forsyth like?' Margaret asked, as though nothing had happened.

'Margaret!' Ron wailed, 'do we have to talk about that now?'

'Come on,' said Margaret, suddenly animated by the stir she had caused. 'It's not often you get a chance to find out what the stars are really like.'

'Yes but . . .'

'Go on. What's he like?'

'He's all right,' Lucy replied in a monotone. 'He's all right. How you'd expect.'

'How's that then?'

'Margaret, leave her alone.'

'Look, why not? Why shouldn't I?' Margaret's face had changed shape. A small spark of life glinted in her eyes and her cheeks were pink, ablaze with curiosity. She was thrilled to actually know someone who had met these people, these enigmas. Television stars were a race unto themselves to Margaret. They were beyond her reach. They all lived in her dream world of big houses, fast cars and money. It was a side of life she could barely envisage, barely imagine. Yet here, with Lucy sitting in her very own front room, she had a chance to find out, first hand, what life was really like on the other side of the fence. Fuck the baby. 'Well? What's he like then?'

Lucy shrugged her shoulders and ran her fingers through her hair. She knew Margaret wasn't going to let her get away without saying anything. She'd never even met Bruce Forsyth. But who was to know that? 'He's quite nice,' she said. 'I don't really know him that well. I've met him at a couple of parties, but that's all.'

Margaret's face lit up. 'Parties!'

'Yes. But . . .'

'What sort of parties?'

'Ordinary sorts of parties.'

'Full of stars.'

'Sometimes.'

'With champagne. Is that what you drink? Champagne?'

'Usually, it depends. I mean champagne isn't such a big deal, you know. Most people drink it.'

'Oh do they?' Margaret looked at Ron and nodded in a 'told you so' way.

'Who else have you seen at these parties then? Do they turn into anything else? You know, like orgies? Or anything else?'

'No. They're just ordinary parties.'

'I bet,' said Margaret mischievously, her imagination working overtime for the first time in months. 'Go on then; tell us about them.'

'Oh God,' Lucy wailed, turning to me for help.

By this time, I had Toby back on my lap, sullenly chewing a magazine. I shrugged my shoulders and grinned. Lucy could get herself out of that one. It was her fault for getting my sister going in the first place. She knew what she was like.

'Look, another time Margaret. I've got to be off now. My

parents were expecting me for lunch.' Lucy looked at her watch. 'Oh God, they'll be furious.' And then she was up, off the chair, into her coat, and out of the door before any of us realised she'd gone.

Annoyed by Lucy's sudden disappearance and lapping up the attention she was creating for herself, Margaret suddenly decided to turn to Toby.

'Let me hold him,' she suddenly snapped. I looked up at her in alarm. 'Well, he is my baby.'

A sadistic smile twisted her thin lips as she took the wriggling child. She held him away from her, as though she didn't want to dirty herself. And as he hung, suspended by her large hands, he began to whimper miserably. 'There you are, you see,' she said. 'Back with Mum.'

Mum suddenly popped out of her stupor and glared at Margaret, who plonked Toby on the end of her knee and held him out at arm's length to joggle him up and down. Tiny spots of perspiration began to prick the child's forehead as he continued to grizzle and stare helplessly at Mum who, in turn, gazed quite as helplessly back.

The next morning was as bright and as crisp as its predecessor. A clear sky allowed the sun to breathe life into a thin layer of dew that shimmered on the beach and glistened from the hulls of the boats.

As soon as I heard Toby squealing next door, I threw off the bedclothes and padded into the bedroom to find him crawling around Mum's bed on all fours, pulling her nose and shrieking with laughter as she threw him into the air. 'Morning.' I sat down on the edge of the bed and smiled, relieved to be met with such a happy scene. I had dreaded the worst. 'How are you?'

'How are we?' Mum asked, holding Toby up and making a face at him. He stretched out his chubby hands and pawed at her eyes. 'We're fine,' she answered.

I presumed my mother remembered what had happened the day before. When we left the bungalow, she had trudged back across the beach behind me, mumbling and still wearing her slippers. I carried a boot in each hand and Toby on my back. Once we arrived at the pen, she stumbled into her room and collapsed on the bed, leaving me to feed Toby and put him to bed. That morning, she was in a nightdress as usual. She must have woken during the night and changed.

As Mum seemed so well that morning I turned my thoughts to Margaret and her plans for the future. When I saw Ron washing his old green Ford Zephyr – almost a collector's item by then – I pulled on a jumper and a pair of jeans and walked across the beach for a chat.

'How's your head?' I asked.

Ron grinned and, pulling himself up to his full height, set his hands on his hips. 'I never get hangovers,' he said. 'Never have done. Not once in my whole life. That always riles 'em.'

'Oh?'

'Well, folks don't like it if you take your fun without paying the price. It gets on their nerves.'

'Does it? Lucky you. If you can do it.'

Ron let out a short grunt and dipped his sponge into a bucket of mucky water which he sloshed over the car windscreen.

'So. You're going to be a dad.'

'So she says.'

'Good news, isn't it?'

'I should say.' Ron seemed embarrassed and dived down behind the car again so I couldn't see him.

I walked round and leant against the door.

'Careful. That's wet.'

'Ron . . . are you pleased about the baby?'

'Of course,' he replied, without looking up at me.

'You don't sound it.'

'Just surprised, that's all.'

'I see. It's just that, well, I'm a bit worried about Toby and Mum. And Margaret. It's just that yesterday Margaret made out she was thinking of taking Toby back. You know what that would do to Mum.'

Ron squeezed out the sponge and started to vigorously rub a hub cap, his huge shoulders moving back and forth like the joints of a great bony ox.

'You know what Margaret's like,' I continued. 'I was just wondering if there was any truth in what she said. I mean, are you planning to take Toby back?'

'I don't know Rosie,' Ron answered slowly. He looked up at me. 'At the moment it's difficult to tell.'

'Well what's she been saying?'

'Not a lot.'

Frustrated, I sighed deeply and said, 'Ron. You know what will happen to Mum if Margaret takes Toby back. You know what those two are like. Margaret doesn't want Toby. She's using him to try and get back at Mum.'

Ron still did not answer. Slowly, pensively, he wiped the driver's door, caressing the bodywork lovingly with his sponge, letting a stream of soapy warm water slither down the door and form a swirling, lathery pool at his feet.

The sun suddenly ducked behind a thick cloud and cast a shadow over the side of Ron's face, accentuating his rough features. A slight gust of wind crept around the car and ruffled his hair, goading it, teasing it up into the air.

I liked Ron. I always had. He was a gentle giant of a man. A cliché. A cliché who was content to remain so. He knew there was another world outside Saltingford, a world that could offer more, but was happy with what he had. 'Why did you marry Margaret?' I suddenly asked.

He looked at me, startled, and then wiped the sleeve of his shapeless old black jumper across his nose. 'Because I loved her of course.'

'I'm sorry,' I mumbled. 'It's none of my business. I don't know why I said that.'

He probably did love Margaret. Ron was the sort of man who could love anyone. There wasn't a grain of hatred in him.

Ron looked up at me and smiled reassuringly. 'Don't worry. Things will settle down.'

* * *

Whether I emerged from the dank corridors of Riggs Road or from our recently renovated Georgian conversion, I still felt miserable to be back in London after a stint at Saltingford.

Seven o'clock in the morning and I was carefully making my way down the slippery steps of the house and onto the pavement of Clifton Road. A steady sheet of drizzle fell from the overcast sky through which a dim light was beginning to ooze, shedding little joy on the morning. The light made the day look worse, it showed it up in all its misery: the concrete flats and their concrete balconies and concrete stairwells, covered in graffiti; squares of yellow light that zig-zagged skywards, inconsistent and all at odds with each other; dog-shit smeared across paving stones, diluted by the rain, sliding into the gutter and the cracks in the pavement where the bears never trod. London seemed to be growing out of itself, like a gigantic foot swelling from a weather-beaten old shoe.

As I walked along Clifton Road, I cursed every car that ploughed past me, splattering my legs with filthy grey water. We could still see the railway tracks, elevated above the waste land that lay around the arches. Trains were flashing by like rolls of film, their carriages crammed with bodies, silhouettes, crushed against the windows. People going to the city. People yawning. People dazed. Tired. Making up. Winding up. Staring into space. At each other. Reading papers. And books. And other people's papers and books. Hung over. Bleary eyed. Drunk. Awake. Ready to set the city on fire. To scuttle a few jobs, a few businesses, or people. To keep competition healthy.

Muriel turned up the steam to heat a jug of milk. 'It's the democratic way of controlling everyone. Build dreams. Make them come true. Make money. Spend money. Borrow money. Borrow more money. And then what?'

'Borrow more money.'

'Right. And then you're trapped. You have to work, to keep it all going. To maintain your lifestyle. And if you work, you haven't got time for anything else. Right?' Muriel slammed the jug of hot milk down on the sideboard. 'Am I right or am I right?' she shouted, addressing Mr George who was sitting at table five.

No answer.

'That's what capitalism's all about for me,' she continued, enjoying her own discourse. 'And it stinks. Stinks like a piece of shit.'

Mr George sat clasping his hands on the table. He was wearing an old brown anorak and a pair of pale blue trousers which hung from his scrawny frame like a sack. He had given up the charade of going to work after he had barricaded himself into his flat at Riggs Road. He never said anything to his wife about losing his job and she never once asked. For a week, he had even found a position as a porter in a block of offices. But it didn't last. He couldn't take orders from men half his age and with a quarter of his know-how. He couldn't stoop to clearing drains and emptying sanitary bins in the Ladies' toilets; he might as well have been a cleaner. He probably would have been paid more.

'Take him a cup of tea then,' Muriel grumbled, nudging me as I stood buttering rolls for lunch. 'He's getting on my nerves just sitting there like that, waiting to be served like it was the Ritz.'

'He only wants a bit of attention.'

'I'm not everyone's mother you know.' Annoyed, Muriel turned around to take another look at Mr George, who had barely uttered a word in the half hour he had been there. 'Pathetic,' she clicked.

'He's upset about something. Go and talk to him Muriel.'

'This isn't the Samaritans you know. You go.'

'He won't talk to me. He confides in you.'

Trying not to be flattered and pretending it was a great inconvenience, Muriel clicked again and poured out Mr George a cup of tea. 'This isn't the Ritz,' she said, plonking the tea down in front of him.

Mr George jumped. He hadn't heard her walk over.

'Come on then. What's wrong?'

'Muriel!' I wailed from behind the counter. Poor Mr George looked in a worse state than I'd seen him for ages. There were times when she could be so cold and heartless.

'Well he can talk,' Muriel quipped, snapping the filter off her cigarette and shoving it into her lipsticked mouth. 'He's not a baby you know.'

'He is a person.'

Muriel shrugged her shoulders as though she didn't really care. She looked down at the forlorn Mr George, up at me, raised her eyebrows and then slid behind the table opposite him. 'All right, what's the matter,' she asked in a softer voice, conceding to his whim.

Mr George was hurt by Muriel's lack of concern. Yes he was upset. And yes he needed to talk. Muriel had always made herself available to him when he needed it before, and now he felt she was pulling the carpet from under his feet. He continued to say nothing, sulkily staring down at the thick milky tea.

Muriel let out a long sigh, pursed her lips and glanced at her watch. This sort of behaviour irritated her. She only had to look at a man and he'd turn into a baby. 'Come on; I haven't got all day.'

He didn't answer.

'Right. Well I've got to get on.' She lodged the cigarette in her mouth and, pushing the chair back, began to stand up.

'No. Stop. Muriel.' Mr George gazed up at her like a sick dog. 'Muriel, I've got to talk.'

Muriel sat down again and began to tap her fingers on the table top. Mr George stared back at his cup of tea, which had a layer of greasy globules floating on top of it. 'I've got crabs,' he quietly mumbled.

Muriel didn't answer for a moment, not quite sure how to react. 'Oh. Well sorry,' she finally said in a very matter-of-fact way. 'Actually, I thought I'd got them off you.'

'No.'

'Well, it's not the end of the world you know. You can get lotion over the counter.'

Mr George looked around the cafe, even though he knew no one else was around. Nervously pulling at his moustache he hissed, 'It's my wife. What if I've given them to her?'

'I thought you never did it with her any more,' said Muriel in a loud voice. She sat back and threw one arm over the back of the chair next to her. Typical, she thought; all they ever worried about was their wives.

'Sssh,' Mr George hissed, surveying the room again.

'Well I'm sorry, but that's not my problem.'

Mr George took a noisy slurp of tea. The conversation had made him so nervous that his mouth had become dry and parched. 'You can catch it off blankets too,' he whispered. 'I got it in the army like that.'

'Then you should know what to do about it.'

'We still sleep in the same bed together.'

'Crabs aren't marathon runners you know.'

Mr George went red. He was dying to give his groin a good scratch; he could feel the little buggers crawling around all over him. It was an abomination. How dare they invade his privates like that? Sometimes he scratched so hard, he thought he'd kill them by crushing them to death. But no. No such luck. 'You haven't got any of that lotion here, have you? If you've got them yourself.'

Muriel began to stand up. 'What's the matter? Too scared to go into the chemist?' Then she stared down at Mr George condescendingly and added, 'All right, give me a couple of minutes and come up to the flat.'

Not unlike herself, everything in Muriel's flat was damp and had seen better days. The rooms were small and squashed together along a narrow corridor which was filled with all sorts of clutter: clothes, piles of old magazines, a battered radio and a mound of paperback books. The flat was airless, filled by a heavy smell of stale cigarette smoke. Ashtrays were everywhere, overflowing with powdery grey ash and the filters that Muriel snapped off her cigarettes. When the ashtrays were full, she stubbed out her fags in the dry, unwatered soil of the plant pots.

Mr George followed Muriel along the corridor, carefully stepping over the mess so as not to disarrange anything and annoy her. By now he was used to her flat and didn't give the chaos a second thought. Anyway, on this visit he was far too preoccupied.

While Mr George was in the bathroom, frantically rubbing the lotion into his privates, Muriel flopped down on the sofa, kicked off her shoes and put her bony legs up. Then she snapped a filter off a cigarette, planted it in her mouth, lit it, inhaled and let her head fall backwards, closing her eyes. What bliss to relax, to take that load off her feet and allow her limbs to become heavy. Absentmindedly, she allowed her hand to slide up the inside of her thigh, creeping upwards until it found the delicate folds of her sex. So comforting. So relaxing. Warm and creamy to touch.

One day Muriel would leave the Peach Melba. She was ready to move out of the city altogether. And the smog and the filth, the neurosis and ill health that went with it. She'd had enough. She didn't have the stamina to keep up with London life any more. She didn't want to. She wanted to put her feet up and take it easy. It was as though her whole body had been battered and bruised by the past fifteen years. Even after a holiday she felt tired, as though the rest had made space for her to drown in. That wasn't what life was about. And now, she'd spent so long grafting in the Peach Melba, she had forgotten what it was about. Not working like a dog for bugger-all, that was for sure.

Muriel had a half-brother who lived near Hastings with his wife. He and Muriel had not been close, but recently she had written proposing a visit. That morning she had received a reply suggesting she spend a week-end with them on the south coast.

So lost in her thoughts was she that Muriel didn't see Mr George poke his head round the living room door, or blush when he saw where her hand was. Instead she fell asleep for half an hour and when she emerged through the door in the wall downstairs, yawning, she asked, 'What happened to him then?'

'He scuttled away hours ago. What on earth do you do to them up there?'

'I didn't do anything.' Muriel picked up a pile of dirty plates that was sitting on the counter and slowly shuffled into the kitchen.

'God this place,' she grumbled. 'Look at it. Have you ever seen such a shit hole?'

'Well . . .' I looked up at the sweaty yellow plaster that was blistering on the ceiling.

'Exactly. Just look at it.' Muriel stuck her hands on her hips and gaped at the cafe. 'Grotty bloody tables, chipped and cracked; greasy filthy bloody floor. I don't know. Sometimes I think I'm going mouldy with the ceiling. Turning green with the Formica. Fuckin' place.' Muriel picked up a piece of cold bacon that was lying in a thick layer of white fat on the grilling pan. 'Look; that's me. Dry and brittle like a piece of old bacon.'

* * *

A few months later, after Margaret had given birth to another boy, she decided to take Toby away from Mum so 'the whole family could be together'.

As I predicted, the results were disastrous. When I returned to the pen, I found all the curtains drawn and Mum sitting in the armchair in her own shit. The air was putrid, reeking of urine and alcohol. 'Oh Mum,' I exclaimed, standing by the door and staring down at her pathetic figure slumped in the chair, bundled up in her brown dressing gown. 'Look at you!'

Barely aware of who I was, Mum stared at me pitifully and then looked away, biting her lip, on the verge of tears, ashamed and utterly, utterly devastated by her loss. Beside her was an empty bottle of vodka, and on the table a full one that hadn't been touched.

'Where have these come from?' I picked the bottles up and glared at the back of my mother's unwashed head. Then, suddenly, I slammed the bottle back on the table and stormed out of the pen and onto the beach.

'Margaret!' I flung open the front door and stormed through the dark hallway and into the living room. 'Margaret. Where the fuck are you?' I stopped, horrified, as my eyes fell on the tiny figure of Toby who was standing like a prisoner in his play pen, clinging to the rails, terrified and, for a moment, quiet. As soon as I walked over to him, he began to wail again, making such a din, I've never heard anything like it. Then the baby began to cry from his carrycot that sat on the table. He frantically flung his tiny arms around, his face distorted and puce from the effort of it all.

Both babies were filthy, their clothes saturated in piss and shit and food and vomit. When I picked one up in each arm, Toby calmed down to a slow, rhythmic whimpering while the baby continued to yell his lungs out. No one was around. No Margaret. No Ron.

Stacked up on the draining board in the kitchen were piles and piles of dirty plates and dishes, cups, glasses and spoons, all balanced precariously on top of each other. I was amazed to see so much crockery and recognised most of it as Mum's. The rest of the bungalow was in a similar state; clothes were everywhere, beds unmade, carpets strewn with bits of food, dirty nappies, newspapers and junk. Everything was everywhere, except Margaret, who was nowhere.

Once I had fed and cleaned the two babies, I sat down on the sofa with one in each arm and they both fell asleep exhausted.

It was comforting to comfort these two tiny things. Sitting there, feeling the warmth of their bodies as their breathing deepened, I felt such love for them. Great love, and security, and a sense of purpose. I saw myself as their only hope.

The quiet gave me time to think. To think what I was going to do about the children. About Mum. And Margaret. Everyone seemed to be going to pieces. And why hadn't the social services done anything? They surely must have been keeping an eye on my sister, though knowing her, she had probably spun them one of her yarns. And then I wondered how often the children were left like that, on their own. How many times had this happened before? And where the hell was Margaret?

About an hour later, all three of us were woken by the crash of the front door slamming. My heart began to bang against my chest, setting Philip, the baby, off again. He seemed to sense my fear and responded to it with tiny whimperings that slowly built up in volume and intensity.

'What the hell do you think you're doing here?' Margaret's huge body filled the doorway. She had put on more weight after giving birth to Philip and looked like Mum at her worst.

'You look just like Mum.'

'I don't remember asking you over.'

'No you didn't. Though it's just as well I came.'

'Oh yeah,' Margaret sneered like an eight-year-old. Under her arms she was carrying two large brown paper bags that chinked as she walked.

'You look more and more like Mum every day,' I said, looking down at her feet. 'Look at that; you even go out in your slippers.'

'So? What's it to you?' Margaret dumped the two brown bags on the sideboard in the kitchen.

'What's it to me? I'll tell you what it is. It's when I find Mum incapable of moving a step out of that pen and pissed out of her head. It's when I come down here and find these two screaming their heads off, filthy bloody dirty and starving. I don't know what right you think you've got to bugger off and leave them. How long have you been out today?'

'Mind your own fuckin' business.'

I pulled myself and the two children off the sofa so that I was upright and in a more defensive position. The baby stopped crying while Toby scrambled over my shoulder like a monkey and planted his thumb in his mouth.

Margaret dived into the large brown sacks and pulled out a stack of plates, mugs, saucers, cups, bowls and God knows what.

'What on earth have you bought that lot for?' I asked. 'You've got enough crockery for an army already.'

'Yes. And look at it.' Margaret nodded at the heap of filthy plates that was piled up on the draining board.

'Well wash it up for Christ's sake.'

Margaret turned to me, widened her mad eyes and, craning her face forward so that it was about six inches from mine, yelled 'No!' I could see her tonsils wobbling around in her throat like the devil's fork. Then, as nonchalant as anything, she pulled out three bottles of cheap American vodka from the other bag.

'Who the hell are those for?'

'Me.'

'You bloody liar. Are you mad or what?' I screamed, so

full of anger and confusion that huge watery globules began to well up in my eyes, and spill down my face.

Margaret smirked and arranged the bottles on the table before screwing up the paper bag and throwing it into an overflowing bin from which there wafted the most revolting smell.

'You'll kill her. You'll kill her for God's sake.'

'Now look.' Margaret turned around and glared at me. Her eyes were shining and wide; I was terrified just looking at them. 'Don't think you can just swan back here whenever it takes your fancy and change everything around. You fucked off. So you keep your bloody nose out of it. All right?'

'I'm not going to just stand here and watch you kill Mum off.' I turned and looked at the three bottles of American vodka, guessing that Margaret had fallen back into her old ways and spent the day at the base. 'How long did you have to spend on your back for that lot?'

'Fuck off you.'

'The state you're in, I'm surprised you got an orange squash for your efforts. Or do you do it for crockery now? A cup and saucer for a wank. Set of bowls for a blow job. Canteen of cutlery for . . .'

'Don't start,' Margaret yelled, sending Toby into a fit of hysterical crying. The baby had fallen asleep again and comfortably nestled under my arm, quite oblivious to what was going on. 'Now bugger off. And you're not taking them with you either.'

'You don't think I'd leave them with you.'

'I'm their mother.'

'Mother! Don't make me laugh. They'd be better off in care. You're never here. They were filthy and hungry when I arrived. And what if something had happened? What if the house had caught fire?'

'Nothing was on.'

'Did you check?'

'Look, just put them down and piss off back to that old

fart over the beach.'

'It's you who made her that way.'

'And a fat lot you've done to help out.'

It was hopeless trying to argue with Margaret. She was standing in the middle of the kitchen, her huge bulky figure planted firmly on the floor, her hands on her hips, defiant, ready for battle, ready for victory. I slowly turned around and wandered into the living room, where I laid Toby and Philip on the sofa. Then I swung quickly around and slammed the stable door to the kitchen shut, bolting both parts of it before scooping up the children and tearing out of the bungalow.

Blindly stumbling across the beach, I could hear the hammering of the infuriated Margaret. After a short while, the noise became drowned by the wind and the wailing of the two infants whose weight was dragging me down towards the stones. I had forgotten it was dark. Whilst I was in the bungalow, night had fallen and I could barely see twenty yards in front of me.

I knew Margaret would eventually manage to struggle out of the kitchen window and head for the pen so, seeing the lights of Miss Stiff-finger's house, I decided to seek refuge there.

'Come in, immediately,' she commanded, instantly responding when she saw me on her doorstep, clasping a baby in each arm. 'Into the sitting room, that's it,' she instructed, pointing the way. 'Now over here.' She puffed up the cushions on the sofa and stood back as the three of us collapsed in a breathless, exhausted pile.

Suddenly I became aware of my heart pounding, of my pulse darting around my body, of my breathlessness, and throbbing head. Both children were still sobbing, tears rolling down their faces, mucus bubbling out of their noses, their limbs frantically flapping and their faces pulled and contorted. I hardly noticed them, but sat back and closed my eyes, clinging to them for my own comfort, breathing deeply and slowly, catching my breath until gradually we all calmed down. Toby stopped crying and hung limply over my shoulder, his tiny body jolting every now and again as tiny pockets of fear released themselves. Philip calmed down too and was shortly fast asleep.

Suddenly, as though woken by the quiet, I opened my eyes. Miss Stiff-finger was looking down at me through her bi-focals in a concerned and rather school-marmish way. Without a word, she handed me a small brandy balloon and I thankfully allowed the honey-coloured liquid to slide down my throat. I dipped my finger in the brandy and put it in Toby's mouth. He screwed up his face and pushed my arm away. And then I grinned at him and held him close. I couldn't let him go for a second. 'Do you have any milk?' I asked. 'These two need something.'

Once the children had been fed and strapped up in the most extraordinary home-made nappies that had been ingeniously put together by Miss Stiff-finger, I collapsed on the sofa in front of the fire and let out a loud sigh. I could relax. Philip was fast asleep in Miss Stiff-finger's table-cloth drawer and Toby was lying stretched out on the sofa beside me, his thumb in his mouth, his dark eyes staring at the ceiling, flickering, closing, opening, staring, flickering, closing, and then resting, sleeping.

Miss Stiff-finger sat in her huge, high-backed red velvet chair musing over what I had told her. I watched the reflection of the flames in her tarnished eyes as she stared absent-mindedly at the portrait of her mother which hung on the wall facing her. As she mellowed with age, Miss Stiff-finger forgave her mother for being the pathetic door-mat she had watched her father stamp on. Her mother was one of those women who didn't feel alive unless she was kicked around and abused like a dog. She disgusted her own daughter. Now, Miss Stiff-finger saw her as a pitiful creature who had probably never known real happiness, who had never shared love. And at least Miss Stiff-finger could claim to have known that painful pleasure, even though it had been her greatest loss.

Brutus, a large ginger tom, stealthily climbed onto Miss Stiff-finger's lap as soon as she sat down and nuzzled against the thick tweed of his mistress's skirt. Brutus, Titus and Nero were now the objects of Miss Stiff-finger's affection. The three of them prowled around the house like hungry predators, one of them always jumping onto the sideboard for a sniff or a nibble of whatever was out of the fridge. Miss Stiff-finger ran her hands down Brutus' knobbly spine and gently pulled at the soft fur around his neck. What comfort these creatures were to her. She had resigned herself to growing old alone years ago; the capricious nature of the relationships she favoured seemed to guarantee it. At least that was how it seemed. Yet with her cats, she wasn't alone. Her three companions were always there. She suspected she preferred them to a person. They didn't answer back.

Neither Miss Stiff-finger nor I spoke for a while. We both sat quietly listening to the loud tick of the grandfather clock and the crackle of the fire as it spat into the hearth. Both boys slept. We were pensive, anxiously wondering what had happened to Margaret. She must have guessed we were with Miss Stiff-finger. So where was she? Why hadn't she come over? It wasn't like her to hold back. 'I've got this terrible vision of Margaret suddenly storming in through the window.'

'You've been watching too many horror films.'

'Maybe.'

'Have you decided what you want to do? You know you can stay here with the boys for as long as you want. I'm certainly not frightened of that wretched girl. Wretched nuisance. Honestly, I don't know what's got into her.'

'I'm going to check on Mum. Then I'll be back if that's all right. I don't really fancy spending the night over there and ifToby wakes up, I ought to be here.'

'Of course. Now then Brutus; I suppose you'd like your dinner . . .' Miss Stiff-finger gave Brutus a shove, and he grumpily landed on the carpet and then wound his way around and around her feet as she walked into the kitchen.

The ramshackle silhouette of the pen against the clear night sky made the beach look like a shanty town. No lights were on, only the television. I could see the darting figures on the screen through the thin curtains. Already, I felt tears welling up as I anticipated the scene. Had Mum thought I'd abandoned her? Did she even remember I was there?

Suspecting that Margaret might have paid the pen a visit, I didn't know what to expect when I walked in. But Mum was still sitting there, in more or less the same position as I had left her, her dressing gown wide open, revealing a pair of huge veiny breasts. Before stepping inside, I peered around the door, half expecting to see Margaret there with a chopper in her hand, waiting to bring it down on me. She wasn't there. And she wasn't in the bathroom, or the kitchen or the bedroom either. No one was there. No one except Mum and another bottle of vodka standing on the table. Obviously, my sister had paid Mum a visit and left her usual calling card.

I switched off the television and knelt down beside Mum, grasping her hand and staring into her vacant eyes. 'Mum, I'm going to leave you tonight. But I'll be back tomorrow and everything will be all right.'

Very gradually, Mum turned her head and stared at me, confused. I was relieved to see some life, some movement, however basic, in that head of hers. What was going on in that wet brain? Could she see? Smell? Did anything register? Did she know I was there? Or who I was? Even the blood seemed to have stopped circulating around her body, her flesh was white and flaccid and lifeless.

I quickly ripped the stinking sheets off Mum's bed and, as I couldn't find a clean one, had to lay a table cloth on top of the mattress. I knew she was in no state to be bathed and, as I couldn't lift her on my own, I gently washed her body with a warm flannel and then led her into her bedroom where she collapsed onto her bed and fell asleep immediately, snoring within seconds. 'Toby's safe,' I said softly, wiping her sweaty rats' tails away from her forehead. 'And so is the baby. They're both safe.' I didn't say where the children were, just in case she was listening. Margaret would easily be able to prise any information out of her.

I left Mum snoring her head off underneath an old woolly brown blanket. The vodka, I decided, would have to stay for the time being. At this stage, there was no way I could get her off the booze without professional help. It would probably kill her off altogether. Maybe that was what Margaret had planned. Who could tell what was going on in that mad head of hers?

As I closed the door to the pen I let out a huge sigh of relief. I had done all I could for Mum; there was no point calling the doctor at that time of night. All he'd do, I was sure, would be to cart her off to the nearest hospital, and that was the last thing I needed. With Mum tucked up and asleep for the night, I was sure she'd be fine. I needed time to sort out the whole situation.

The night was cold and dry and a soft breeze blustered across the shingle as I crunched over the pebbles towards the sea. I could see that lights were on in the bungalow, but that didn't mean anything. Margaret could be anywhere. Again, I had grown unaccustomed to the silence that enveloped Saltingford. As I tried to regain my equilibrium, my thoughts were calmed by the steady, rhythmical fall of the waves as they plunged into the shore. Always there. Always falling. One after the other, after the other.

From the clear night sky burst a great fat moon that radiated a tremendous light across the shimmering grey sea. Straggling clouds wafted across the sky, obscuring the moon for a moment until they were chivvied on their way by the wind. And way out to sea were five tiny black ships that slowly moved along the pencil-line horizon, leading from north to south and south to north.

I breathed in the thick salty air and then suddenly froze. Not because of the wind, or the chill or the eerie silence that surrounded me, but because of the footsteps I could hear crunching across the beach behind me. There was a time when I had felt no fear on that beach; it was my beach. How the 'smog' had changed me.

I could never have mistaken the gigantic figure of Ron as he lumbered down the bank towards me. 'Moonbathing?' he asked.

'Can you?'

'I don't know. Is there ultra-violet in moon beams?'

'You should know that.'

'Not really. My expertise don't go much farther than greasin' pipes and checkin' the odd nut here and there.' Ron bent down and picked up a handful of slithery wet sand in his huge palm. He ran it through his fingers. Water gave life, turning it into a slimy living organism.

'Have you only just got in from work?'

'An hour or so ago. There was an alert at the plant. Some bugger was looking for a fault with a candle and set all the cables alight.'

'Oh my God.'

Ron shrugged his shoulders. 'There was no danger. They were cables that control the monitors so all sorts of disasters began to register, although it was only the controls at fault. If that happens, the reactors shut themselves down.'

'Isn't that dangerous?'

'Not in itself.'

'Radiation must leak though.'

'Well . . . another of our blokes has gone down with leukaemia. But it's hard to tell what causes it. It turns up in small clusters all over the place. It could be here, there, anywhere really. Most of the radioactivity in the atmosphere is left over from the weapons testin' in the Fifties. The power station don't let out much at all really.'

'Then why all the fuss? There must be an element of danger.'

'The element of danger is human error, Rosie. That's what caused Chernobyl.' Ron took a deep sigh and sank his hands into his pockets. 'These plants only have a limited life span, you see. Ours is past it already. And if anything did happen, well, to be honest, I don't know what they'd do. They're not equipped for an emergency at all. They'd evacuate people inside a mile and a half radius of the plant, and what good would that do? Not a lot, I can tell you. That's the problem, though of course none of us like to say much. Don't you repeat this to your Miss Stiff-finger.'

'Speaking of whom, she's got your kids.'

'Ah.' Ron slowly nodded his head.

'Have you seen Margaret?' I asked.

'Earlier. She said you'd taken the children.'

'You should have seen them. Hungry. Filthy. Tired. Screaming their heads off and Toby stuck in that playpen as though it was a cell.'

Ron pursed his lips and strode over to the bank, where he picked up a handful of pebbles. One by one he began to hurl them into the sea.

'Why on earth didn't you let me know what was going on, Ron? Why didn't you do something? You must have known what was happening.'

The answers were stuck somewhere in Ron's throat. If I'd turned to him I would have seen tears in his eyes. But I never looked. Finally he said, 'I . . . er . . . well, Rosie, I don't rightly know what did happen to tell you the truth. I just thought that things would change, you know. That she would change.' He swallowed and looked down at his boots.

He'd seen what was going on, but hadn't wanted to acknowledge it. He thought that if he ignored it, it would go away. Everything would be all right. 'Every night I spend at the pub,' he slowly mumbled. 'I can't stand being at home you see. It's too painful to watch her . . . with them. Mind you, she's got worse since she had the baby.' Ron shook his head pensively. 'That she has; got a lot worse since then. Of course, I expected it to a degree, but I didn't think it would be like this. I thought she'd just snap out of it.'

'She's gone mad, Ron.'

'I know. I know she has.'

'You should have waited really, before having the baby.'

'Well . . .' Ron slowly moved his head to face me again. 'Well Rosie, to be honest, I couldn't rightly say that that baby was mine. To be honest.'

I didn't reply. The sea filled the silence as it gently lapped against the shore.

'She's still up to her old tricks on the base, so who's to know?' Ron stooped and picked up another handful of stones which he sent skimming across the waves, one by one, watching them disappear into the black sea.

I didn't know what to say. His life with Margaret must have been miserable. 'What does she say about Philip?' I asked.

'Oh, she says he's mine. Of course she does. But I've got my doubts, Rosie. I mean, you know what she's like.' Ron took another deep breath and holding back the tears stared vacantly out to sea again. Poor thing. I wanted to put my arms around his shoulders and mother him.

Though neither of us were wearing coats, we both seemed oblivious of the chilly wind that was blustering around us. 'Those ships look as if they're being pulled across the horizon by a piece of string,' I said.

Ron smiled. 'Are the children all right with Miss Stiff-finger?'

'Oh yes. She's loving it. Makes a change. She seems to have given up on people these days. The place is swarming with animals.'

'That's a good one for a butcher.'

'Cats. Poor thing. Imagine ending up like that, all on your own.'

'It needn't be so bad. It sounds bad, but it needn't be. It depends on how you want to look at it, doesn't it?'

'Does it?'

'It's the right way for her. If it wasn't, it wouldn't be like that.'

I looked at Ron's calm face. Upset he was, but underlying it by an aura of well-being, as though he instinctively trusted that everything would be all right in the end. He reminded me of Mum as she used to be.

'I think hope is the most important thing. When you lose hope you have nothing.'

'I agree.'

I wondered where on earth I was the next morning when I found myself rolling around on the soft spongey mattress of Miss Stiff-finger's guest bed. It was Toby who had woken me. When I opened my eyes I saw him crawling eagerly towards me, his mouth open, panting like a dog, his eyes wide and shining. 'Come here, I'm going to eat you up,' I laughed, hauling him over by his hollow little armpits.

We both lay cuddling, like two young lovers, until I began to worry about Philip and wonder why I hadn't heard him cry. 'Come on, up we get,' I said, ruffling Toby's hair and throwing back the bed covers.

'Oh, you're up,' I exclaimed, surprised to see Miss Stiff-finger sitting in the kitchen with the baby on her lap, feeding him with an antiquated baby bottle.

'We've been up for hours, haven't we?' Miss Stiff-finger looked down at her charge and kissed him gently on the forehead. 'Come and have some breakfast.'

Toby and I sat down at the huge pine table that covered a large part of the tiled floor.

'Help yourself,' Miss Stiff-finger instructed, nodding at the spread she had laid out for us: bread, jam, two different sorts of marmalade, butter, cereals, milk and sugar. 'And if you want toast, the grill's over there. Did you sleep all right?'

'Fine thanks.' Suddenly I was starving, and greedily leaned across Toby to find some bread for him and then for myself. 'Where did you manage to dig that bottle out from?'

'I have nephews and nieces you know,' Miss Stiff-finger snapped as though I had insulted her. And then she added in a softer tone, 'Not that I see them much. Of course, this bottle was made for another vintage of baby, but it seems to be doing the job.'

Miss Stiff-finger had washed out the children's clothes the night before and hung them up in the airing cupboard to dry. So once Toby and Philip were safely installed in their crunchy clean romper suits, she and I sat quietly at the kitchen table, each cupping a mug of coffee in our palms and wondering what to do next.

'You can leave the children here as long as you like,' said Miss Stiff-finger. 'It really is no trouble. A pleasure. A pleasure for an old bat like me to have them.'

'Thanks,' I said, taking a loud slurp from my mug. 'Sorry.'

'What?'

'Nothing. The problem is that the only way we can secure any proper protection for the children is if we call in the authorities. And if we do that, what's going to happen to Margaret?'

'There's no doubt that they'd certify her. Of course, she's always been mad.'

I didn't reply. We both examined the state of the walls.

'And of course, there is the possibility that they would take the children into care.'

'I don't see why they should. Not if Ron can prove he's a capable father.'

I wondered whether to tell Miss Stiff-finger what Ron had told me the previous night on the beach, but then decided against it. Sometimes I thought she knew far too much about everything. 'Mum's bound to be taken in to be dried out.'

'Well you can't possibly expect her to look after them.'

'No. I really ought to go and see if she's all right.'

'Anything you'd like me to do?'

'Just look after the children if you don't mind.'

'Not at all.' Miss Stiff-finger shuffled on her chair and peered over at the morning paper which was sitting on the table. She pretended to read it while I tried to fathom out what to do. Ten years ago she would have taken command immediately. But by now, she too felt she knew too much about everyone. She was fed up with having to make everyone's decisions and now tended to hang back and let people make them for themselves. 'Let people make their own mistakes,' she said to me during one of our weeding afternoons. 'Otherwise they'll never learn anything.'

As I walked across the top of the beach towards the pen, I hoped that Ron would be around. Surely he wouldn't have gone to work with a crisis on his hands. I hoped he'd be in the pen waiting for me. I hoped he might have miraculously taken charge of the whole situation and that everything would have returned to normal: Mum would be sober, happy and content, living in clean and tidy comfort at the top of the beach. Margaret would be sane and stuck in front of the television eating. But then that wasn't normal either. Something had to break.

There was hardly anyone around at that time of the morning; only the postman doing his rounds and George Jarvis plodding along the back road, pushing a wheelbarrow. George's home life may have been empty, but he certainly had plenty to do during the day. There were always odd jobs to be done, either in his own garden or for others. He was glad to be on the safety of dry land. With his nerve, he had lost a touch of dignity too, and had given up caring what they thought of him for deserting the lifeboat.

At some point during the night, Mum must have woken and struggled out of bed in pursuit of her bottle. By the morning it was rolling around the floor, empty. She was sprawled across the bedclothes with her mouth open and snoring. She looked like a witch.

I decided not to move her. Miss Stiff-finger was ringing the doctor and I knew that when he came, he'd call for an ambulance and they'd take her away. Meanwhile, I decided to clean up the pen and went round pulling the curtains and picking up the dirty cups and plates and bits of cutlery that were strewn all over the place. Then I filled the sink with hot soapy water and started to wash up. I picked up a complete jumble sale of filthy clothes and shoved them into a large black rubbish sack to take down to the bungalow, where there was a washing machine in the garage.

Ron was in the garden, trimming the edge of the grass as though nothing had happened. I was relieved to see him; I hadn't seen Margaret since taking the children away and the prospect of a confrontation terrified me.

'Is she back?' I asked.

'Oh yes. She's back. She's back all right.' Ron looked at me and raised his eyebrows. His face seemed a lot more relaxed. 'You're going to get a shock you are.'

'Oh?'

'Go inside and take a look.' Ron took a huge stride over the weedy front path and opened the front door for me. 'Go on,' he said again, 'take a look.'

I don't know what time Margaret returned to the bungalow the night before, but she can't have got any sleep at all. It would have taken her hours to clean the place up like that. Everything had been dusted and polished, buffed, puffed and Hoovered. All the dirty plates and cutlery in the kitchen had disappeared and the windows were open. It was the first time I had known the bungalow to smell so clean and fresh.

Margaret looked better too. When I walked into the kitchen she was cleaning the top of the cooker, vigorously rubbing it with a Brillo pad. She had bathed, washed her hair and I even detected a dab of powder which sat like flour on her bloated cheeks.

'You're scared,' I said, taking my sister's favourite stance and leaning against the doorway with my arms folded. I decided that attack would be the best form of defence and tried to be as calm as possible.

'What's that supposed to mean?'

'Playing the innocent are we?'

'I don't know what you're talking about.' Margaret smiled at me creepily.

I shrugged my shoulders and picked up the black bag that was full of washing. 'I've got Mum's washing here.'

'Leave it on the floor, there.' Margaret nodded at a patch of worn linoleum that sat between the table and the doorway. 'I'll do it later.'

'How do I know that? You should have done it weeks ago.'

'Give it here then. I'll do it now.' Margaret threw the Brillo pad into the sink, snatched the bag from my hand, and swept it out through the hallway into the garage.

While Margaret was sorting out the washing, I stepped back into the sitting room and sat down cautiously on the sofa. Her behaviour was making me feel very uncomfortable. At least I knew where I stood when she was screaming and mad. When she was like this, it was impossible. Who knew what she was scheming in that devious brain of hers? She was ill, obviously. But if anyone came to visit, they'd never know. It was one person's word against the other, and I was sure that would never be enough to make the authorities take her away, or even keep the children out of her clutches.

'You're ill Margaret,' I said when she went back into the kitchen and took up with the Brillo pad again.

'Don't be so daft.' She turned and grinned at me like a

naughty child. 'Hung over more like.'

'You weren't pissed yesterday.'

'Want a bet?'

'You need to see someone Margaret. A doctor. A psychiatrist.'

Margaret gaily laughed. 'Oh well, thanks very much. Is that what you say to all your friends up in London after they've had a few drinks?'

'They don't leave children on their own for hours on end, filthy and hungry.'

'I was only gone five minutes.'

'It takes longer than that to get to the base and back.'

'I'd only gone up the shop.' Margaret looked at me, her eyes wide and innocent, the sickly smile still smarmed across her face.

'Oh? I didn't know they sold American vodka there. Getting very cosmopolitan, isn't it?'

Margaret didn't answer. She turned back to the cooker and carried on cleaning. 'Where are the children?' she asked, as though in passing.

'Safe.'

'They're my children.'

'Well you're not fit to be their mother.'

'Oh. And who do you think you are to be a judge of that? How come you suddenly know so much about motherhood?'

'You don't give a shit about them. All they are to you is pawns in your game of revenge with Mum.'

'Oh, Mum,' said Margaret calmly, as though she hadn't heard me at all. 'You know Rosie, I'm worried about Mum. I think she's got a drinking problem.

'Of course she's got a drinking problem,' I shouted, leaping up from the sofa and storming over to the kitchen door. 'She's had it for years and all you do is buy her bloody vodka.'

'Now don't get so excited,' said Margaret calmly. 'Yes, I admit I buy Mum the occasional drink, but what else has she got? It's the only thing that gives her any pleasure these days.'

'She did have Toby. Until you took him away, you cruel bitch.'

'Toby's my son, Rosie.'

'And stop talking to me like that for fuck's sake. For fuck's sake, you're ill.' I was so angry I was almost frothing at the mouth. Never, never had I hated anyone as much as I hated Margaret them. She was evil. She didn't deserve to be a part of the human race. I felt I could kill her without the slightest compunction. I would have been doing the world a favour.

'We've got to do something about Mum.'

'You don't care about her. You're using her to take the attention away from yourself. It's you that needs help.'

'I've been trying to get her off it. But what can you do with people like that? They never want to know, do they?'

'She's mad.' I slammed the front door and stormed along the path. 'Mad, bad and evil.'

Ron looked up from his edges in surprise. 'Oh?'

'She's crazy for God's sake.'

'I thought things seemed a lot better. The house looks neater.'

'Oh for God's sake Ron. What's wrong with you? You've put those bloody blinkers on again. I thought you took them off last night.'

Ron pursed his lips and looked away from me, ashamed. 'I know,' he finally mumbled.

'Do you? Then why don't you do something about it?'

He didn't answer. He stood staring down at his edges like a naughty child.

'I need some help with Mum. She needs a bath before the doctor arrives.'

Ron dropped his clippers on the ground and lumbered after

me, back to the pen.

After the doctor came, the ambulance arrived and Mum was taken away, a shivering terrified wreck. I didn't know what to do, whether to go to the hospital with her or to stay in Saltingford and sort out the children who were still with Miss Stiff-finger. I decided that Mum would have to go to the hospital on her own. If I went with her, I couldn't get back until the evening and if Ron came to pick me up in his Zephyr, we would be leaving Margaret on her own.

I tried to explain all this to my mother as they wheeled her out of the pen but not much registered. A look of terror spread across her glazed face and both her hands were trembling underneath the brown blanket that had been wrapped around her like a huge bib. I felt terrible letting her go like that. It made me cry.

After I had seen Mum safely into the ambulance, I wandered back to the pen where her washing was flapping around like ghosts on the line. The first thing I saw when I walked into the front room was an empty vodka bottle poking out from underneath a cushion on the sofa. I bent down and pulled it out, then brandished it in the air at Ron. 'You know what Margaret spends all your money on, don't you?'

Ron looked at me guiltily.

'It's her fault Mum's got so bad. God knows what she's trying to do to her.' I glared at Ron. For some reason I was blaming him. His complacency infuriated me. How dare he stand back and let that crazy bitch slowly kill my mother? 'I just don't understand how you let it happen,' I continued, my voice beginning to tremble. 'I don't. Really I don't. And if you couldn't do anything, why didn't you call me? At least. It's the least you could have done.' Suddenly, a tremendous wave of anger surged through me and I clung onto the back of a chair for balance. 'Why the fuck didn't you do anything?'

I bawled. 'Are you blind or what?' And then I stormed into the bedroom and slammed the door.

Ron sat staring vacantly through the window at the sea. He didn't know why he hadn't done anything. Of course he had seen, but nothing had registered. He had heard but never listened. Everything went in, then out again. And somewhere in the middle of it all he clung to the hope that everything would change. Everything would change if he left it alone. If he was patient and waited. Sitting there, it suddenly dawned on him that Margaret was sick. Really sick. She was mad. And he had never realised. Perhaps he was going mad too. Or maybe he was only blind.

Ron opened the bedroom door. 'There's nothing I can say,' he meekly said, touching my shoulder with his huge hand. 'I don't know what happened. I really don't. I'm sorry.'

Listening to his pathetic apology made me weep even more. I knew he wanted to comfort me, I wanted his comfort. But he was too awkward and embarrassed, and it just didn't seem proper. So he rubbed my shoulder backwards and forwards until the howling and the sobbing gradually wore down to intermittent sniffles and finally subsided into hiccups.

'She really started drinking as soon as Margaret took the children away,' said Ron a few minutes later, after he had installed me at the table next door with a cup of strong, milky tea. 'She used to creep down to the bungalow and peer through the window. Poor thing. I suppose she used to stand there for hours.'

The mere idea of poor Mum staring through the window at the helpless, miserable children made me burst my banks again.

'It's all right,' said Ron, putting his arm around me this time. 'It's all right, I'm here. I can see now Rosie. Rosie, I can see everything.'

Miss Stiff-finger was as sad to see the two children taken

out of her care as Margaret pretended to be happy to have them 'home' again. Ron and I wrapped them up in bundles and smuggled them across the beach like contraband. Their mother welcomed them back with open arms and both Ron and I stood watching, disgusted, as she hugged them. She may have been their mother, they may have grown in her rotten womb, but she had never given them the sunlight babies need to really grow.

After Ron and I had left the house, Miss Stiff-finger wistfully closed the door and slowly walked back into the kitchen, where she began to pick up the magazines, books and coloured cooking bowls Toby had been playing with on the floor. How different her life would have been if she'd had children.

Once she had even considered having a child and raising it alone, or with Martha. But then she'd still have had to find a father, still go through the sexual ritual and, even then, one could never be sure it would work. What if she went through all that and found out she was infertile? What if the man suddenly became difficult and wanted access to the child? Men often did, she knew that. These were questions which rambled around Miss Stiff-finger's mind when she was younger. And then, suddenly, she passed into her mid-forties and was too old to have a baby any more. Years of procrastination had left her nowhere and finally she was able to drop the issue.

There were times like this when Miss Stiff-finger regretted never having children. But she had her cats instead, and at that moment, she could hear them all wailing outside in the back courtyard. Of course she had forgotten to give them their milk that morning. How could she? she tutted, and quickly cleared the breakfast left-overs from the kitchen table and went to the fridge for the milk.

As Miss Stiff-finger was pouring the cats' breakfast, she saw Nero pacing along the top of the outside wall. He was screeching and wailing and making the most terrible din, his fur wet and standing on end. Sensing that something was wrong, Miss Stiff-finger quickly banged the milk bottle down and rushed outside.

Titus was patrolling the opposite wall; both cats stalking across the rough brickwork, the fur on their backs raised like hackles, their mouths hissing and distorted to expose their sharp white fangs. And from a hook on the shed wall hung Brutus. A piece of grey rope was around his neck, his eyes and long tongue popping out of his head as though he'd been making funny faces for the children.

Miss Stiff-finger recoiled onto the kitchen step in horror and grasped the door handle to steady herself. Only last night he'd been sitting, purring happily on her lap. It was the most appalling thing she had witnessed in her life.

'What the fuck's going on down there?' said Muriel when I called her up for the second time to say I had to stay in Saltingford even longer.

'Everything. I'm not going into details now; I'll never get off the phone. Anyway, I hope to be back in a couple of days or so.'

'O.K. Will you still be down there at the weekend?'

'Maybe. I don't know.'

'I was thinking of a visit. Just to get out of this shit hole.'

'You wouldn't find it very relaxing right now Muriel. Maybe another time.'

She sounded put out, upset even. 'O.K. Well I hope it all works out.'

'It will. So I've been told.'

I put the phone down and pushed the heavy door of the telephone kiosk open. I couldn't imagine Muriel in Saltingford. God knows what I would have done with her there. She'd look completely out of context. As though one of my worlds had invaded the other. And what would all the old boys down at the King's Head make of her toppling into the public bar in her stilettos, and done up to the nines?

She did sound low. Muriel's future always looked so bleak: one long round of bacon sandwiches.

'You've got to get a phone in here,' I said to Ron when I arrived back at the bungalow. 'It's ridiculous. What if something happened and the kiosk is out of order?'

'We could always borrow someone's.'

'You can't keep doing that.'

'Never had to so far.'

'Well don't talk too soon.'

Ron scratched the back of his thick hairy neck and looked around at Margaret, who was playing the perfect mother and patiently feeding both babies at once. Toby was sitting grumpily in his chair and refusing to open his mouth and Philip was nestling in the crook of her arm, greedily sucking from the bottle. 'I suppose it might be a good idea,' Ron concluded.

'It also means I can get hold of you easily. And you can ring me. Then I won't have to come running back here every five minutes to make sure you're still all alive.'

'We like to have you back Rosie.'

'I know. But I still have my life in London.' What a fraud. London seemed so far away, a dream. I could barely believe that another life sat waiting for me to join it.

The day changed dramatically when Miss Stiff-finger arrived at the bungalow huffing and puffing and blubbering and ranting in the most terrible state. Margaret stood calmly by while our guest recounted the sordid sight that had befallen her, and then sympathised with the poor cat's mother along with the rest of us. Of course, when accused of the deed, she flatly denied it. We all knew she was lying. She knew we knew she was lying. But we were powerless to do anything about it. We had no proof. And even if we did produce evidence, what could we do? Hang her?

Ron accompanied Miss Stiff-finger back to her house and unhooked Brutus from the shed wall. He then dropped him into a V.G. bag and buried him in the back garden, leaving Miss Stiff-finger alone with her grief.

Dinner, therefore, was not a happy occasion. Prepared by Margaret, both Ron and I sat picking at the stew wondering what was in it. Rat? Cat? No. The meat was red, like beef. Margaret was enjoying it, chomping away, leaning over the pot and greedily helping herself to more, totally oblivious to the atmosphere. 'Not off down to the pub then?' she said, chewing loudly between words.

'Not tonight.'

'Oh? What's up with you?'

'Nothing.'

'Takes a visit from Rosie to make you stay in of an evening, does it?'

Ron looked at Margaret and didn't reply.

Margaret continued to gobble away like an old turkey until her dish was empty. Then she wiped it clean with a large chunk of bread. 'That's better' she said, letting out a huge sigh and patting her distended belly. 'I needed that.'

That night, I lay in Mum's bed listening to the sound of the waves lapping against the shore outside. If there was a moon, it was obscured by the clouds. The night was perfectly black and the darkness frightened me, as it always had. I left the curtains open so that I could see the lights in Miss Stiff-finger's house; it was comforting to know that she was still up and awake. I had dropped in to see her after supper and found her sitting looking most subdued, with Nero on her lap and Titus restlessly wandering around her feet.'Such a pointless and cruel thing to do,' was all she could say. 'Who could dream of such a thing? To what end?' I sat with her for an hour or so and, not knowing how to console her, finally left and slowly walked back to the pen, which was so empty. No Mum.

God, what a day that was.

The next morning, I decided to take the children up to the village for a walk and dumped Philip in a huge perambulator which was known as 'the tank'. Margaret stayed behind, cleaning obsessively. She'd only been doing it a couple of days and already it was driving us mad. None of us could move without her hovering behind us, waiting to pick something up, or smooth over the carpet, or puff up the pillows.

'Are you planning to invade with that thing?' said Vera at V.G. Stores, nodding at the tank which was sitting outside on the pavement.

Toby was going through a stage when he could only eat crisps and chocolate. There was no point trying to shove anything else into his mouth, he just spat it out. So when I paid for a couple of packets of crisps and a Milky Bar, Vera looked at me. 'That's not much of a diet for a child.'

'He won't eat anything else.'

Vera shrugged. 'Oh well. Anyway, now you're here, you can pay your sister's bill.'

'How much is it?'

She pulled out a small red exercise book. 'Fifty-four pound and twenty-seven pee,' she said. 'And I'm not giving her no more credit neither. She's owed me that for months.'

'Well I can't pay it. I haven't got that much on me.'

'Send Ron up to pay it then, will you? Not her. Stroppy bitch. She's got a right mouth on her, she has.' Vera rang up the till and stood impatiently waiting for me to fish some money out of my purse. Then she blurted out, 'And what's happened to your Mum? I hear she got taken off to hospital.'

'That's right.'

'Everything all right is it? Nothing serious I hope.'

'Nope. Everything's fine.'

Vera gave me my change and slammed the till drawer back, furiously chewing her lips. She'd never liked me much,

I knew. Never liked any of us. Thought we were all the same, Mum, Margaret and me.

'That sister of yours has gone off her head, Rosie,' she shouted as I left the shop. 'Tell her she owes me some money. And probably a lot more than what I've accounted for too. Know what I mean? I've seen her put things into her pockets. Why else would she wear a big woolly coat in the middle of July?'

'You should stop her then.'

'Huh! Stop her! I wish I could. She runs off. In bare feet what's more.' Vera folded her arms and grinned smugly like a barrister who had just rested his case. Then she raised her eyebrows in a knowing way and said, 'If you see what I mean.'

'No. I suggest you call the police then, Vera. I'm not responsible for her.'

'Oh. Well I will then. If that's all you can think of. What a way to treat your own sister. You won't mind then, having a member of your own family locked up?'

'Not at all.'

Leaving Vera seething behind her counter, I slammed the door, and unwrapped the Milky Bar for Toby, who had scrambled up into the tank and was sitting at the other end, bouncing up and down. It didn't seem to bother Philip at all; he'd slept through the whole journey.

As I pushed the tank along the High Street, I was aware of curtains being pulled back from the windows and faces appearing from behind the smeared panes of glass. I felt as though I were leading a procession, even though we were only three.

Vera, of course, would never tell the police about Margaret. She loved the drama too much. My sister's activities kept the whole village going in gossip. Without her they'd have nothing to talk about. Vera liked the idea of being the long-suffering shopkeeper; it distracted her from having to look at her own miserable life.

Even though Vera was not much older than me, she'd been middle-aged since adolescence. Her parents had more or less handed the running of the shop to her when she left school, and she immediately took on all the attendant responsibilities. Not that it's unusual to be middle-aged in adolescence. After all, we live by our parents' values. The difference is, most teenagers grow out of middle age. Vera never did.

As I slowly made my way home, I noticed some activity in the church hall. According to a scruffy home-made poster that was pinned to the notice board, there was a bring-and-buy sale the following day.

'Maybe a good chance to clear out that garage down at the bungalow.'

I jumped and turned around to see George Jarvis standing behind me, grinning. George always looked a lot older than he actually was; the harsh North Sea wind had dried out his face and his wiry ginger hair had turned prematurely white. It had been like that for years. We used to laugh at it crawling out of his nose and ears and Mum used to say it was because his head was stuffed with straw. He tipped his imaginary hat to me (a habit that began when I moved to London) and bent down to examine the two boys through his cloudy, bloodshot eyes.

'Bit big for that old pram, isn't he?' He nodded at Toby, who was watching him very attentively.

'Philip doesn't seem to mind.'

'Used to be Ron's pram, that did.' George then turned his attention to Philip, who was still fast asleep, and peered at him as though he were examining some strange phenomenon. He sniffed loudly and pulled himself up again. There was nothing Jarvis about him, George concluded to himself. 'Hear you've been having some trouble down at the bungalow,' he said, sniffing again and wiping the length of his sleeve, from the elbow to the cuff, across his nose.

'You can say that again. You know Mum's in hospital.'

'I heard. Doing all right, is she?'

'She only went in yesterday. I'll call later.'

'Well let me know.'

George grunted and stuffed his hands into his trouser pockets. 'Look; I know you've got trouble down there; so if you want anything, just say the word. I'm not one to stick my nose into other people's business though, so don't expect me to come knocking on the door every five minutes.' George tilted his head upwards and looked around the sky. Situations like this always made him feel awkward – he wanted to help but never knew what to do.'So I'm there if you need me,' he grunted in conclusion.

'Thanks George.'

By the time we got back to the bungalow, Margaret had disappeared again, so I set to and fed the children before putting Philip down for his nap. Toby stumbled out into the garden with me to join Ron, who was rather enjoying his time off.

He'd made great progress with the hedge. It was already looking a lot neater where he had pulled out the rubbish and given it a good short back and sides. 'Where's Margaret?' I asked.

'She's not in the house?'

'No.'

'Oh. Then I don't know where she's taken herself off to.' Ron began to drag a tangled bundle of dusty branches and twigs over to the bonfire which was crackling away in the middle of the garden.

By seven o'clock that evening, Margaret still hadn't appeared. After I put the children to bed, I went into the kitchen to put some food together while Ron sloshed around in the bath, scrubbing away the dust that had stuck to his leathery skin.

'I'm worried about her,' I told Ron when he wandered into the kitchen rubbing his wet hair with a towel, making it stick up like a loo brush.

'She'll be all right. She's done it before. She's always

disappearing like this.'

'Not till this late, surely?'

Ron shrugged his shoulders and turned his back to me while he cut a slice of bread from the large loaf that was sitting on the table. 'Sometimes.'

'Well, how often?'

'It depends.' He spread butter and jam on the bread and took a huge mouthful.

'How long does she stay away for?'

'Depends.' Ron munched away, staring vacantly through the window at the pitch black night outside. A deep furrow meandered down his forehead as he stood silently wading his way through the bread. I could see it was painful for him to face up to his marriage. We both knew perfectly well where Margaret was.

Like most of the local men, Ron hated G.I.s and still thought they were overpaid, over-sexed and over here. He couldn't stand the way they swanned into the King's Head as though they owned the place, thinking they could have any girl they wanted. The problem was, that they could, more or less, do just that. Local girls loved the Americans. They could offer the world. What could a poor boy like Ron offer? Not a lot.

After a very quiet and picky dinner, Ron went to bed. Even though neither of us missed Margaret, her absence left an uncomfortable gap that we could only fill with negative and painful thoughts. Sleep was the best remedy.

The next morning, Margaret had still not appeared, so I decided to take the children up to the bring-and-buy sale, as advertised.

Most of the women in the village were involved in the endless rounds of jumble sales, bring-and-buy stalls, coffee mornings and the like. All except Miss Stiff-finger that is. She was only interested in putting the anti-nuclear case. To every other cause she gave a generous donation which could have been received with better grace. Of course everyone cooed their thanks, yet behind her back ground their teeth; to just give money wasn't entering into the spirit of it at all.

The first thing I saw when I lugged the tank into the village hall was Margaret. She was frenetically rummaging through a pile of old underwear that was lying on one of the trestle tables. It was obvious that the villagers were giving her a wide berth. Even the four serving women who stood in the middle of a square made up by tables were keeping their distance. They greeted each familiar face, cheerfully taking the money and diving into nose bags they wore around their necks for change. They loved it, to be orderly and efficient. To be useful, to contribute something to the community. And now Margaret had appeared and was bound to spoil it all.

I pulled the pram towards my sister and was almost knocked over by a sickly body odour that was lurking around her like an evil shadow.

'Oh it's you,' she said, holding up a ragged vest that had turned brown with age. 'That would do for him, wouldn't it?'

'Who?'

'Ron of course.'

'You can't buy that for him. It's too small for a start.'

'It'll stretch.' And to demonstrate her point, Margaret pulled the vest out at both sides. 'There. Perfect.' She rolled it up and stuffed it into a battered carrier bag she was holding.

One of the servers glared at her but didn't dare say anything; it wasn't worth it for that old rag. They were all terrified of my sister: no one knew what she might do.

Margaret then moved on to another table which was piled up with old plates and bits of broken crockery. Three dinner plates with brown rims went into the bag, followed by a chipped bowl wiith flowers on it and a pale green milk jug.

One of the women turned to the others, a look of alarm on her face. They couldn't just let Margaret get away with whatever she wanted. They'd never make a penny for the vestry. 'Um, I say,' she said, leaning forward and pointing at Margaret. 'I say, I hope you intend to pay for those items.'

'Oh fuck off.' Margaret continued to rummage through the bric-à-brac, ignoring the stir she was causing around her.

'I don't know what you think you need that lot for,' I said. 'The house is overflowing with rubbish already.'

'You fuck off too.'

'Fuck off yourself.' I didn't know what else to say. And then she did fuck off. And I stood there, gripping the tank handle, staring at this great clumsy oaf of a sister as she stomped out of the church hall. 'Are you going home?' I shouted.

'How the fuck should I know?' And she stormed out of the door with two fingers up to the lot of us.

Margaret finally wandered in that evening as though she'd just returned from the village shop. She offered no explanations of where she had been and went straight into the bathroom for a bath. Then she fed Philip and Toby, bathed them and put them to bed. All as gently as could be.

Neither Ron nor I could take our eyes off Margaret; we were both waiting for her to do something. What I don't know. But we still waited.

'Will you be around tomorrow?' I asked her.

'Of course.'

'Good. I must go and see Mum.' I looked at Ron and raised my eyebrows. Of course we could never rely on Margaret to be there. He would have to stay home to look after the children again.

I wasn't allowed to see Mum at the hospital. After I'd been sitting in the stuffy waiting room for almost an hour, I was told that she wasn't up to a visit. I guessed that my arrival had upset her and she was playing up like a naughty child. Relations were meant to have this sort of effect on the patients.

So I had to spend the rest of the day wandering around the gloomy streets of Ipswich, plodding from one café to another, drinking one coffee after the other, waiting for the bus to get back to Saltingford. Everyone and everything seemed so drab and dreary in that town. Somehow, poverty was more depressing in Ipswich than in London. Everyone seemed deprived in one way or another. Young girls scuffled along the road pushing prams. Women were fat and men were thin. Women wore clothes hitched up around their arses, exposing knee-less legs that had blown up like balloons. And men wore their dull, lifeless clothes like wire coat-hangers. There was no hope. Whereas in London poverty was fringed by opulence and there was always something to set your sights on.

Rather than linger in the gloom of the bus station, I decided to walk through the town centre and wait on the road which led out of town.

Jean Grantham saw me standing there, shivering, but decided not to stop. She had seen Margaret's performance in the village hall and was horrified by her behaviour.

Lucy was sitting in the front seat next to her mother, looking blankly out of the window, seeing nothing. Her sudden return to Saltingford was an emergency mission. She had telephoned Jean that morning to inform her of her arrival and expected a welcoming party at the station. She looked terrible: pale and washed out with tiny red pimples popping out of her face like mole hills.

The next morning, Lucy and I were sitting in the deserted public bar of the King's Head, huddled around a few meagre flames that flickered behind a large damp log. Lucy was crouched on her knees, glass in hand, while she stared gloomily at the dusty hearth. She had recently acquired a new man, Brian – a straggly-looking character who reminded me of our neighbour's Irish terrier. On hearing about Brian, Samuel had threatened to reveal her as never before to the gutter press. 'Bastard,' she muttered. 'Well, I suppose it was all my fault. My fault for being so naïve. I never should have posed for the bloody things in the first place.'

'You enjoyed it at the time.'

Lucy turned around and scowled at me. 'Not very comforting when one's all is about to be exposed to the public.'

'Sorry.'

She drained her glass and let her head drop backwards. 'I don't know what to do, Rosie, really I don't. I feel so bloody powerless.'

'Everyone will know he's only done it out of spite, wreaking his revenge.'

'What does it matter what they think? If those pictures are published I'll lose my job.'

'I thought the series was on the way out anyway.'

Lucy let out a long wail. 'Rosie! What the hell's wrong with you this morning? You haven't made a single helpful suggestion yet.'

'Sorry.' I was quiet for a moment and then said, 'Have you still got keys to his flat?'

'No. He demanded them back as soon as I told him about Brian. Bloody hypocrite. I know damn well he screwed that Sarah Johnson in our bed.'

'His bed.'

'Oh, who cares whose bed it is? Bloody thing gave me back-ache anyway.'

'You'll have to get Brian to break into his flat and steal the pictures.'

'Steal them! Why should I have to steal them? They're mine.'

'Well, get him to break in and take what's yours.'

Lucy grunted gloomily and stood up to get a refill from the bar.

That was at eleven thirty. By twelve thirty the two of us were well on our way to total inebriation and Lucy was becoming more and more aggressive with every drink she took. 'Oh my God, look at that, they've even put horse brasses in the public bar,' she announced loudly, so Randalls could hear her.

Randalls ignored her. He didn't like women and certainly not her type who thought they were the Queen Mother and screamed and screeched like hyenas all the time.

As lunchtime approached and Lucy and I got more and more pissed, a few old men shuffled in and glared at us, annoyed at finding two women in 'their' bar. 'You did a good job on that lounge bar, Randalls,' said one of them. 'Most of the ladies favour it now. They can sit and chat in there and it's just like being at home.'

'Who goes out to go home?' Lucy quipped. 'You might as well stay in if that's what you want.'

'Shame to waste it, when Randalls has been to such trouble to make it nice.'

'Why don't you go in there then?'

The old boy looked down at his beer. Then he turned to Randalls and raised his eyebrows. 'Women,' he clucked. What else could he say?

'Stupid old prat,' said Lucy, picking up a cigarette and lighting it. And then, in a loud voice, she added, 'English men don't like women. I'm convinced of it. None of them, whatever class they're from. They stick together like frightened little animals, spending all their time at work or down the pub and never wanting to go home. Have you noticed that? I see it all the time.'

'Perhaps they're scared of them.'

'Maybe. I just don't think they like them.'

All the men had stopped talking and were staring at us. 'We've got us a heckler in here,' said one, grinning at his mates. 'A women's libber.'

'That's what the smog does for ya.'

'It's true, isn't it?' said Lucy. 'When do any of you lot see your wives?'

'At night. First thing in the morning.'

'And at the weekend.'

'Yes. And at the weekend too.'

'Big deal. Well you don't like women in here.'

'Now we never said that. We said it's more comfortable in the other bar, that's all.'

'Oh bollocks. You've never wanted women in here.'

'Well now . . . '

'A man's got to have a place he can go to for a bit of peace and quiet. For a drink with his mates. Hasn't he?' The other men nodded their approval.

'Why?' Lucy snapped, working herself up. She threw the rest of her drink down her throat and sat clutching the empty glass.

'Well . . . because. That's all.'

'And where does your wife go?'

'Well, she's at home all day, isn't she? She's got her own place.'

'Yes, stuck there all day, like a prisoner, with a handful of kids. And then you leave her there on her own all night too. Selfish pigs.'

The men looked at each other and, without uttering a word, decided to bail out. 'No need to get personal,' said one, before he turned his back to us and shakily lifted his glass.

'And they wonder why we spend our time down the pub,' one mumbled to his neighbour, ensuring that he was well out of Lucy's earshot.

The next person to walk into the public bar was Margaret. She'd come to buy a couple of bottles of light ale to tide her over the afternoon. Lucy, who was completely drunk and knew nothing of what had been going on, greeted her like an old friend and insisted that she join us for a drink.

By this time, both Lucy and I had run out of money, so we decided to carry on drinking and put everything on Ron's chit. The men at the bar were quietly outraged by our behaviour. But what could they do? Randalls didn't care. As long as he was selling his booze, he wasn't bothered who paid.

'Where is Ron anyway?' said Lucy, beginning to slur her words. 'We should at least drink a toast to the old bugger, seeing as he's paying.'

'At home,' Margaret replied, by now well stuck into her light ale.

'Not looking after the children?'

'That's right.'

Lucy and I fell about laughing, clutching each other, spraying the room with alcohol. Margaret wasn't quite sure what she'd said, but sat looking very pleased with herself.

'Oh God, if only you knew how funny that was,' said Lucy.

'If only we knew how funny that was,' I added. And we both spluttered off into more uncontrollable laughter.

A couple of minutes later, Lucy decided to try to persuade me to go back to London with her the following day. 'Come on,' she said. 'Everything's all right down here. Margaret can cope, can't you Margaret?'

'Of course I can bloody well cope,' Margaret growled, as though there had never been any question of it.

'There, you see.'

The atmosphere changed. The alcohol gave me a strange sensation, as though nothing were real. I was looking in from the outside.

Of course Lucy was too far gone to notice anything. 'If you don't come back to London now Rosie, you'll stay here forever and rot.'

'I won't.'

'You will. You'll rot and die. It's just one excuse after another. Everyone is coping perfectly well without you.'

'You're not.'

'What's that supposed to mean? I'm all right. I don't need you you know. I only thought you might like to live in my flat as you had nowhere else to go. If you don't like it, you can fuck off.'

'Thanks very much.'

'Well it's true. You try and run everyone's life and they can do perfectly well without it. Ron and Margaret don't need you down here interfering, do you Margaret?'

'Telling me.'

'I know you; you'll hide away down here, making one excuse after another, and that will be that. You'll never go back to London and then you'll miss everything.'

'Like what?'

'Life.'

'Oh very profound. There is life here too, you know. People don't keel over and die the moment they cross the North Circular.'

'Oh don't they? Look at this lot! Is this the sort of life you want to lead? Stuck in some backwater with an oaf of a husband who spends his whole time down the pub and only fucks you once a fortnight.'

The men at the bar turned around again and stared at Lucy, who was too enraged to realise what a rumpus she was causing.

'People here turn into vegetables,' she hissed, leaning over towards me and spraying me with saliva. 'Cabbages. They've got nothing. Look at them. What have they got in their lives? Nothing. Nothing to look forward to. Nothing to live for. Just the same old monotonous, dreary life. Day in, day out.'

Despite the fact that I was beginning to feel queasy, I was vaguely aware of Margaret digesting Lucy's every word. Unlike us, she was still more or less sober and sat with her head cocked to one side, fiddling with the bobbles on her duffel coat.

'You're not even giving yourself a proper . . .'

'Oh shut up Lucy,' I snapped, infuriated. 'How dare you assume that just because we don't have the same as you we're miserable? Not everyone wants what you want. Just because we're not all film stars doesn't mean to say we're all failures. Or all miserable. So don't be so bloody arrogant. I'll come back when I'm ready. You'll have to wait, that's all.'

Lucy didn't say anything but stared sulkily down at the fire. 'I feel sick,' she finally grunted.

'So do I.'

* * *

Much to Lucy's annoyance, the burnt-out shell of an old Ford Anglia had been sitting in front of our house in Clifton Road for over a week. It lay there like a dead animal, slowly breaking up before our eyes. On its death bed, the car had been pounced on by the local vultures who had stripped it of any parts that could be used or sold. The empty carcass was left for the 'slat' boys to use, abuse and finally desert, leaving it to rot like a heap of rusty shit.

'Nice of you to drop in,' Muriel sneered when I emerged through the steam of the Peach Melba.

'That's not fair. You said I could take as long as I wanted.'

'Within reason. I didn't think you were going to take the whole year off.' She turned away from me and grumpily shoved the big teapot under the still. 'Well I can't pay you for the whole time you were away,' she added. 'I just can't. I haven't got the money.' A gush of boiling water whooshed out, spitefully spitting at her arm. 'Bastard!' she screamed, leaping back. 'Bastard. Cunt. Fuckin' thing. For Christ's sake.'

I took off my coat and wandered into the kitchen. The

place was a pig-sty. Bits of stale curly bread, old buns and half-empty pots of marmalade were everywhere. Eggshells and opened packets of bacon had been left on grill-pans, work surfaces, anywhere there was a space.

'What's up Muriel?' I asked, wandering back into the cafe.

She ignored me and carried on frantically washing up in the sink behind the counter.

'Muriel. Something's wrong. What is it?'

'Nothing.' She dried her bony red hands with a grubby tea cloth and, pushing her hair away from her face, said, 'I'm going upstairs for a while, all right?'

'Fine.' I shrugged my shoulders and watched her disappear up to her flat through the hole in the wall.

According to the customers, it was the third day that there had been no 'special' and if we didn't change our tune they'd start going to the pub for their lunch. I promised a choice of two 'specials' the following day, and while I was in the middle of the lunchtime service, Muriel appeared from her flat looking bleary-eyed and washed out.

'Where the fuck's this lot come from?' she said quickly, tying her apron round her waist and making a vain attempt to straighten her hat-like hair style.

'Feeling better?' I had eight lots of cups and saucers lined up on top of the counter and heaved the teapot across them, blessing each in turn.

'I'll take those.'

'Table four and table two.'

Muriel went over to table four to deposit two of the cups. Then she screamed. The builder sitting beneath her had a tiny black spider crawling across the dome of his dusty bald head.

I stared at Muriel for a moment and then stormed over, grabbed her arm and roughly pulled her into the kitchen. 'Now what's wrong?' I demanded. 'And don't say it's nothing. It's written all over your face.'

'A fine time for a confrontation' Muriel jerked her arm away from me.

'I don't care what time it is, Muriel. I want to know what's up with you and what's been going on while I've been away.'

Muriel glared at me, defiantly pursing her lips. She gritted her teeth and held on. Her jaw was set. Tight. Tense. Every muscle in her body clenched. And then the flood banks burst. Her skeletal body began to quiver and shake and, suddenly leaning forward, she grabbed my arm and stood there sobbing her eyes out. As I held her, I tried not to notice the wig slowly slither down the side of her head, revealing a large white marble bowl, criss-crossed by a labyrinth of tiny red capillaries. Without her noticing, I managed to get the wig back into position by stroking her hair. It didn't seem to be fixed on properly at all.

Muriel had been raped. Up in her own flat and by a man she used to do it with, Bill Wyatt. He had rolled in drunk one afternoon and was so pissed Muriel couldn't get rid of him. The only way to get him out was to sober him up. So, having plied him with coffee, she took him upstairs for a lie down. He crashed out on the sofa in her living room while she got busy with the housework. When she went back to check on him, she found him three-quarters of the way through a bottle of whisky, and as soon as she began to have a go at him, he grabbed her and raped her, right there on the living room floor.

'I just feel so disgusted with myself,' she sobbed. 'So fuckin' disgusted. Of course it was all my own fault. There's no one to blame but myself. I shouldn't have been stupid enough to take him up there in that condition.'

'You were trying to help him.'

Muriel pulled away from me and, wiping her nose, put up her hand defensively. 'Well I won't do it again, I can tell you that. Not if that's what helping does for you.'

Never before had I seen Muriel so frail and vulnerable. Usually she seemed such a tough old boot. She let men use her when they couldn't get satisfaction from their wives. She loved the power, she loved to be desired. This bastard had taken everything. He had helped himself. He had invaded her.

I tried to get Muriel to take a few days off while I looked after the cafe. But she refused, saying there was no point in her sitting round moping. It was far better for her to keep her mind occupied. And anyway, it wasn't such a big deal. She didn't know why she was making such a fuss. It happened to married women all the time.

Later on that evening, while I was sitting on my own in the flat watching television, the buzzer downstairs sounded and made me jump.

I looked out of the window but could only see a vague, lumpy shape shuffling around on the steps below.

'Who is it?' I asked through the entry phone.

'Me.' A woman's voice answered.

When I saw Margaret standing on the doorstep I froze in horror. 'Margaret! What the hell are you doing here?'

'Don't sound so pleased to see me, after I've come all this way.'

I led her up to the flat, where I took her coat and stood there, staring at her, hardly able to believe what I saw.

'Well then? Are you going to stand gawking all night?'

'No. I . . . er . . . well, sit down. You'll have to sit on cushions; we haven't bought a sofa yet. I . . . er . . . well, I wasn't expecting you, that's all.'

Margaret cautiously began to lower her huge body and then suddenly toppled and crashed onto the floor. 'Well, I've left them,' she mumbled, looking very awkward on the floor and wondering what to do with her legs. 'I've had enough of that bloody lot; they can look after themselves from now on.'

'But Margaret, you can't just take off.'

Margaret had already switched her attention to the game show on television. 'Oh I like this. I like Bob Monkhouse.

Mind you, it's all fixed. If you watch it regular, you can see they only win on every other show.'

'Does Ron know you're here?'

'I don't know.' Margaret shrugged her shoulders and put her hands behind her so she could settle back and watch the programme.

Furious, I switched the television off and stood in front of the screen, glaring at her. 'You're not going to avoid this one Margaret. Does Ron know you're here or not?'

My sister scowled and shrugged her shoulders again. 'I don't know. Maybe. He might have guessed if he had more of a brain.'

'Right.' I marched over to the phone and started dialling.

'I'm not going back to that shit-hole,' said Margaret, rolling over onto one side and struggling to pull herself up from the floor. 'I'm not staying there to rot like a cabbage. I'm going to live here, in London. Get a good job, earn some money, go to parties . . . and do all sorts of things. Let's go to a nightclub. Shall we? Now. Tonight. Let's go out on the town, Rosie. You and me. We could go down to Oxford Street and find a couple of blokes. Make them pay.'

She looked ridiculous. Somehow, she had managed to squeeze into a black lurex evening top and a green skirt, under which she wore a pair of multi-coloured tights. On her face she wore heavy turquoise eye shadow and thick red lipstick that made her look as though she'd been snogging with a pot of jam. She looked like a clown.

I was grateful Lucy was with Brian, and not around to witness such a sight. I would have died of embarrassment.

Margaret saw London as the answer to all her problems. This was where she could really live. Where all the action was. Where the real people were, the sort of people you saw on the television and in the papers. Not like those boring old farts in Saltingford.

'Hello.' Ron's voice sounded strange. The phone rang six times before he answered it, and I could imagine him standing holding the receiver and wondering what this thing was that rang and rang, demanding to be picked up like a baby.

'Ron, it's Rosie. Margaret's here.'

'What?'

'Margaret's here Ron. It's Rosie.'

'Where?'

'In London.'

Silence. I could only hear Ron's thick breathing down the phone. 'She's in London?' he asked.

'Yes.'

'Well, when's she coming back?'

'I don't know. Hang on.' Margaret had managed to pull herself up from the floor and stood leaning against the kitchen doorway with her arms folded, staring at me. It was just like home. 'Do you want to talk to him?' I asked, cupping my hand over the receiver.

Margaret shook her head, furious that 'they' were being pushed on her already.

'She doesn't want to talk to you Ron,' I said.

'What else is new?' Ron sounded such a country bumpkin, his heavy Suffolk accent seemed to dredge the words from his mouth. 'Look Rosie, what's she up to?' he asked, beginning to perk up a bit.

'I don't know.'

'Well I'm at the end of my tether here. I'm having to take days off work all the time and they're beginning to get really short with me. If I'm not careful, I'll lose my job.'

'Why? What's going on?' I looked over at Margaret, who was glaring at me.

'She keeps taking off, sometimes for a couple of days at a time. I go off to work in the morning and everything's fine. But then I come back at night and she's buggered off again, leaving the kids on their own, all hungry and dirty and screaming.'

'Mum will be out of hospital soon,' I said. 'Mind you, she won't be up to much to begin with.'

'So what about Margaret? Isn't she coming back?' There was a note of desperation in Ron's voice.

'Yes of course she's coming back. She . . .'

'I fuckin' ain't,' Margaret barked.

'I heard that.'

'Look Ron, why don't you contact the social services and see if you can get the kids into a day nursery? At least it will take some of the pressure off you.'

'Do you think they will?'

'They might. Of course, you will be alerting them to your problems.'

'Well, what other choice have I got?'

'Not a lot. Leave it till tomorrow Ron and I'll call you in the morning. Margaret's here now, so maybe we can sort something out.'

After I put the phone down, Margaret said, 'You're not going to make me go back there you know.'

'You're such a selfish cow, aren't you? If I had a choice, I wouldn't put you in charge of a wet match.'

'Well you haven't got the choice, have you?'

Every evening, Margaret would leave the flat dressed up like a dog's dinner and not return until the following morning. The first time she did it, I was frantic with worry and blamed myself for not going out with her. After all, it wouldn't have killed me. But then she made it a regular habit and after a week I never gave it a second thought. 'Where on earth do you go?' I asked her one night.

'Piccadilly Circus.'

'There's nothing there.'

'You've obviously never looked.' And off she stomped, heading for the bright lights, with no idea where she was going, how she would get there or even where she was in the first place.

As Margaret rarely arrived home until after I'd left for

work in the morning, I thought it better to keep her contained in my room, rather than let her spread out across the flat and upset Lucy. My bedroom door could be shut, and Margaret forgotten about until she re-emerged, pig-eyed and dopey, later in the afternoon.

'How long's she staying?' Lucy hissed while we were both standing in the kitchen.

Margaret had just stumbled through for a cup of tea, leaving a pile of tea-making debris in a little heap on the draining board.

'Don't worry. Not long.'

'Good. Because she gives me the creeps. Nightmares even. Last night I woke up sweating, expecting her to charge through the door with a meat cleaver in her hand and that loopy smile on her face.'

'She wasn't even in last night.'

'No. Thank God. She's like a were-wolf.'

'She'll get bored soon and go. I know she will.'

'But how do you know? I know people like that who just swoop down on you and never move. They grow roots and attach themselves to your life.' Lucy poured out a cup of tea and stood leaning against the kitchen sideboard, cupping the mug in her hands and noisily sipping it. She had just come back from work and for the first time in months, her skin looked alive and healthy. She hadn't heard from Samuel for a couple of weeks and was hoping he had forgotten about the pictures. 'You know, Brian's asked me to audition for a new play he's directing. On the fringe.'

'Great. But what about the series?'

'I think it will fold. Really I do. It's just not getting the ratings they hoped for. It's too old hat. Too Coronation Street.'

'So what will you do?'

'Move into the theatre I hope.' Lucy put a cigarette in her mouth, lit it and deeply inhaled. 'As an actress, there's no future for me in this series anyway. Basically, I looked right for the part but that was about it. It would be easy to stay and rot in that series. It pays well. Demands little. Just turn up and switch on. I'm a jobbing actor, that's all.'

One morning, Margaret stumbled through the front door with a deep gash across her forehead and blood dripping down her. She was filthy, her clothes half torn and her hair matted and sticking out all over the place. She looked as though she'd spent the night with the rats in the barn.

'What on earth's happened to you?' said Lucy, terrified.

'Lend us a tenner, will you?' said Margaret. 'I had to get a cab.'

As soon as Margaret was out of the door again, Lucy called me at the cafe. 'You've got to come back,' she hissed down the phone. 'Something's happened. She looks like one of those gargoyles that hang from the roof of Notre Dame.'

When I arrived, Margaret had lumbered into my room and collapsed on the bed where, sometime during her restless sleep, she had managed to smear blood all over my new duvet cover. Afraid that she might throw some mad fit and attack us if woken, Lucy and I decided it would be better if we left her to sleep her ordeal off.

'Look, I really ought to go back to work. Muriel's having another one of her depressions today.'

'You're not leaving me on my own with that.'

'She'll sleep for hours.'

'How do you know? She probably suffered some awful brain damage. More awful brain damage.'

When Margaret eventually woke up that afternoon, she didn't give us a single clue as to what had happened.

'Come on Margaret,' I said. 'Who did that to you?'

'No one,' she grunted as she heaved herself off the bed and began to ferret around the floor like a smelly old stoat, picking up her things and stuffing them into the two tatty carrier bags she had arrived with.

Lucy and I were huddled together by the door staring at her, afraid to go too far into the room. I was disappointed to have taken a whole day off work and not even be told why. 'Margaret,' I insisted. 'The police should know.'

'Bollocks.' Margaret sat on the bed and suddenly clutched her head as a deep pain seared through it. 'Shit!' she shouted, violently banging her fist against the headboard. Lucy and I grabbed each other, and then let go, embarrassed in case she saw us.

Keeping our distance, we watched the wounded animal. Then, when the pain had gone, she finished stuffing the rest of her things in the carrier bag.

'What are you doing?' I asked, knowing perfectly well what she was doing.

'What do you think? Going of course.'

'Why?' I asked, ashamed to hear myself say this when I knew she was going because neither Lucy nor I could stand her.

Margaret stared at me and pursed her lips. 'That's what you want. So that's what you're getting. I know you don't want me here.'

'That's not true,' I said, blushing with more shame. 'The real problem is space. The flat's not big enough for the three of us.'

'Well I'm fucking off anyway. And I know you're glad.'

'You can't go like that.'

'Why? I'm all right.'

'You're not. Look, stay and let's sort this out.'

'No. I'm going.'

I felt compelled to implore Margaret to stay because I felt so guilty at wanting her to go. I couldn't stand the thought of being responsible for her departure.

Muriel never did fully recover from being raped. She became more subdued in her appearance as well as in her behaviour and her effervescent well of quick retorts almost completely dried up.

'Why don't you go and see someone?' I suggested time and time again.

'What about?'

'About what happened.'

'What for?'

'It might help to talk to someone who's been through it too.'

'Like fuck.'

For weeks, she tortured and blamed and punished herself. She thought she was weak, pathetic, and that it was only a matter of time before she would snap out of it, just like that. All she needed was a good kick up the arse.

And then, one Monday morning, everything did change. I opened the cafe door and saw Muriel already sitting at table four, smoking a cigarette and reading the paper. She looked up and smiled.

'Morning.'

'Morning,' I replied, slightly suspiciously. I went into the kitchen, where I hung up my coat and changed into a pair of old moccasins I wore for work. When I went back into the cafe, Muriel had poured herself another cup of tea and put one out for me.

'Come and sit down,' she said, beckoning me over to the table. 'I need a chat.'

I don't know why my heart began to beat so fast, but it did. Apprehensively, I pulled out a chair and sat down, my face rigid and ready for defence.

'Listen to this,' said Muriel, her eyes gleaming as she leant over to face me square on. 'You know my brother?'

'Yes. Well no, but I know of him.'

'Right. Well, I went down there yesterday. Down to Hastings. And we went for a walk along the prom, you know.'

I nodded like a sulky child who knew it was about to be deserted.

'And there we saw a cafe. Well I went in and it was perfect. Smaller than this place, with only eight tables, but perfect Rosie. Really perfect. It's called The Sea View. . .'

'. . .That's original.'

'Now, now. And it's got a flat above. Overlooking the sea. You can see right along the beach and miles out to sea. Well, you'll never guess, and I don't know why I did it, but I did. I put an offer in for it there and then. Can you imagine? There and then!' Muriel sat back in her chair and stared at me, a huge grin on her face. 'Well, we haven't actually agreed a price,' she added. 'But we will. If I've got to, I'd be willing to pay the whole whack. But what's the point if you can do it for less?'

I didn't know what to say. Any words stuck in my throat and I just sat there, staring at Muriel and swallowing hard. I thought I was going to cry.

Sensing this, Muriel tried to tone down her excitement and continued in a more soothing fashion. 'I can't stay here you see Rosie. Look at me. I'm miserable. I'll turn into a cabbage and rot if I stay in this place forever. You know, in some ways what happened was the last straw that pushed me over the edge and made me do something. I haven't been happy for years, but I could never be bothered to do anything about it. And maybe if it wasn't for the rape, if I hadn't sunk so low in my own mind, I wouldn't have even thought about a change. But that's what I need and I really believe that. I really do.'

'It's all right, you don't have to justify it to me. I think it's great. It's just what you need Muriel,' I said, almost choking on my own words.

Muriel looked down at the table. 'The thing is of course, Rosie, this place. Now I don't really want to sell it. Not yet anyway. So I was wondering how you would feel about taking it over. You pay me rent and take all the profits yourself.

That way you can build it up to what you want. I haven't done badly from it, I can tell you. I mean, I haven't made a fortune, but I haven't lost out either.' Muriel pursed her lips together and sat back to gauge my reaction. 'And of course you'd get the flat upstairs too.' She lit another cigarette and stared at me. 'So, what do you think?'

There was a silence, a very long silence while I tried to digest what she had said and imagine what future the Peach Melba might offer me. Of course, it would be a great opportunity to build something of my own, virtually from scratch considering the state of decay the place was in. There were all sorts of possibilities. I could convert it into a trendy wine bar, a smart restaurant, a shop. Anything really. And, of course, it would be my chance to make some money. Real money. Money that could be invested. I would probably end up owning my own empire.

'Can I think about it?'

'Sure.'

* * *

It was quite apt that the day should be dismal and gloomy, even though it was the middle of August.

The wind was so cold, it badgered against me like an irritating child, ruffling my skirt as I plodded down towards the sea. The sky was a very pale grey, almost white and very dreary. It went on forever until it crashed into the murky grey sea at the horizon.

This was the perfect day to see Margaret off. Dismal, dark and gloomy. Real funereal weather.

Tiny white crests danced across the top of the waves. Such movement. Such motion. Closing my eyes, I tilted my head back and allowed the sea to spit on my face, spraying me with tiny drops of water that bit into my cheeks.

I was at one with it all. Nothing was definable. Everything was. It all existed, as it was, without explanation or cause. And I was one with it. With the sea and the sky, the wind, the pebbles and the sea-weed. All of it. We were all part of the cycle; none less important or more powerful than the other. We were all participating in the wheel of existence that knows no past or future. That only exists. I existed only to further the cycle. Like the waves and the sun and the sea-weed and the stones. When I died and decomposed, plants would grow from the soil. Animals would eat the plants and humans eat the animals. This is how it is. This is how it is for Margaret too.

My shoes were beginning to sprout salty,white rims. And then, as they dried, the leather would shrivel up and go crinkly, like a pair of old leaves.

When I arrived back in Saltingford from London, I let Ron off the hook for a few hours while I baby-sat. Margaret had not been home for three days and he was frantic; not so much about where she was (we all knew she was holed up on the base) but because he couldn't leave the children. Luckily Mum was a lot better and had been able to help out, but she still wasn't back to normal and certainly not up to coping with two toddlers on her own. All those years of drinking had left her tired and washed out, as though they had sapped her of her strength. In time, she would gain it back again. But until then, Mum needed almost as much care and support as the children.

Ron couldn't wait to get out of the bungalow. As soon as I arrived, he was pulling on his anorak and barely managed a grunt of welcome. It was most unlike him. But I knew he was desperate to escape. The bungalow was closing in around him, imprisoning him. He felt trapped like an animal.

Margaret's obsessive tidiness obviously hadn't lasted. Every room was a shambles, and coated by a thick layer of dust that was only disturbed by toys, books and clothing that had been flung across the room.

Despite the circumstances, both Toby and Philip were on fine form. Toby was picking up everything we said and spluttering out his own interpretation of his new identifiable world. And Philip was crawling, bounding around the floor on his hands and knees. I put both boys to bed, read them a story, and another, and another. And then switched off the light and, leaving the door ajar, went into the living room where I began to clear the place up.

After I had thrown the toys into a battered old plastic washing basket, I sat down and began to aimlessly leaf through a magazine. Margaret always had hundreds of them all over the house. She stole them from doctors' waiting rooms and bus seats, people's shopping baskets and newsagents. She had magazine mania, and when she found a new one, she'd sit flipping through it, throwing a cursory glance at each page. Of course, she never read anything. Her concentration simply wasn't up to it.

On that evening, my concentration wasn't at its best either. I scanned each page without digesting a single piece of information. I felt itchy and irksome. I wanted something to happen, something explosive, but I didn't know what. Nothing I could do, would do. The telly was no good; the magazine useless. The children, no; Mum, no. Everyone, no. I wanted to tear down the beach and scream. I wanted something earth-shattering to happen. I wanted the heavens to open and the sea to part and God to blow us all out of existence. I couldn't stand just sitting there, so I stood up and walked over to the window. I breathed in, and out again. Loudly. I let the strong salty air fill my body, blow up my chest so I could float up and away, out of that place, away from the earth altogether, to somewhere else that I'd never heard of.

Then I saw Margaret standing by the shore. A rotund and solitary figure that wobbled in the wind, barely able to keep her balance.

There was no moon, no stars. Only a dark sky that was streaked by cloudy mucus.

'The sea's rough tonight,' I said as I took my place next to her. She wasn't surprised to see me. 'Rough for August. Look at those waves. I wouldn't like to be out there tonight, would you?'

Margaret didn't answer me.

I turned and peered at her face. It was covered by a thin layer of perspiration and her eyes were vacant and glazed.

'Margaret.'

'What?'

'What have you taken?'

'Nothing.'

'You're lying to me. You know I can tell when you're lying.'

Silence. And then: 'A red pill, a blue one and one with lots of bits in it.'

'Who gave them to you?'

'Bobby. He told me they would make the earth move.'

'And have they?'

Margaret put out her arm and grabbed my sleeve. 'Yes. Look. The beach is moving. It's going to swallow us up. It's like quicksand, Rosie. Look, we're going to drown in the sand.'

I steadied her. 'It's all right. The beach is still.'

Margaret grabbed my arm with the other hand and stood there for a moment, clinging to me. Every time a gust of wind came along, she began to wobble and lose her balance, thinking the sand was moving.

'Where've you been, Margaret? We've been worried about you.'

'No you haven't.'

'Well that's true. We know where you've been. You've been up to the base, haven't you?'

'Might have.'

'Screwing some desperate bugger. What do they see in

you?'

Margaret didn't answer. She stood staring out to sea, her eyes glazed, tiny drops of sea water clinging to her bloated face.

'I'm amazed you haven't latched on yet. None of them are interested in you. Why should they be? Look at you. They just think you're some poor wretched sow. They only fuck you because they pity you.' I nodded at the sea. 'There is someone though. Someone out there. Did he tell you that?'

Margaret nodded.

'He's out there. Waiting for you. It's your only hope. You'll never survive here. You'll never survive in London. What a disaster that was. Not quite what you expected, was it?'

'No.'

'So do you want him?'

'Yes.'

'Well he's waiting for you.' I pushed the hair away from my sister's eyes and caressed the side of her face with my palm. 'Go on,' I said. 'He won't wait forever.'

Margaret stared at me for a moment and then, lightly clenching my hand, removed it from her face and began to walk towards the water.

She walked, then she waded and then she began to swim, like a brown hippo bobbing out to sea. Further and further until I could only see a dark shape rising with the waves; sinking and swimming, sinking and swimming and sinking and sinking and sinking.

Now we could all be at peace.

There was an air of excitement as we all got ready for the funeral. Even the children seemed to sense it and were leaping and jumping around the place, flinging their arms about and dancing, constantly imitating each other. Mum looked a million times better; she had lost weight – hospital food she said – and her face had shed its puff-ball appearance. She still didn't look healthy, but she didn't look poisonous either. She came and collapsed on the sofa next to me and then bent down and scooped up Philip, who was zooming past her on all fours.

'You O.K.?' I asked. I wasn't sure what sort of effect Margaret's drowning would have on her. The hospital had been very dubious about her chances if she drank again. But she seemed fine. Perhaps she would have a delayed reaction. Perhaps we would all have a delayed reaction.

Mum nodded her head and gestured towards Ron, who had just wandered in in a suit and tie. He didn't look bad at all, especially in the red and grey tie I had bought him for his birthday; it gave him quite a sophisticated air.

'Nice,' I said, looking at him admiringly.

'Very nice,' Mum echoed, nodding her approval.

'The tie looks good. It suits you.'

'Yes, it suits you that tie.'

Obviously feeling pleased with himself, Ron returned to his bedroom to give the suit a final brushdown. Mum and I looked at each other and raised our eyebrows. 'There's hope for him yet,' said Mum, nudging me.

When the time came, we all emerged from the bungalow and made our way up to the coast road in a sort of mini-procession. Ron led the way, followed by Mum, and I pushed Philip in the tank. Toby skipped on ahead, gunning down a helicopter every time one passed over us. It seemed appropriate that the base was on some sort of manoeuvres that day; huge great iron monsters clattered by, some so low we had to put our fingers in our ears to block out the row. It was a final salute to Margaret, for her services to the men.

The loss of Margaret had not been the loss of a mother to Toby. It had simply been the loss of Margaret. She had let him down too many times for him to ever secure any attachment to her. Ron, who was more of a father to him, told him that Margaret had gone away and wouldn't be back. He didn't understand. I told him Margaret was dead and that seemed more tangible somehow. Dead meant 'not able to come back'. Gone away meant 'could come back but doesn't want to'.

Margaret was already at the church, waiting in her coffin at the head of the aisle. Thankfully the lid was down. I didn't want to be confronted by her icy features. None of us did. Not even when she was fished out of the sea by a couple of early morning dog-walkers.

Not surprisingly, few people attended the funeral. Those who did, came for Ron or Mum. Or for a chance to participate in a real life drama or the tea we were laying on at the King's Head. George came and stood beside Mum, holding her arm throughout the service.

No one was surprised by Margaret's death. No one questioned it or wondered why it had happened. It seemed only right that someone like her would die young; she wasn't for this world. Death was the only answer for someone like that.

After Father Armitage had droned through the service, we filed out of the church and across the sodden grass to the grave which lay gaping like an open wound. Mum had heels on and kept getting stuck in the soil. Arthur Matheson had no reason to be at the funeral at all, other than to offer moral support to George. In appreciation of this, George stood with Arthur for this final part of the ceremony. Both men stood there in suits that must have been a hundred years old. During the last blessing, I noticed them move into their pub formation.

When it began to drizzle, the vicar quite shamelessly began to speed up his monologue. Ron didn't notice. He stood vacantly staring into the coffin as it was lowered into the ground. Mum didn't notice either; she was miles away, staring into the distance at a tractor trundling along the side of a hill. George and Arthur noticed. And so did I. Arthur's wife didn't. But it didn't really matter. No one cared. It was only a formality. I don't think it meant anything to anyone.

In the distance, I could see a thin veil of mist descend like a net curtain over a line of trees; you couldn't see in, only out. And above the mist, the sky had grown darker, blotted by heavy charcoal clouds, pencilled in by Margaret.

When we stepped forward to throw soil on the coffin, I peered down into the earthy hole. I could hardly believe it was her in there, dead. She would be left there forever. For ever and ever and ever. And then, in a few years, when her grave was covered in grass and moss and lichen, no one would know who she was. People would trample over her. Dogs piss on her. Flowers would grow, die and grow again. I stepped back, away from the hole, and wondered who I was standing on.

Once the service had finished, everyone rushed over to the King's Head as slowly as possible. Randalls could not have been relied on to serve a decent tea, so Ron had called in a couple of the local ladies to do the honours. Unfortunately, when we arrived, no one had thought of putting the heating on because it was August, so the room was cold and miserable.

The local ladies had made a valiant attempt at turning the King's Head into a suitable venue for a funeral tea. White nylon squares had been thrown over the circular tables to cover the stains left by glasses and tankards. Most of the ashtrays, especially those advertising beer, had been hidden and neat little glass ones strategically placed around the room. On each table sat a plate of minute sandwiches together with a selection of rock-hard fairy cakes that had been bought in advance but gone off during the wait. On the bar was a stack of cups and saucers. One of the ladies stood behind it armed with the most gigantic iron tea pot. It was bigger than the ones we used at the Peach Melba.

Suddenly all heads turned as Lucy made her grand entrance.

'God, I'm sorry,' she said, marching straight over and grabbing me for a peck on the cheek. 'I've just been up to the church and . . .' she shrugged her shoulders and looked at me guiltily.

'You didn't miss anything. Have a sandwich.'

'No thanks.' Lucy looked anxiously around her.

'What's the matter? You're very wound up.'

'I know. I've just got Brian to break into Samuel's flat. That's why I'm late.'

'Did he get the pictures?'

'No. He did manage to break a window though.'

'Oh God.'

'Oh I don't care. The bastard deserves more than a broken window.' Lucy looked around her anxiously. 'I don't know why, Rosie, but he scares me. It's as though he's obsessed with me. All those letters and phone calls. It's weird.'

'Well what does Brian say?'

'Oh he's no good. He thinks it's all a laugh. I wish he'd do something about it.'

'Why should he? It's your problem.'

'Oh God. Don't you start. That's what he keeps saying. Well, I'm not going back to the flat till you come back. I'll stay at Brian's. He won't mind.'

She looked around and stared at Ron for a moment. 'Poor thing,' she said. 'Have you ever noticed how everyone always sticks together at these dos? Huddled together like limpets on a rock.'

I looked around the room. Lucy was right. Everyone had moved into little clusters where they were talking in low, monotonous tones, wondering whether they might get a drink, but not liking to ask.

'Are we going to get a drink?' Lucy asked.

'I don't think so. Randalls isn't around.'

'Oh.' Disappointed, she looked around again. 'Well at least no one's pretending she's missed.'

I looked at Lucy and nodded. 'I'm just going outside for a moment.'

'Are you all right?'

'Yes, fine.'

By this time it had stopped raining. The thick grey clouds had lightened up and were beginning to let through a stream of sunshine that glistened on the wet path, bringing alive a spectrum of colour in the oily puddles. I opened the wooden gate of the churchyard and crossed over the soft wet grass to Margaret's grave.

'Ah'er'non,' said one of the two grave diggers who were strenuously filling in the hole. He looked at his colleague, who stared awkwardly at me and then, shrugging his shoulders, carried on.

'It's all right. Don't bother about me. I'll just watch,' I said.

'Do you want to arrange the flowers?' one asked as the other patted down the soil.

'O.K.' I moved forward and picked up the few drowned anemones that had been put to one side. Miss Stiff-finger must have paid Margaret a visit while we were down at the King's Head. I noticed a wreath from her, sitting beside the other flowers. She had not wanted to attend the funeral, I knew. She had never forgiven Margaret for hanging Brutus.

As I bent down to arrange the flowers, I was flooded by a great sadness. Not for the loss of my sister but because of the loss of an era in my life that was drawing to a close. It occurred to me that I might pray. But I wouldn't. Just in case she was watching. I would never give her that satisfaction. And I would never repent or blame myself. Not for one single thought or action. Never.

'Are you all right, Rosie?'

I turned around. Lucy was standing behind me, clutching her bag. 'Fine. Fine,' I said. For a moment, I saw her as the Lucy I had always known, with frizzy red hair and a freckly face. And I realised that despite all the trimmings, she was still that person. She hadn't really changed. If anything, she was like me. She'd gone all the way round the world to end up where she started.

'Look, I'm going back to London tomorrow.' She shifted awkwardly on the spot. 'I mean, I know it's early days but if you want a lift back . . .'

'No thanks. I'm not coming back.'

Lucy stared at me for a moment. 'What do you mean?'

'She's staying out here now, aren't you Rosie?' Miss Stiff-finger slid out from behind a small cluster of pines which cast a dark shadow across the graveyard.

Surprised, Lucy and I swung around and watched her walk towards us.

'I'm sorry. I didn't mean to startle you. I was just leaving by the south gate when I saw you approach.' She moved towards me and rubbed my shoulder reassuringly. 'Rosie's staying with us now, aren't you Rosie?'

The tone of her voice made me feel uneasy. 'Yes,' I replied cautiously.

'But what about the cafe?' Lucy blurted out.

'The Georges are going to take it over. I don't want it.'

'When did you decide that?'

'A few days ago.'

'You didn't say anything.'

'How could I? You're never at the flat. You're always at Brian's.'

Lucy grunted and stared down at the grave. 'What are you going to do here?' she asked quietly.

'Nothing. Just stay here. With Ron.' I shrugged my shoulders and looked down at the flowers I had arranged across the side of the mound, aware of Miss Stiff-finger's hand that was still on my shoulder.

'I see.' Lucy was obviously taken aback and didn't know what to say. 'Well it's your decision. I can understand in a way. In a way I almost envy you. Though I could never do it.'

'Of course you couldn't.' I pulled myself up to face her and smiled.

'Well, I'd better get back. My parents . . . you know?'

'Of course.'

Miss Stiff-finger folded her arms and we both smiled as we watched Lucy turn and walk slowly across the graveyard. 'Fuck!' she yelled. The heel of her shoe had got stuck in the grass.

Fiction from Honeyglen Publishing

THE DAWNING *by Milka Bajic Poderegin*

A family saga evolving against the turbulent background of a province in southern Yugoslavia as it emerges from five centuries of enslavement in the wake of the collapse of the Turkish and Austro-Hungarian empires.
The dramatic outline of the novel, in which romance and tragedy, intrigue, melancholy and iridescent vitality create a penetrating portrayal of a family, reflects subtly the old customs and way of life, the fight for national identity and the historical events resulting in the First World War.

'An assured and moving record, written in a transparent, evenly-paced Russian realist style, of the provincial hinterland of nationalist aspirations that lay behind the portentous assassination at Sarajevo.'

The Observer

'*The Dawning* offers the foreign reader much more than the attractions of a colourful traveller's guide to quaint folk customs and exotic traditions. The comparison it suggests is with the pure lyrical quality and pervading melancholy of the rich corpus of Balkan folksong which captures with absolute truth the moods of the people under centuries of foreign oppression.
"Mothers and Daughters" might have been a better title for this remarkable novel, for it is the moving portrayal of successive generations of Serbian women, whose stoical strength holds their families together in the face of overwhelming odds, which is one of the book's greatest assets.'

The Spectator

'Milka Bajic Poderegin left behind only one book – but sufficient to remain forever in literature.'

NIN – Belgrade